WILDER'S WOMEN
a novel by PD Watts

Greed, corruption, financial duplicity and sex at the heart if the British Establishment. Few had the funds, the know-how or the audacity to challenge it; fewer still the tenacity or the skill.

Mike Carlow has made millions exploiting the selfishness, greed and corruption at the heart of the British Establishment. Following his breakdown and indiscriminate sacking of staff at his company, Carlow Mason, his preoccupation with power and money ends in his beautiful investment broker wife, Laura, leaving him, and Geoff Mason, his business associate of twenty years, coercing him into applying himself and his millions to the task of changing the *System* by which Britain is governed.

The book is essentially English. It had to be. The author makes no secret of the fact that it was born of many years of disappointment followed by a growing sense of despair. A parliamentary system that hands the keys to the nation's future to a collection of cynical bigots and their so-called *Parties*—Parties which by their very structure encourage these people to indulge in juvenile confrontational games and farcical posturing at the taxpayers' expense, to say nothing of holding sway over our lives—ought not to exist, never mind prevail.

The power to change this, however, is vested in this confrontational farce and those same groups of individuals. And yet their conduct is rarely questioned by us or effectively challenged by a supposedly *free* Press, which continues to collectively demonstrate its unwillingness to emphasize our concerns by demonstrating an unwavering desire to maintain the status-quo.

The ballot box can thus measure nothing but our impotence, leaving successive generations of the British people powerless to intervene.

Wilder's Women is therefore a necessarily fictional account of how Mike Carlow—a millionaire many times over—is coerced by his business partner, Geoff Mason, into setting out to harness the shameful pursuit of self-interest at Westminster, and by exploiting the predictability of our news-media, make a desperate bid to rid the United Kingdom of political wastrels and an archaic *System* of government that has succeeded in bringing a once confident and independent group of nations to its knees.

Copyright © PD Watts 2012. All rights reserved.

This work is copyright. Apart from uses permitted under the Copyright Act 1968, no part may be reproduced, copied, scanned, stored in a retrieval system, recorded or transmitted in any form or by any means without the prior written permission of the author.

The Book is a work of fiction. Names, characters, places and incidents are either the product of the author's imagination or used fictitiously. Any resemblance to people living or dead, events or locales is entirely coincidental.

Ebook cover design by Philip Walters.

www.ladybird-design.co.uk phil@ladybird-design.co.uk

For my father, Arthur Watts (1910-1967)
—the wisest and perhaps most intelligent man
it has been my privilege to meet.

PROLOGUE

Gordon Templeton couldn't remember the last time he'd been at the wheel of his car this early in the morning. His brother Andrew—had lived he now reminded himself—in what had originally been the family home; the house they'd shared all too briefly with their parents before being sent away to school. He'd gone up to Cambridge after his time at Eton, while apparently hell-bent on self-destruction, Andrew had dropped-out to use the in phrase of the time; a period which had begun as a gap year and continued unbroken for the rest of his life.

The passing of their parents had financed his debauchery for a time; giving him the house along with investments and savings yielding more than enough income to support him had his addiction to alcohol and drugs not intervened. Of course, fathering a child out of wedlock and surrendering a fortune to a predictably sluttish ex-wife hadn't helped.

Had his brother really taken his own miserable life? Templeton supposed he must have if that was what the police were now saying.

He turned into the driveway, the sound of tyres on gravel stirring memories of childhood as he circled the forecourt and brought the car to a halt opposite the open front door. It was the first time he'd been back there in years.

A uniformed constable intercepted him. He introduced himself, explaining that he was there at the behest of Chief Superintendent Keen.

Keen came out to meet him. "My condolences, Sir Gordon,"

he said, stifling a yawn. "Thank you for coming."

Templeton noticed the policeman studying him minutely. "Not a pretty sight, sir. Best not to go in," Keen added quietly. He continued to study him. "Your brother shot himself with a Purdy, Sir Gordon—one of a quite handsome pair, perhaps I should add. He left a note saying he couldn't meet his financial obligations."

Templeton frowned. "I see."

"Yes," Keen added. "but what would you say the property's worth, sir? I am right in thinking it did belong to him?"

"Indeed, you are, Superintendent. But it'll be mortgaged to the hilt, whatever its value. He had—how shall I put it—several habits to support?"

Keen considered what he'd said. "*Habits*, you say?"

"An alcoholic addicted to heaven knows what else and cursed with an insatiable appetite for the wrong kind of woman—need I say more? I washed my hands of him a long time ago. Thank God our parents didn't live to see this. I was thinking on the way over, the world will be a better place for his passing.

Hardly a brotherly reaction, I suppose, but I'm sorry to say it's a reaction he earned."

ONE

It had surprised everyone at Carlow Mason when Mike Carlow began dismissing the staff—the ultimate sin as far as Geoff Mason was concerned. Hundreds had gone; a growing number driven from home, family and friends in search of work that where it could be found at all, was more often than not part-time or impossibly low paid. He'd all but begged Carlow to reconsider, and failed. Now, a mere couple of months later, the hardships reported didn't bear thinking about.

If something needs saying, best get it said. How many times had he listened to Carlow reciting those words? And yet he'd agonized for weeks before contacting Laura, when she too had surprised him, condemning her husband not just for his recent behaviour but for very much more, insisting that it perfectly illustrated what he'd become—what he'd degenerated into.

Mason had introduced them to each other at a colourless, fund-raising thing, he remembered—the kind of so-called party it's difficult to imagine yourself coming to the moment you arrive. Six feet plus an extra couple of inches tall, good looking even, in a well-used sort of way, Mike Carlow had been in his mid-thirties at the time; by turns disarmingly laid back and single-mindedly intense; by common consent the best catch in town.

Almost ten years younger than him, Laura had laughed when he called it their *enchanted evening*. She was the kind of woman most men dream about but lack the good fortune to experience. According to Mason, her life was *'a succession of genetically choreographed acts of seduction designed by the almighty to give him a permanent erection*—so *orgasmically* perfect, as he'd chosen to put it, that he couldn't see how any red-blooded male could fail to be mesmerized by that body, not to mention those fantastic legs. They'd pledged their donations, offered their excuses and left.

Her marriage to Carlow had made the front pages, after which, following a honeymoon in the sun—an all too brief honeymoon as far as she was concerned—Carlow hadn't much liked taking his eye off the business—they'd moved into a refurbished manor house in a pleasant, country village an hour and a half by car north of London.

But the couple who had everything were soon to find themselves asking was it her, was it him? the question repeated until tests and investigations confirmed it was her, it was physical and there was nothing to be done. A second opinion had echoed the first.

Laura had dismissed the idea of mothering another woman's child out of hand—a point of view with which Carlow had been tempted to agree. Life without children was hardly the end of the world. Adoption might have improved a young life, it was true; made a child happier than it would otherwise be, but he'd been quick to decide it might be best to say nothing.

Mason was convinced there was more to Jane Garside than was allowed to meet the eye. He'd long since discounted the *comfortable* shoes and clothing to match—even attempting to seduce her. But that had been five years ago now. It had intensified his curiosity about what she would be like in bed, but achieved nothing more—unless her subsequent decision to avoid or ignore him at every opportunity could be called an achievement. He'd excused his behaviour by saying that Carlow's secretary was *'a sexual volcano—seething beneath the surface waiting to erupt.'*

He helped himself to a mug of coffee from the pot on the filing cabinet in the corner of her office. "Your meeting's at eleven," Jane informed him, "And he said to tell you not to be late."

"And a good morning to you," Mason muttered.

Yes, and why had he chosen to resurface today of all days? Why return to his desk for the first time in months exactly to coincide with his long-suffering business partner inviting a lady-friend to lunch—that too *for the first time in months*?

He returned the mug to the tray in the corner and went into the boardroom. He'd no idea what Carlow's problem had been given his refusal to talk about it, but when he'd been overtaken by his *upset*—he'd not only *lost the plot* where the staff were concerned, he'd added new *Directors* to the Board, two of them: the final straw in Mason's eyes.

Indeed, he was finding it hard to believe that he'd recently been heard to claim, admittedly in an uncharacteristic burst of enthusiasm—that were Carlow to arrive in the office one morning saying, '*sell everything and sink the proceeds into yak shit*,' he'd be arse deep in the stuff before the smell reached his nose.

Yes—and he wouldn't be writing off Laura Carlow any time soon. Not that she was aware of it. Oh no—not a chance. She added a whole new dimension to the concept of *heaven on Earth* —the closest to female perfection he was ever likely to see.

So where the fuck *was* he? The clock on the wall already laid claim to ten minutes past.

For his part, Carlow had finally accepted that owning eighty per cent to Mason's twenty of a company which had made them *obscenely rich at other people's expense,* wasn't an achievement to be proud of. Thanks to people like him, unemployment was epidemic when the official books were uncooked, too many lives being '*cynically sacrificed to selfishness, greed, and a mindless dedication to an economic delusion,*' to use Laura's words.

Yet no one else would have called him a mercenary. He'd become part of *the scene*—too much the obviously *good chap* to be tarred with the same brush as others they could name. With Laura on his arm, he spent long afternoons at Wimbledon and Ascot plying his carefully selected guests with lavish hospitality, including the increasingly mandatory vintage champagne. *'One would feel positively desolate without one's champers, daahling —and such an awf'ly good year.'*

Summer also saw him entertaining the *frightfully proper* City bankers who grew ever more eager to provide him with funds. An invitation to join him for the Saturday of the Lords Test match was a coveted prize; very much part of the social calendar to which the financial community aspired. His villas in exotic places, yachts, aeroplanes and the like, were what Mason called his *social* investments; his *friends* quick to fund their acquisition, granting him licence in the process to virtually name his own terms.

Mason attended to what he would have found tedious, freeing him to concentrate on what he did best—acquiring vulnerable companies for throwaway money, hiving-off their real-estate assets and anything else worth the effort, and having used their former shareholders and managers to extend his circle of influence where he could, going on to swell the ranks of the unemployed by closing most of them down.

Carlow punched Laura's number into the car telephone. Finding the line busy, he paused before punching it again. "Who's that?"

"Marian, sir."

"Who?"

"Marian, Mr Carlow; Mrs Carlow's secretary."

"Ah—yes—of course—er, Marian. Is my wife there?"

"She's no doubt held up in traffic. Have you tried her mobile?"

The lie came to him easily. "I have. Ask her to call me, will you? I'll be at the office."

Yet another argument with Carlow had left Laura running late. Her meeting with Sir Gordon Templeton—the Cabinet Secretary—had been scheduled for nine-thirty. She'd managed his investment portfolio and the remnants of his brother's for almost five years. They'd recently liquidated the bulk of their holdings, but his contacts at Lloyds and in the City, added to those at Westminster and, of course, in Whitehall, made her understandably anxious not to damage the connection.

Selecting a pair from her extensive collection of stiletto-heeled shoes, she smoothed down the dark skirt she'd chosen for the day and thinking *late* was almost certainly unexplored territory for the fussy civil servant, hurried downstairs.

She called her secretary on the car phone.

"He hasn't arrived," Marian said blandly. "Oh—but Mr Carlow rang. He said he couldn't get you on your mobile so would you please return his call. He'll be at the office."

Laura filled with apprehension as Jane connected them. "Hello, darling," he said cheerfully. "Thanks for calling back. I rang to apologize and to thank you." It was as if they hadn't argued. "That's the hardest my arse has ever been kicked—and you were right—I deserved it."

What could she say, he still assumed she'd forgive and forget.

"Let's make a night of it," he added. "I'll put a couple of bottles on ice and organize some food. Seven o'clock at the penthouse—what do you say?"

She considered refusing, but could see little to be gained.

Carlow took his seat at the head of the table as one of Jane's girls delivered their coffee. He drank too much of the stuff and rarely refused it. He couldn't recall seeing the girl before, and might not have noticed her at all had she been less familiar with Mason. Mason had agreed to avoid relationships with women in the office, albeit ready it seemed to make an exception in her case.

"I'll come straight to the point," Carlow said when she'd gone; no reference to his recent conduct or long absence from his desk. "We have to go public. France has been good to us, but becoming a European force to be reckoned with more or less demands a public quotation." He'd registered a company for the purpose, he told them—Carlow Mason Europe—CME. It rolled nicely off the tongue.

He went on to promise shares to Robert Barker and Graham Wright—the pair new to the boardroom. A token of appreciation, he said, for their consistent hard work. Fucking nerve, Mason thought—they hadn't been with the company for more than five minutes. As with everything else lately, Carlow had failed to consult him.

"I'm sure we're grateful to you, Mike," Barker gushed. "Er—and to you, too Geoff, of course," he added, conscious of his oversight. "This is typical of your generosity—both of you—" At least he was consistent. "—and, if I may say so, the right approach to Europe."

"Graham?" Carlow enquired.

Wright was quick to demonstrate the kind of man he was—tight; mean; close—there weren't enough adjectives. His bony fingers twitched at the pencil-thin moustache underlining his nose, going on to absent-mindedly smooth down the hair long since departed from the crown of his head.

"All right on the face of it," he said, anxious to say what he thought Carlow wanted to hear.

He was a good accountant—competent; well respected in the City. Why, Mason wondered, was the tight-fisted bugger so blatantly two-faced? Perhaps jokes about tight-fisted accountants weren't jokes after all.

"I'll need to look at the underwriting implications," Wright continued, "but I can't think why it wouldn't come together—and as Robert has said, we're delighted by the prospect of owning some shares."

He paused, hoping to give the impression that the shares were incidental to his train of thought.

"Good," Carlow said, "because I'd like CME up and running by the end of this month." As always, he made do it or else sound like a friendly suggestion. "That's it for now, then, unless you've something to add?"

The two men looked at each other before shaking their heads.

Mason waited for them to leave before speaking. "So how are

you feeling?"

Carlow Mason was arguably the biggest private business in Britain. Carlow had enjoyed building and running it with Mason; sometimes obsessive about it perhaps, but it had made him rich beyond his dreams; given him everything he'd ever wanted—everything he'd striven for. Now he was at odds with the world, his re-born conscience constantly reminding him of things long forgotten—things he was finding it hard to believe he'd allowed himself to do.

Mason took a swig of coffee and picked up the telephone. "Jane? Jane, some kind of disaster has overtaken this coffee. Do you think one of your young ladies could make us some tea? For Mike and me," he added solemnly. "The others have gone."

He put down the phone. "And since when flotation—why lie—we both know you won't let the City within a mile of the business?"

"There's no mystery about it," Carlow said. "I've had enough. I don't want all this anymore."

"So why CME?" Mason asked calmly.

"A vehicle to take my shares off my hands—unless you want them, of course?" he added as an afterthought.

Mason found the suggestion mildly insulting. "Such generosity. I pay you top dollar for control—not that I could—and you up stumps and leave."

Carlow shrugged, forced into silence by the arrival of their tea.

"Look," Mason said, studying the girl. The bodywork was average, but he was sold on the legs. "I've never hassled you, have I, and I have to agree it's a bit late to start, but you do realize, I trust, that throwing in the towel won't turn back the clock?"

Carlow was miles away. Twenty years was a long time. He'd taken a wrong turn, surely Mason could see that—easy to do given the pressure he'd been under. "I realize it's no consolation for some," he announced, "but it's time for me to quit."

"Too right it is," Mason muttered to himself.

He'd always played second fiddle to Carlow—to his genius for making money, that is. They'd organized themselves that way—a logical division of labour. But what he was about to demand was going to feel good—exceptionally good—a fitting final chapter to their time working together. "But not before you've made an effort to give something back," he added firmly.

Carlow laughed. "And how do you suggest I do that?"

"Try changing the way the UK is governed."

"Oh, come on," Carlow groaned. "I was good, yes—but never that good. Watching each others' backs is what *honourable members* do—it's what they're about. An army of Carlows couldn't change that. They'd close ranks to the last man and woman at the first sign of somebody questioning their right to short change us—particularly if that somebody happened to be me. They represent the people they always represent—themselves. That's why we're forced to listen to their hypocritical babbling. Anyway, *sad-case multi-millionaire attempts to salve conscience by trying to change the world*—I don't think so."

"You can stop there," Mason snapped. "I'm not asking, I'm telling. For once in your life you're going to do what you're told."

Carlow raised an eyebrow. "And if I refuse?"

Mason laughed. "Simple—the Great-British public get chapter and verse on the real Michael Carlow."

"Shouldn't you consider what that would do to you?"

"I don't give a shit. But I do know Laura could kiss her fancy clients goodbye. So—go ahead—fight me—if you want her name added to the list of lives we've screwed up. I really don't care. Either way you are going to do this."

Their heated exchange continued over lunch, Mason's invitation to his latest woman forgotten. Ignoring Carlow's protests, he'd insisted they meet with their bankers that afternoon. Whatever the pros and cons of the demands he was making, CME was going to need funds.

Welcomed at the Bank with open arms, Mason was soon

outlining what he called the *Carlow Mason European Project*. He lent a wonderfully convincing ring to it by trotting out every fancy sounding cliché to which he could think to put his tongue: European expansion, monetary union, escalating profits—the *golden dawn* of a new millennium. They loved it. He wanted fifty million from them, he told them—fifty per cent of what he estimated they'd be needing to fund their campaign.

Sensing their indecision, he went on to offer a tongue in cheek assurance that there'd be no hard feelings if they preferred opting out. If fifty million was too rich for their blood, he could always approach their competitors. Why not? They'd been trying for years to get a foot in the door. Given agreement now, on the other hand, and valuing the relationship as he assured them he and Carlow did, it would be less disruptive all round if things stayed pretty much as they were.

Intervening only to confirm or reinforce Mason's arguments —still furious at being blackmailed by him, Carlow listened, fully entering the conversation to end it by hinting at flotation —whetting their appetites without committing the company to anything in so many words."

TWO

Adrenaline had begun to flood through Carlow's veins when they returned from the Bank. Parking the Rolls, he recalled for the first time in years how he and Mason used to drive all over town looking for places to park simply to avoid the cost of the multi-storey car-park. Impossible these days, he imagined, with so many meters, restrictions and hideous yellow lines—in addition to which, the modern parking fine was enormous and petrol much too expensive to waste it driving round town.

Mason's performance at the Bank had been impressive, but he'd obviously convinced himself that pressurizing sections of Westminster and Whitehall would produce what he wanted— when, intense though it couldn't be denied they had the ability to make it and regardless of an excess of skeletons over cupboards along the corridors of power, they'd be challenged at every step.

He was refusing to acknowledge that Party politics was a game—an elaborate game, maybe, but a game nonetheless—a game played by people desperate to prove, not least to themselves, how important they were.

An added modern complication was that the politically ambitious female of the species was better versed in its arts than most of the men; which perhaps explained how an increasing number were managing to find their way into the House of Commons. This, when Westminster and Whitehall were invariably quick to repel anything and anyone they saw as a threat to their cosy co-existence—safeguarding our Great-British democracy, or so they would claim.

But nothing had changed, or was likely to. In order to be considered for selection these women had still to prove to their respective Parties that they were even more bigoted and conformist than their male counterparts—guaranteeing they'd be a bigger threat to the welfare of the nation than the men they replaced.

Carlow was also aware that a significant percentage of the population were instinctively opposed to change, political or otherwise. It disturbed them; made them feel anxious and insecure. Even if he did succeed in recruiting an outstanding team and they were beneficiaries of unrealistically large and timely slices of good fortune, the odds were heavily stacked against them. Success was not just unlikely, it was almost certain to remain so.

The lift doors opened on to the air-conditioned opulence of the fifteenth floor. Carlow left Mason and the atmosphere between them, stretching his legs across the familiar dark-blue carpet, through the softly lit foyer to his office, the touch of a button on his desk causing blinds to rise and fall, curtains to slide back and forth, denying the late afternoon sun while preserving the panoramic view over London they were designed to preserve.

He was beginning to formulate a strategy with the potential to succeed—*if*, he'd little need to remind himself, such a strategy existed.

"Hi, Jane," he said, determined to appear confident and relaxed. "How are you?"

When you saw that certain something in his eye or heard it in his voice, it was no time for questions. It was advisable on these occasions to do precisely as he asked. "Fine," she said hesitantly. "Is there anything you want?"

He smiled and shook his head. "No, but you can tell young Richard Wells I want him here tomorrow morning at ten o'clock sharp."

She screwed up her face. "He doesn't work here anymore."

His eyes registered surprise. "Since when?"

"Since we—*you*, kicked him out."

He spun his chair. "Do what you can, then, eh?"

The third floor were certain to have thought themselves threatened by Richard's successes in France. He should have seen it coming. "NO!!" he snarled. "Get it through your thick skull, cretin—this is all down to you."

Jane reappeared round the door. "Did you call?"

"What? Er, no—No—just talking to myself."

She closed her office door and rang the IT section twelve floors below. "He was thrown out with the others," the sarcastic voice said. "Or have you forgotten already?"

"I don't suppose you happen to know where I might find him?" she asked mildly.

"At his local job-centre I shouldn't wonder—if he hasn't left this godforsaken Country."

Briefly unemployed herself, she remembered, she'd been recommended to Mike Carlow by a mutual acquaintance. He'd had little to say at her interview—little that was that seemed to make sense at the time; peering across his desk as if trying to read her mind, then offering her the job.

It was unusual for her to make up her mind about anything quite so quickly, but she'd surprised herself by accepting without even a moment's hesitation. Months had passed, however, before she finally came to terms with the sheer magnitude of his wealth. He'd created a vast fortune from nothing—against all the odds.

Happily married in what had soon become a complicated, part-time sort of way, her relationship with her husband had been overshadowed by her dedication to her position with Mike Carlow. He seemed to wield power with consummate ease —albeit not a man to whom it even occurred to her to think she might be physically attracted, even if she had felt excluded when Laura came on the scene. She'd never consciously envied Laura Carlow as she was soon to become. Later, when her marriage collapsed, he'd been understanding and considerate, oblivious to the fact that her attention to him was the principal cause. She was his secretary. That was how he saw her, and how she invariably behaved.

A model of self-control, she thanked the sarcastic voice for its help and ended the call. Desperate for cash after losing his father and his job, Richard had traded the family house for a two bedroom flat and tried to move his life on. She'd no difficulty finding him.

"His brother has shot himself," Marian announced. She'd finally managed to contact Templeton's private secretary only to be told the police had called him to his brother's house at dawn and he was apparently still there.

It would be to understate Laura's reaction to say she felt anything but a sense of relief. She'd disliked Andrew Templeton with an intensity sometimes bordering on hate, and but for Sir Gordon's importance to her business would have rid her client list of his creep of a brother a long time ago—objectionable pervert.

But she hadn't expected him to take his own life. As far as she was concerned he'd always been psychologically unbalanced. Full of himself, too, so hardly the suicidal *type*—whatever that was. He'd liquidated what was left of his portfolio to cover losses at Lloyds, or so she'd been led to believe. She was no stranger to the irrational decisions clients sometimes made, especially clients like him, but it now seemed probable the events were connected.

Anxious to begin preparing for the evening ahead, she dictated a letter to Sir Gordon—more out of a sense of duty than sympathy—cancelled lunch with a client, pleading pressure of work, and swallowing what proved to be an unappetizing sandwich, spent the rest of the afternoon finding an *appropriate* new dress.

She visited the West-end stores only rarely, her presence an open invitation to their PR/advertising people; photographers instantly on hand to record every move she made. She had no real objection, especially as she was never called upon to pay for what she chose. Her photograph monopolizing the fashion pages was good for business and a small price to pay.

It was still early when she made her way across the City and took the lift to the penthouse. Carlow called it *the film set*, claiming that it had become so fashionable and spotless under her direction that he found it impossible to relax and put his feet up without feeling guilty. According to him it was the most luxuriously exclusive overnight accommodation in the world.

Examining the new dress in a full-length mirror, she smiled, holding it against her. She'd never worn or owned anything quite so revealing. It was totally perfect for what she had in mind.

Six o'clock saw the arrival of the caterers. Finding the champagne ready chilled, she smiled at a particularly attentive young man; flirting; the desire in his eyes and the sudden bulge in his trousers leaving no room for doubt about what he was thinking. She raised her eyebrows knowingly at him before heading for the bathroom with bottle and glass.

Her hands had a will of their own as she threw off her clothes. She reached her first orgasm in front of a mirror, her second two glasses of champagne later lying in the bath. She'd never experienced such desire; such an intensely powerful need for a man.

She pressed her body close to Carlow as soon as he arrived, the dress accentuating the curve of her hips, the jut of her breasts and the long sweep of her legs. "What are you waiting for?" she whispered.

He was taken off guard. "Whoa now—whoa," he said defensively. "How long have you been drinking?" He removed her arms from around his neck, conscious of the kitchen door and the caterers beyond it. "Pour me a glass of that stuff, will you?" he said over his shoulder, escaping to the shower, "Before you drink the whole bottle.

You know, darling," he said when ten minutes later she

handed him the glass—he was sitting in front of a mirror in the bedroom drying his hair—"we should get some time away together, don't you think?"

Getting no response, he looked for her reflection. She'd returned to the bed and was sitting, legs crossed, the hem of the dress high up her thighs. He turned to feast his eyes. Making no attempt to cover herself, she swayed across the room on extravagantly high heels and dropped to her knees at his feet.

He said nothing about developments with Mason and what he'd been pressed into doing, doing his best to introduce some kind of normality to the situation as they sat down to eat; raising the subject of CME and his retirement; explaining how the new company would enable him to part with his shares at a fair price—an often complicated not to say impossible proposition where private company shares were concerned.

Intent on demonstrating her disinterest, she pulled him away from the table as soon as the caterers had gone. Emptying her glass at a swallow, she allowed a shoulder strap to slip, exposing her breasts; promising him everything but making him wait—knowing the effect this was having—moistening her lips, exciting him further, reminding him of the bedroom and her warm, eager mouth.

She began to laugh—trembling with excitement; making him burn; taunting, teasing, playing with every emotion he possessed, to say nothing of her own. "Do it," she insisted.

He hesitated.

She mocked him with her eyes, slid to the rug in front of him and spread her legs wide.

Carlow woke from what had been a fitful sleep just before eight. Exhausted and hung over, he dragged himself out of bed, leaving Laura asleep, her hair partly obscuring her face, her smooth, sun-tanned body only half covered. God, she was beautiful.

Her unashamed lust had excited him, of course, but it had succeeded in troubling him last night and he was still troubled by it. What had prompted it? he wondered. And more to the point, what had prompted it now? He needed time just to talk to her; to hold her; to rediscover the woman he'd married.

Waking at nine o'clock, after he'd gone, Laura walked into the shower easing her limbs after the exertions of the night; stretching and remembering; feeling her body and enjoying the sensation. She'd set out to shock him, surprised by the number and strength of the orgasms she'd experienced; astonished by the intensity of her need to surrender her body to sex. She crossed the room to the telephone. "Hello, darling," she purred, her voice husky and dark; intentionally seductive. "Why don't you come up and help me get dressed?"

He was slow to reply. "Your prize client's brother has committed suicide," he finally offered. "I heard it on the radio."

Her reply was dispassionate. "I know."

He seized the opportunity to escape. "Sorry, the other phone's ringing. I'll catch up with you later."

She replaced the receiver as the lift doors opened in front of her, no time to cover herself with the towel she'd abandoned on the floor.

THREE

Richard Wells had met Jane Garside for the first time three years earlier. Instructed to acquaint the Board with the company's new, state-of-the-art computer, he'd asked with some trepidation if she minded his taking the afternoon off. His father's illness had been diagnosed the previous day—cancer. He'd promised to be at the hospital to await the outcome of more tests.

His rapport with Jane had proved to be instant; she the mother he'd never known, he the son she would now never have, when with hope cruelly short-lived and computers forgotten, he'd exhausted himself emotionally and financially trying to make his father's last days the best he knew how.

Following the funeral had come the exercise in France and redundancy, after which even she couldn't have changed his opinion of Mike Carlow. "He wants you for his latest project," she'd explained on the telephone, carrying out Carlow's instruction to do the best she could. "It's confidential," she'd added, picturing the disbelief on his face at the other end of the line.

"I'm beginning to think there's no understanding or compassion left in this world," he'd eventually replied. "When Dad died and your man threw me out, I consulted the local Social Security people—had to, I was skint. I was subjected to a never ending list of fatuous questions, ending in them describing me as a halfwit, or words to that effect, for squandering the last of my savings. Yes, *squandering*, the insulting bitch said."

He was twenty-eight years old, brilliant with computers, industrious, personable; and his work prior to expulsion from the company had generated a small fortune. Jane had taken his dismissal personally. "Will you talk to him at least?" she'd asked, not for a minute expecting him to agree.

"Why?" he'd grumbled, his exasperation showing. "What would be the point?"

She'd gritted her teeth. "Here at ten in the morning, and don't be late. Use the penthouse lift. The access code at the moment is ten sixty six."

"I'm so sorry," he said to Laura Carlow, his face registering many things, none of them sorrow. "My name is Richard Wells." He stepped back into the lift. "I'm here to see Mr Carlow."

She's magnificent," he told Jane sixty seconds later. "I obviously pressed the wrong button and went all the way to the top." He pointed to the penthouse directly above them. "The lift doors opened and there she was—naked as the day she was born and hell-fire is she gorgeous." He shook the fingers of both hands as if they were burning. "I'd run up all sixteen flights—"

"So it would seem," she interrupted. "Surely you've seen Laura Carlow before?"

He grinned. "Of course I have. But never as much of her as I was treated to just now."

Already anxious about his meeting with Carlow, she was annoyed by her involuntary reaction to his comments about Laura, wondering if she was beginning to think and behave like a frustrated old maid. "I'll tell him you're here, but I don't think you should talk to him the way you do to me. I understand how you feel, and you're probably right, but don't get into an argument. If that's why you've come, you might as well leave now."

He kissed her on the cheek. "You're a good woman, Jane Garside, but he asked me to come so I'll handle this my way."

Pressurized by Mason and considering a number of theoretical strategies while going through the motions of recruiting a team, Carlow would have preferred to meet Richard without a barrier between them. As things were, they'd be wasting their time. Richard was a young man with an innovative mind. His work in France had demonstrated that. What had been obvious to him but clearly not to those responsible for the Carlow Mason sawmills, had seen him reprogramming computers, modifying work procedures, cutting costs and enhancing efficiency, his endeavours improving the potential for overall profitability by what in one instance had turned out to be as much as ninety per cent.

"Do sit down," Carlow said. "Can I ask Jane to get you something—tea, coffee—something cold?"

Richard was tense but determined. "No thank you, Mr Carlow."

"Do call me Mike," Carlow added. The odds were against, but this was a skirmish he needed to win. For some inexplicable reason he hadn't opposed Richard's dismissal, a decision which remained as difficult to understand now as when Jane had originally explained what he'd done—if, indeed, it had been a conscious decision at all. By some miracle she'd convinced Richard to come into the office, but if he'd made up his mind not to listen; unless he was at least curious about what might lay ahead, there was no obvious way forward. "You know, Richard," he said. "Running a company's not as easy as it looks. We rectify our mistakes where we can, it's the least we can do—but there's no going back."

"Look," Richard said. "I promised Jane I'd listen to you, and I shall, but I ought to make it clear I'm not doing it from choice."

"Point taken," Carlow said, steeling himself.

Emerging from behind his desk, he threw off his jacket, loosened his tie and dropped into an armchair, beckoning Richard to follow. Despite his having refused it, Jane came in with coffee, serving Richard's exactly as she knew he liked it—strong and black with a single heaped teaspoonful of demerara sugar.

"There is an explanation for what happened," Carlow began. "Jane told me you'd gone when I asked her to call you, and I was forced to accept that it was all down to me." He shrugged. "Not how you describe it, I'm sure, but I'm ready to admit to an *un-*

fortunate mistake. God knows we're crying out for people with the ability you showed in France."

He sipped his coffee in silence. "Since then," he eventually continued, "and I do recognize what I owe you for that—I've attempted to analyze Britain's social, financial and political development since I formed Carlow Mason—at the same time attempting to assess the merit or otherwise of my personal performance. Had things changed for the better? Had I made a meaningful contribution? Those and others—the kind of questions I imagine the majority of people ask themselves at one time or another."

Richard remained silent, watching him closely.

"My sins are well documented," Carlow continued. "I've been ruthless, unscrupulous, fixated on profit—not altogether surprisingly I would argue considering I started with nothing—but it is true to say that other people's aspirations have rarely featured in my plans. You see, Richard, if you allow money and power to possess you as I did—to become your mother, father, lover, king, queen and God—there can only be one priority in your life: *yourself*—forget other people."

Foolishly, of course, he'd realized that a long time ago, he'd ignored the opinions and discounted the values of too many of the people with whom he'd grown up—his parents, teachers, relatives and most of his friends, for example: the man from the corner shop in the village—the baker, the shoe mender who'd taught him to play chess, the butcher and the milkman; people he used to meet on the street and in the pub; good people; real people; English, Irish, Scottish and Welsh as distinct from nondescript *British*; people to be admired—envied even.

"I was blinkered," he added grimly, "blindly committed to making money. I was convinced there was nothing I could do about sleaze and corruption, and nobody gave a tinker's shit about what I said or did. So I set about turning the situation to my personal advantage."

Richard broke his silence. "There's nothing new about people like you doing that."

"My point exactly," Carlow added ruefully. "The tragedy is that when our balance sheets begin to suffer, as most very soon will given what lies ahead, we'll liquidate our assets and go—to hell with what happens to those left behind."

This was so far from what Richard had expected from Carlow that he found himself wondering how often the world turns on preconceived ideas about other people; especially when so few appear to believe or have faith in anything. Having lived most of his life without a second thought for anyone but himself, here was this super-capitalist filled with remorse. "So why do you need me?" he asked him.

"It seems to me that helping to misappropriate a rather large sum of money before disguising where it goes and how it's used when it gets there, is right up your street." He grinned. "We're going to harness the twin powers of self-interest and greed by adding bribery and blackmail to the equation. They fuel the British *System* and they'll bring it down."

"Yes—but why do you want to bring it down?"

Carlow laughed. "That has to be obvious. The Governments of Europe, including our own, operate beyond our control—obscenely expensive to maintain and too often corrupt. Think about it. We can do nothing about the rest, but with vast sums being thieved or squandered by them here at home, the proverbial man in the street is encouraged to live way beyond his means, aided and abetted by bankers whose greed and incompetence beggar belief.

And how will the *Honourable Gentlemen* react when the shit hits the fan—when our naïve man in the street can't repay what he owes?"

Richard shook his head.

"Well, I'll tell you," Carlow went on. "They'll abandon him in favour of bailing out the money-lenders using our cash. They won't hesitate. They specialize in misusing what doesn't belong to them. Take their salaries and expenses, for example—especially their *so-called* expenses—and that's to forget the golden handshakes, pensions and god-knows what else. Indeed, they're totally relaxed about raiding the public purse to fund the good-life for themselves and their *friends*—and more incredible still, they've managed to convince themselves they have the right.

I know this sounds rich, if you'll pardon the pun, coming from someone like me, but somebody has to stop them. I've worked with Geoff Mason for twenty years and, rightly or wrongly, he believes that *somebody* ought to be me."

The sun was burning into the rooftops; shadows knifing over parapets and gutters into the streets far below as Richard got to his feet and crossed to the window. He was astonished and at the same time intrigued. He'd found himself agreeing with most of what Carlow had said. What he was contemplating was unacceptable in a democracy, yes—to say nothing of illegal—but he was certainly right—somebody had to do something even if the chances of succeeding were a long way from clear.

Had his father's lifelong refusal to succumb to selfishness and greed done anything for him? he asked himself. Had day stopped rolling into night since his passing—had the seasons stopped turning? Of course not. The world went about its business still very much in the hands of people who were happy to demonstrate their concern for nothing and no one but themselves. Nobody challenged them.

He watched mountains of snow-white cloud crossing the summer sky like an armada of chariots carrying used-up lives to far-off destinations known only to them. His mind was made up. He would accept Carlow's offer. Yes—if the terms were to his liking, he would definitely accept. Life was too short to do otherwise—the merit of the decision at the whim of the fates. "So you formed Carlow Mason twenty years ago," he said as Jane served fresh sandwiches and coffee.

"Roughly," Carlow said. He'd been studying Richard closely as he stood at the window.

"When you were twenty five?" Richard added.

"Twenty-six, I think—yes, twenty-six."

"Was that when you thought you were ready to take on the

world?"

Carlow hadn't thought about it much, and never in those terms. "Not really. I just wanted to be rich."

"I'm an only child," Richard continued. "I never met my mother." The tension between them eased as they laughed. "I mean she died when I was a kid and I grew up with Dad. What I've experienced at first hand doesn't add up to much. My education, such as it was, came pretty much from the classroom, from books and what I've learned from the box. I'm bright, I suppose, but my ability has never really been put to the test."

"What about France?"

"A straightforward reorganization."

"A bit more than that, surely?"

Richard shrugged. "Well—maybe a bit. Anyway, I enjoyed the experience—for all the good it did me. I've had one or two women, though—in between times." He said it as if stating it openly might have the power to change something. "My point is that everything passes you by if you don't jump in with both feet. That's why I enjoyed France so much—out in the real world; real problems; real people—I'd started to live." He frowned, pausing to think.

"I thought I was doing rather well until you kicked me out. That's how it is for people like me. Things usually turn sour if we're ever too confident or dare to relax."

Carlow understood what he meant. "We're not so different, you and I," he said, continuing to observe him. "There was simply less pressure to contend with when I started out. We were given licence to be young; irresponsible, too, if that was how it turned out. We weren't called upon to wrestle with an educational sausage-machine so consumed by its own insecurity that it only adds to the chaos waiting to devour us.

I've no axe to grind—other than to object, I suppose, to the tendency these days to forget basic human values. We're presumed guilty of just about everything unless and until we prove otherwise. And why would anyone waste his time trying to do that—unless for some obscure reason he wants to be accused of one politically incorrect *ism* or another?

Added to which, as I said, everyone knows Governments the world over are riddled with liars and cheats; that corruption is equally universal and that the Great-British infrastructure is not so much falling apart as being systematically dismantled by intellectual pigmies who couldn't survive if it weren't for our apathy.

My father *dragged* himself up by his bootlaces. Like so many of that generation he was a trustworthy man, neither eaten up by greed nor envious of anyone. It simply wasn't in his make-up to let people down. He was poor and sometimes unhappy, which might have been different, but he pressurized no one—certainly not for cash. In fact, he owned virtually nothing of value if you exclude self-respect. 'It's hello *slippery slope to oblivion* if you let money rule your life,' he once said. Soon after that I married Laura and from a purely mercenary standpoint have never looked back. Sadly, I was quick to forget just about everything he taught me."

He'd not just failed to listen to his father, he'd underestimated him.

"Where was I?" he continued. "Oh, yes. We form a new company—Carlow Mason Europe—and establish its headquarters in the chateau at Blaye. Were our intentions as we shall claim, CME would need capital, so we spread rumours of the flotation of the Group as a whole."

The initial moves would be simple. They'd buy the attention of the political Parties with contributions to their funds. Then, having established their bona-fides in this way, they'd move on to using every means at their disposal to bribe or blackmail every politician, civil servant, banker, diplomat or the like, whom they thought might be usefully *persuaded* to propose, promote or support their programme for change.

The financial transactions involved would be concealed behind a well publicized campaign designed, as far as the rest of the world was concerned, to enhance their trading profile with Europe. In practice, they'd be doing whatever proved necessary to ensure their success; enticing targeted individuals into their net. "Remember," he continued, "these people fantasize about a European bureaucracy with themselves in control. Once we have them hooked they'll be only too willing to promote our ideas. It may take longer than we'd like, but a period of hard work and a serious pot of money ought to see the dawn of the Single Transferable Vote, the removal of adversarial Party politics from a democratized Westminster, and no House of Lords."

Richard had only been half listening. "I'm with you until you begin laying out cash."

"Questionable transactions require creative accounting," Carlow said.

"I expect they do," Richard said quietly.

"You'd be employed by CME," Carlow went on. "Ostensibly to service and maintain its computers—hardware and soft. The installation in France, I've code named it Servant, will play second fiddle to another right here. I call it, Master. Our reported activities, some real, some not, will enable us to operate anywhere and in currencies of choice. We'll schedule the legitimate ones using Servant, confining the full picture to Master.

To be frank, if we could know in advance how complicated it's going to get and how long it might take, I'd forget Master altogether."

Richard stared up at the ceiling, his hands behind his head. "Something of a leap, I'd have thought, from bribing or coercing a few people to generating support for constitutional change, especially with Westminster and Whitehall lined up against you? Somebody's certain to blow the whistle before you even get started."

"On the face of it, yes, but there are more people on the take in high places than you might think—heaven knows I've dealt with enough of them over the years. Target them initially and it ought to be possible to escalate from there."

Richard sat up. "Is there something you're not telling me? Something you're planning to do to balance the odds?"

"Possibly," Carlow said, wishing it were true. "If I manage to recruit the team I want and get this thing off the ground, I'm prepared to offer you a million pounds; five hundred thousand up-front, the balance if we win."

Richard was amazed. "The money to be paid by you personally, disassociated from the companies, in sterling, into an offshore account of my choosing?"

Carlow smiled. "You certainly learn fast."

In for a penny, Richard thought, trying to contain his elation, "Make it a million up front and another when it's done—win or lose, and you've got yourself a deal."

"You're on," Carlow said instantly.

A few minutes later, Richard left Carlow questioning everything; even double checking the few pounds in his pocket before hailing a cab. Two million pounds and the Single Transferable Vote—an end to orchestrated bigotry and corruption at Westminster—astonishing.

But why come to him—go out of his way to do so, in fact? Carlow had spent twenty years of his life rubbing shoulders with people who ate and drank intrigue and double dealing. Why not use them?

FOUR

Carlow's journey home was bursting with summer. It was Friday; an early-June evening lying warm and content across the inviting prospect of a weekend with Laura uninterrupted by work.

He abandoned his briefcase on the umbrella cum hat stand that enjoyed pride of place in the hall. Laura had complained when he first brought it home, calling it too big, cast-iron and ugly; and saying she didn't want it in the house.

'It's Victorian and I like it', was how the conversation had ended; the first significant disagreement of their marriage. It had stayed. Arguing with Carlow had been as futile in those days as it was now. She'd grown as attached to it as he was.

"I'm on the terrace," she called when she heard him.

He dropped into the chair beside her, sniffing the air like an adolescent schoolboy released from school for the long summer holiday—happy to be home and free just to breathe.

The terrace extended the full width of the building, access to it via French windows in each of the library in the East wing, the dining room, drawing room and lounge in the main house, and the swimming pool in the West wing. He'd overcome all kinds of objections to obtain planning permission for these additions, his ingenuity where the planning committee were concerned, or shall we call it, *persistence*, finally prevailing.

At the outer extremities of the terrace was a low, stone-capped, brick wall with bow-fronted, stone steps down to the lawn at intervals along it. They'd added a pergola to the rear wall of the house; Laura's idea—roses, clematis, honeysuckle;

the ever present ivy a guarantee of shade should an English summer demand it. They already had reason to be grateful for its presence.

The back of the sprawling manor-house faced west of south overlooking the river, the lawn tiered three times as it sloped down to the water since Carlow's refurbishments, each tier bounded by a matching wall and further stepped access to the level below.

Beyond the West wing was the walled kitchen garden once so vital to the household and which now enclosed the tennis courts. He didn't play tennis, but when the sun was high and hot in the sky, he often came to sit with his back against its south-facing wall, its warmth through his shirt reassuringly therapeutic. He'd never known why, but he had some kind of affinity with old buildings and walls. They seemed to exude a strength that defied the passage of the seasons, creating an illusion of permanence, a sense of well-being. *God was in his heaven and all was right with the world*—although nothing had ever convinced him of that.

Adjacent to the East wing stood the old coach-house and stable yard which had once been home to the mighty shires that worked the Estate for generations before the advent of tractors. He pictured them snorting back there at dusk after long days at the plough. He loved its timelessness; its rough-hewn beams fashioned straight from the tree, its worn entrances and brickwork; its enduring, weather-beaten roof tiles.

He mourned the passing of the sounds and smells of the days when its bricks were fresh from local brick kilns, its beams confident in their new found importance; a time when people exalted in nothing more sophisticated than the smell of clean hay, thick walls around them conjuring the illusion of security.

According to Parish records, the last Lord of this Manor, an unsavoury character by all accounts, had owned the land for miles in every direction, controlling the lives of those for whom it had the capacity to make the difference between life and death—harvests filling granaries to overflowing or providing insufficient gleanings to supply the surrounding villages with flour throughout the long winter. In either case, *His Lordship* had never gone without.

Carlow was content with the sixty acres that remained; he and Laura having jurisdiction over none but themselves, with the exception, of course, of their small contingent of helpers. Mr and Mrs Williams lived in. She did the cooking and he was their man about the house. They employed a maid to assist her, three ladies came in from the village to clean, and two full-time gardeners looked after the grounds. Carlow enjoyed driving, limiting the opportunities of the owner of the local garage —their occasional chauffeur—who made no secret of his eagerness to take the wheel of the Rolls.

Carlow pulled down his tie, threw off his jacket, and headed for the kitchen. "Evening, Mrs Williams," he said, opening a cold beer. "I could eat a horse."

"Horse a la carte, Mr Williams always says," she chortled, her ample bosom heaving with amusement. "Begging your pardon, Mr Carlow. No—a whole salmon from Tesco; reasonably priced and plenty left over for the week-end. Mrs Carlow said with a salad—oh, and some wine—least, she put some in the fridge."

He smiled, retracing his steps to lean back in his chair, his head in the shade, his feet in the sun, looking forward to a cool shower before Mrs Williams' salmon and the evening with Laura. "I've invited a few people to stay next weekend," he announced. "A *bit of a do* to launch the new company, after which I'll dispose of my shares and call it a day. I won't bore you with the detail, but some of it's time-critical and could take some months—here." He handed her the guest list, not bothering to ask if the weekend was convenient for her.

Sighing in resignation, she began reading the list aloud. Consulting her first had clearly been too much to ask. "Geoff, of course; Graham Wright and Robert Barker—plus wives, Betty and Joan, the Chancellor of the Exchequer Peter Forrest and his wife—er, Fiona; Giles Morton your PR man. Do I know Tony Morrison—?"

"Son of Lord somebody or other. One of Geoff's contacts. I understand her Ladyship prefers to be known as plain Geraldine Wilder—in spite of the scandal."

"I don't think you should invite that sort of person."

"What sort of person?"

"Her sort—people who've been involved in public scandals."

"No politicians, then?"

She glared at him. "You know what I mean."

"I told you. She's one of Geoff's guests."

Laura shook her head, conscious that she was wasting her breath. "Wetherby—yes, Harry, isn't it? I remember him from Geoff's."

He nodded. "A yorkshireman; Chairman of the Labour Party—a surprisingly decent sort of bloke for a politician. He consumed vast quantities of beer, I remember, happily admitting that he prefers scotch and claret. Daren't be seen drinking it, though—it's bad for his image. And there are two at the bottom there, to be flown in from France."

"At the bottom where?"

"There." Carlow prodded the paper. "Andre from his father's Chateau Darrieux and what's-her-name, the girl?"

"Danielle Chappon."

"That's her—from the Chamber of Commerce in Bordeaux."

She handed back the list. "That's the lot then, is it—including Jane and Richard Wells?"

"No—for security reasons there are two more not listed. First the Prime Minister—"

She jumped as if he'd hit her. He reached for her hand. "What on Earth's wrong?"

She took a deep breath, struggling to regain her composure. "You arrange to fill our home with people without consulting me, including the likes of Lady whatever her name is—*that*—*that Wilder* woman, and then as if to deliberately add insult to injury, you invite the Prime Minister to join her for lunch."

"How many more times?" he insisted. "I didn't."

"Well, you agreed to her coming."

"Look, I'm trying to tie some loose ends. That's what this weekend is about. I told you—I'm going to retire. Anyway, the final name on *our* list is *your* friend Gordon Templeton. I intend to offer him my financial assistance—if you're sure he still needs it?"

"Ask him yourself."

"I'm going to need a couple of people with clout. Who better than him? Just mention my offer and ask him to give me a bell or drop into the office in the week. Oh, and before I forget," he concluded, "Go ahead and buy Chateau Darrieux for me, will you? The pension fund the real estate, the company the business."

"What do I know about French real-estate," she spluttered angrily—"or their vineyards?"

"It's not like you to turn down a lucrative commission," he added. "Why not fly the frogs back next week?"

"Mike, please! Do I have to be treated like one of your wretched minions?"

"Richard Wells is going," he added quickly, as if it justified something. "He'll hold your hand. Incidentally, when do you think you'll be speaking to Templeton?"

"When I can. You may not think so, but I've better things to do."

"Seriously—" he grunted, "Are you sure nothing's wrong?"

"I'm fine," she said sullenly.

He swallowed a mouthful of beer. "Look, why don't I put up the cash for that parasitic partner of yours to buy you out?" he said irritably. "Then both of us can quit."

Laura screwed up her face. "First you decide to offer money to a man you don't know—a civil servant, at that—not your favourite human beings—then in virtually the same breath you suggest assisting my *parasitic partner* as you call him, to buy me out.

Mike—what's going on?"

FIVE

Gordon Templeton wouldn't have been in Carlow's office but for his need for hard cash. Carlow had seen him on television and in newspaper photographs, and Laura had more than once described him—but their paths hadn't crossed.

He was grey-haired and grey-eyed, and mildly effeminate, but Carlow was quick to decide that rumours about his sexuality probably stemmed from a fastidiousness bordering on prim. However, he thought arrogant and ruthless was a more useful assessment.

"Extraordinary weather," he said, breaking the silence between them. "It makes you wonder about this global warming business, doesn't it? Are they right, do you think?"

"I tend to reserve judgement, these days, where so-called expert opinions are concerned," Templeton said. "Lloyds a case in point."

Carlow smiled. "Ah—good; Laura mentioned my proposal."

"She did."

"Too late for your brother, I'm afraid." He moved quickly on. "Debt, I understand?"

Templeton sighed. "Indeed—Lloyds had become a problem for us both."

"I see," Carlow said. "Rest assured, you're not on your own."

"One listens to one's advisors, I suppose," the civil servant added.

Carlow remembered how stubborn Laura had been when he'd advised her to avoid several of the syndicates at Lloyds. "I don't listen to any of them," he said, consulting his watch. "Still, best we press on."

"I can't pretend to understand the mathematics of these things," Templeton said, "but I'm told it could add up to as much as two million pounds over the coming three years. I've liquidated most of my investments as Mrs Carlow can confirm—" He paused. "A mere drop in the ocean, I'm afraid."

"So when do you retire?"

"Two years from now."

"Ah—but there's a decent pension, I imagine?"

Templeton smiled grimly. "Fortunately, yes."

"Right then," Carlow continued, "You can leave Lloyds to me. Are your family involved?"

"Not since my brother—but why would you do this; it's a great deal of money?"

"Mason and I founded the business to put a roof over our heads in the short term and make us rich in the long," Carlow explained. "And we succeeded on both counts, predominantly by exploiting the dishonesty of people in positions of trust—to be frank, Sir Gordon, individuals very much like you. The Great-British public don't know the half of what goes on in Whitehall and the City, do they? And that's to forget the shenanigans surrounding Parliament itself."

Templeton shifted in his chair but said nothing.

"We recently decided to arrange for the nation's future business to be properly conducted," Carlow went on. "To put the national house in order, I suppose you could say; clearing the way for a new generation of public servants to keep it that way."

He hesitated before going on. "A good many problems should evaporate overnight, and you, Sir Gordon, are ideally situated to make sure they do. It's a straightforward deal. I bail you out financially and you give me the benefit of your knowledge and influence—until you retire, at least."

Templeton shook his head. "Very much as I feared. I'm grateful for the offer, of course, but my answer has to be no—it would compromise my position."

"Your position was compromised a long time ago—we both know that," Carlow insisted.

"You won't rid the nation of corruption by blackmailing me," Templeton said wearily.

"Why on earth would I want to do that? As far as I'm concerned you accept or you don't."

Templeton sighed. "And what makes you think Parliament and Whitehall will work to *your* blueprint?"

"I don't have a blueprint; merely a new approach to government which seems to make sense."

"The United Kingdom won't become more equitable simply because it's obvious it should," Templeton added. "People the world over are inherently greedy, including British politicians and people like me. How could it be otherwise? You of all people should appreciate that." Carlow was amazed—a man in his position and so insecure.

"And you think I don't?" he said dismissively. "Look, I break a bone in my leg and I'm carried to a surgeon. Can he heal it? No. So will I be crippled for the rest of my life? Possibly—even though he knows better than most how to encourage fractures to heal.

You see our surgeon's no god. He has no power to heal. And you and I are very much like him. Who else could put a team together with the necessary training and experience, for example? Who else do you know with the capacity and will to initiate and fund this? And it's obvious if you think about it. A hundred years of political baggage has to go—along with the shameful misuse of public resources successive generations of *Honourable Members* seem to consider their birthright. That's when we're going to need people like you to step in. But not to line your own pockets," he added sharply. "Oh, no—to serve *real* people at last; forget the mythical species fabricated by politicians and their conveniently formulated statistical glue. They don't exist.

No—for the first time in your lives you and your cronies will be called upon to support a genuine democratic process—and that means accepting it and working at it until the majority of people accept it and work at it too."

Templeton produced a handkerchief and began cleaning his glasses. "You're nothing like the man I warned myself to expect," he said, carefully replacing them. "Altruistic, yes—like most entrepreneurs, but as improbable as it may seem, I find your argument persuasive. I'd very much like to assist, but I have to be sure you're fully committed. A failed attempt would cost both of us dear."

"And that's supposed to be news to me, is it?" Carlow said. "Jesus, man, I haven't banked five hundred million by being quite so naïve. With people like you at the helm it's no wonder the Country's in such a god-awful mess. I know you've checked me out—well, as far as you could—so we both know a successful outcome is possible if the right cards are played."

Templeton remained outwardly calm. "Even so, you're asking me to risk everything, including my pension. Why would I do that?"

"Oh come on," Carlow said derisively. "You're fucked—mentally, financially and I've little doubt in ways you'd rather not mention—or were you intending to spell those out for me too?"

Templeton screwed up his face. "I appreciate that success is more likely if we attempt this—"

"Bullshit—" Carlow interrupted. "—We do this now or see it imposed later by economic disaster. Logic may suggest that failure's inevitable, but a successful outcome is the UK's only hope—to say nothing of your own."

"So what's my collaboration worth?" Templeton asked. "In addition, I mean, to your covering my embarrassment at Lloyds?"

"Are you suggesting two million's not enough?"

"I'm simply stating the obvious. My cooperation will save a great deal of money and more importantly, time."

"Look," Carlow went on, "I'll pick up your tab at Lloyds as agreed, and throw in an extra half million if we're successful. But that's my final offer. And don't think I won't break you if you try to short change me."

Templeton visibly relaxed. "You need have no fear on that score. For the first time in my life profit to the nation would equate to profit for me. I'd find that spiritually uplifting."

He paused, his eyes fixed on Carlow. "Imagine for a moment that you've taken control of the family company following your father's untimely death."

Carlow frowned. What was he banging on about now?

"Having been employed by it for years," Templeton continued, "it's suddenly yours to manage as you choose. Bear with me," he insisted. "I promise you it's worth it. Then—a bolt from the blue, you're invited to tender for a Government contract—a demanding baptism and there's no time to lose.

Supplying the British Government has long been an activity in which the firm has excelled. So, you reach for the telephone —lawyers to examine the form of contract, accountants to consider the financial pros and cons—and with all that in hand, you analyze the demands it will make on your workforce and invite cover figures from sub-contractors you will use if you win. Then —preliminaries complete, you sit down with your staff. Double checking as you go, you add sensibly for overhead and sparingly for profit until it's ready for signature and subsequent despatch. You're on your way, confident your bid is the most competitive on Earth—nothing to be done except sit and wait.

So—?" he added quickly, "—do you think you could win?" He paused. "You see, this hypothetical example is to illustrate that where Government contracts are concerned, the answer would have to be no.

Why? Well, would you believe there are some forty organizations, for the sake of argument let's call them *brokers*, most using London as a permanent base, one or other of whom decide who wins each Government contract? Indeed, nothing of substance is ever *won* unless and until it's sanctioned by at least one of them. I'm also led to believe no other financial centre in the world is as accommodating to them as London, where they've *recruited* a small army of *helpers*—coerced into providing their services, or suitably rewarded with no questions asked.

These *brokers* are multi-national *fixers*, bribery and blackmail the principal tools of their trade, which means that having failed to make the telephone call your father used to make to agree their percentage, your tender would be disqualified—the contract awarded to an alternative name on their list."

"So are you saying all this is fact—these people exist?"

"I am and they do; their *helpers* strategically located to ensure their success. Hard to believe, I know—to say nothing of expensive given we all foot the bill."

"I doubt bribery and blackmail ever come cheap," Carlow said thoughtfully.

"As good fortune has it," Templeton continued, "one of these *brokers*—a certain Desmond Yarwood—happens to be a member of my Club. He specializes in the placement of Government contracts and has been active for years."

Carlow thought about it. "You're serious, aren't you? These people exist."

"Oh, yes."

"So are you suggesting what I think you're suggesting?"

"Probably. You see he can call upon politicians, diplomats, civil servants, bankers, lawyers—domestic *and* international. In short, an influential group of people listen when he speaks. As I said, bribery and blackmail are the principal tools of his trade."

"I still find it hard to believe. And this man will instruct his people to act on our behalf?"

"If you're prepared to pay his price."

Carlow rang Mason. "Are we ever invited to tender for dubious Government contracts?"

"Oh, come on, Mike, just about every Government contract is dubious in one way or another."

"No—I want to know if we've ever been offered a contract you knew to be fixed?"

"Of course we have, and before you ask, the answer is no. Look, you know as well as I do—we're not contractors and we've never worked for Government. Bought things off them, maybe—but invariably at public auction.

Now you mention it I saw something about this on TV—a while ago now—a documentary, I think. It suggested there are organizations which, not to put too fine a point on it, specialize in *inducing* Government departments to award contracts to those they represent—their *friends*. There was nothing in the press after the broadcast, which I seem to recall thinking spoke volumes in itself."

SIX

The weather was at its June best when the first of Carlow's weekend house-guests were delivered to the Manor. Mason had been at a planning meeting out at Reading, and had volunteered at the last minute to collect them from Heathrow. Jane had been arranging a car when he called, his offer doubly surprising given his often stated dislike for the French—the male of the species, that is. She'd assumed he was out to steal a march on the other male guests—adding spice to the weekend as he might have put it.

The object of his attention, Danielle Chappon—was a provocative, intriguing young women. Sun-tanned and slender, she was twenty five years old, her short, mousy hair accentuating her round face, full lips and insistent blue eyes. And to describe her voice as merely *sexy* would have been to understate its impact.

Mr Williams relieved them of their luggage and showed them up to their rooms, Carlow saving his welcome for when they came down, before leaving them with Mason and Laura on the terrace.

Ignoring Mason's efforts to impress, Danielle was soon discussing the house with Laura who spoke fluent French. But if exploring old buildings wasn't to everyone's taste, the need for something less academic hadn't been overlooked. Big and rangy with something of historic interest round every corner, the house was ideally suited to accommodating guests. You could swim in the indoor pool, work out in the gymnasium or play snooker and tennis, while the less ambitious could stroll in the grounds or take a boat from the boathouse on the undemanding river.

Alternatively, if you preferred to do nothing much at all, you were free to settle for television or the library.

By seven o'clock everyone was dressed for dinner and enjoying drinks on the terrace; the meal scheduled for eight. Far beyond the trees along the river, the vast, overarching dome of East-Anglian sky was changing from grey, pink and orange to black, red and gold as the dying sun slid slowly but inexorably off the edge of the world.

Accompanied by the ring of crystal and the intermittent popping of champagne corks, conversation and laughter floated down to the river on the warm evening air, the ducks congregated below the boathouse objecting to the impertinence repeatedly and loudly.

Laura circulated, followed as ever by every male eye, coinciding with Jane and Richard at the bar by the pool. "Hello, Richard Wells," she said, smiling up at him. "Have you ever seen such a sky?"

"Hello yourself, Mrs Carlow," he said, not even glancing at the sky. "I hardly recognized you with your clothes on."

Jane prodded him in the ribs.

Laura laughed. "And it seems I have to put up with him next week in France. Behave yourself," she whispered, taking his arm and leading him on to the terrace, Jane instantly abandoned to follow in their wake.

Laura interrupted Lady Morrison. "Forgive me Geraldine, but I don't think you've met my husband's secretary, Jane Garside?" They exchanged greetings. "And this is our computer expert, Richard Wells," she continued, nodding in his direction.

"Jane, this is Andre. Andre's family own Chateau Darrieux. We'll be sampling their wines at dinner." Andre bowed stiffly. "I believe you know each other?" she aimed at the two men. "Richard will be with us next week, Monsieur. I expect you'll have much to discuss. Now, if you'll excuse us, we ought to find Danielle."

She shepherded Jane away, Richard sorry to see her go.

"Geraldine can be too much of a good thing," she whispered to Jane. "Overbearing at times—at least, so I'm told."

Carlow was in conversation with the unlikely combination of Harry Wetherby and Sir Gordon Templeton, pouring a Darrieux claret from a crystal decanter. "Try this," he said to Wetherby. "It's the '82—decanted this morning."

He offered a glass to Templeton. "Sir Gordon?"

"Thank you, no, Mr Carlow," the civil servant said. "I'd prefer to confine myself to a small glass with dinner."

Carlow nodded, happy to wait for Wetherby's reaction. "We hope to acquire the Chateau to house our European headquarters," he added—"not to mention supplying us with this." He held his glass up to the light.

"Aye," Wetherby said, looking Templeton in the eye. "Fizzy stuff's overrated. Made *for* poofs *by* poofs, my old man used to say."

Unmoved, the Cabinet Secretary continued to sip his champagne.

"Far side of river may be unfashionable," Wetherby went on, "But my money says Carlow's just the man to give it a boost. Expect y'like a drop of the good stuff y'self, eh, Sir Gordon?"

Templeton smiled. "I drink very little, actually, Wetherby; a dry sherry before dinner—rarely more. Although I freely admit to a weakness for single-malt whisky."

On the opposite side of the room Mason was suffering the insult of being assigned to nurse-maid Robert Barker, Graham Wright and their wives, introducing them to everyone as Carlow had insisted. He'd been tempted to refuse, "your dirty work as usual," his disgruntled reaction. "*Barker, Joan, Wright and Betty,*" he kept saying to himself. "Sounds like a bloody vaudeville act."

The French girl having gone out of her way to make clear her disinterest, he'd chosen Fiona Forrest as an alternative target.

He invariably set himself targets at functions like these. It was an essential part of the fun. When they'd last met she had yet to become a politician's wife, and he'd never had one of those. She was better to look at than he remembered, and according to Wetherby her indifference to her husband's presence was par for the course.

And he found himself rapidly warming to the idea; formulating a plan of campaign as they went in to dinner. If he ever managed to rid himself of the music-hall act, he'd concentrate his aim.

Carlow waited for everyone to settle. *"For what we're about to receive may the Lord make us truly thankful and ever mindful of the needs of others,"* he recited—satisfied that the only words he knew were entirely appropriate.

Overcoming her initial misgivings, Laura had delighted Mrs Williams by giving her a free hand with the food, killing two birds as it were—avoiding the formal atmosphere caterers can bring to an occasion. There was hired help with the bars and for serving at table, but people from the village had been recruited to generally fetch and carry, there being no shortage of volunteers keen to *nose round* the Manor.

Their motivation aside, it was thanks to Mrs Williams they were there. She had most eventualities covered, and now excelled herself with a four course meal that did more than full justice to the Darrieux wines. They'd variously reached the cheese, the port, the cigars and the brandy, when Carlow decided it was time to play the good host. He knocked on the table and got to his feet. "Ladies and Gentlemen. I believe Carlow Mason Europe is our twentieth company." He saw Graham Wright nodding confirmation. *"CME,* as I'm sure we shall call it, is the vehicle we've chosen to embrace the new Europe."

Richard smiled at the smattering of hear hears, listening with interest as Carlow suggested that Government appeared less than enthusiastic at times, but it was clear our future lay with the peoples of Europe. He believed none of it, of course. Who seriously thought joining forces, so to speak, with France and Germany had anything to commend it? The fatuous arguments in favour expressed by politicians, to say nothing of European so-called *commissioners* pressing for the expansion of a wholly undesirable bureaucracy, were difficult to accept. In practice, these people were salting away millions at the expense of taxpayers right across Europe, while, here at home, Westminster and Whitehall happily continued on their profligate way.

"On Monday, Laura flies out to Bordeaux to discuss our acquisition of Chateau Darrieux," Carlow continued. "We've used it before as some of you will know, but we now look forward to it becoming our permanent European headquarters." Another burst of hear hears of an unmistakably Wetherby vintage. "Mademoiselle Chappon and Monsieur Darrieux—Danielle and Andre—have come from Bordeaux in this connection, especially to be with us." The welcome they were given was less enthusiastic. "Tomorrow, the Prime Minister and his wife will be joining us for lunch to mark the occasion, so I take this opportunity to invite you to raise your glasses to CME, the future, and our friends across Europe."

Everyone got to their feet and joined in the toast.

He ended by informing them that the terrace and grounds were floodlit if anyone cared for an after-dinner stroll, but whatever their preference, he and Laura were happy to welcome them as guests in their home. Acknowledging polite applause, he made his way to the kitchen to thank Mrs Williams. "Make sure your helpers are well fed and refreshed, won't you?" he ended. "Tomorrow's certain to be a very long day."

She nodded, beaming her satisfaction.

Returning to the terrace, intent on another glass or two of claret and a few frames of snooker, he was accosted by Tony Morrison who was taking full advantage of their hospitality. "Carlow, old son," he slurred. "A privilege to take wine with yourself and old Geoff. Hand it to you, m'dear fella—brilliant—no other word—abs'lutely brilliant."

"It's very much fingers out, these days, Morrison; Europe

or no Europe. Mustn't let Johnny Foreigner get away with too much."

"Might have said it m'self, dear boy. Give 'em an inch, eh? Eh?"

"D'you know." Carlow slapped him on the back, "You're just the sort of chap we need for a project like this."

"Abs'lutely, old son—jus'say the word."

"I'll mention it to Geoffrey, then, shall I?" Carlow winked and tapped the side of his nose. "Discuss it tomorrow."

"Oh, quite," Morrison mumbled.

Carlow ended the conversation. "Let's join the others. Get ourselves a drink."

Morrison might have forgotten his own name by morning, and needed no second bidding. Carlow left him at the bar and spoke briefly to Mason. "I'm off to play snooker. Get Morrison to meet us in the library after breakfast, will you? Early, mind; the Prime Minister's unlikely to be late."

Had the media witnessed events at the Manor that Friday evening—free hospitality to be followed by a Prime Ministerial visit; politicians and the most senior civil servant enjoying *jollies* at a multi-millionaire's country mansion, the newspapers would have been filled with suppositions and accusations too wild to imagine. And that was to ignore what they might have made of Tory Chancellor of the Exchequer Peter Forrest and Chairman of the Labour Party, Harry Wetherby, joined in mortal, snooker combat with the Cabinet Secretary in tandem with their host.

Carlow re-spotted the black yet again for the surprisingly talented civil servant—helping himself to another glass of claret, secretly complimenting himself and Mason on gathering so many of the people they were going to need under one roof this early in the proceedings.

"By God—no wonder Government's got problems," Wetherby said in mock disbelief, "Cabinet Secretary plays snooker all day. Forrest, have words with your mate at Number Ten, will you? The Whitehall wonder here's too good by half."

Everyone smiled, with the exception of Forrest who was finding it hard to accept that a socialist could have the capacity to amuse. Even the fussy Templeton was enjoying the Wetherby sense of humour, albeit ably assisted by a bottle of good malt.

"As a matter of interest, Forrest," Carlow said casually, "how do you see us coping with the threat from the East—terrorist, I mean, as well as economic?" He was tempted to press for an answer, but could see little point. Anything passing Forrest's lips in the guise of a personal opinion had almost certainly first to be sanctioned by the Party.

"Well played, partner," he added, interrupting his own train of thought as Templeton ended another frame, this time easily at the brown. "Fancy another wager, Harry? That's a fiver you owe me."

Wetherby screwed up his face. "What, against you and Steve Davis here? Not bloody likely." He handed Carlow five pounds. "So, Forrest," he went on as they re-racked the balls, "Carlow's asked a fair question. What does your lot intend to do about what's brewing in the East—if we're not blown to smithereens while you're thinking about it?"

"I'd call that typical of a socialist," Forrest replied, the affected, public-school accent somehow uncalled for.

"That's as maybe," Wetherby added, lighting a cigar. "But what price y'so-called *inward* investment then, eh? Wages'll have to be slashed by eighty pence in't pound if we're going to survive—whatever your Right Honourable friend likes to think." He shrugged. "Either way we lose. And you can bet your bottom euro no bugger in Brussels is capable of dealing with it, either."

"We have to become more efficient," Forrest blustered, "police the money supply and public expenditure, maintain low inflation and ensure public sector wages are strictly controlled. Then we can look forward to sustained economic growth and low unemployment."

Wetherby shook his head. "So how does that stop terrorists?"

"Our security services are second to none."

"Dear God," Wetherby growled, looking round the room. "We really do have a problem; and it ain't civil servants playing snooker all day." He looked hard at Forrest. "This ain't a minor annoyance, y'know—and you're bloody mad if you think it is."

Jane and Laura were drinking champagne by the pool with Danielle Chappon, Giles Morton and Morrison still at the bar. Mason's vaudeville act had taken a final encore and retired to bed at last, leaving him in the lounge with Andre, Richard, Fiona Forrest and Geraldine Wilder.

"Would you care to see the old stables?" he asked Mrs Forrest. "No horses I'm afraid, but a delight nonetheless."

"Isn't it too dark?" she asked.

"No—Mike's proud of his floodlights and I see there's a moon."

And he was right; the night was as warm and almost as bright as the day preceding it. She took his arm to negotiate the steps at the end of the terrace in her high heels, hardly a leaf stirring as they strolled under the archway at the entrance to the yard, the old buildings and beech trees behind them stencilled in sharp relief against a full moon.

Mason found himself whispering. "What a marvellous night."

"Isn't it," Fiona Forrest echoed softly, "Listen to that silence." As they stopped to listen the silence was broken by the hooting of an owl. "What an incredible place."

"You have to hand it to Mike," he said. "Everything's been perfectly restored. I keep telling him it ought to be used, but he insists he wants to keep it as it once must have been. Laura was the last to keep a horse here, but that was years ago."

"Are we allowed inside?" she asked.

A heavy door swung smoothly open on recently oiled hinges, revealing a steep wooden staircase. Mason tried the switch he found immediately inside and a light sprang to life.

Fiona hitched up her skirt and started up the stairs. He followed close behind. "I'm not dressed for this," she complained. He could see nothing to complain about.

They walked the length of the long hay loft overlooking the yard on one side and the stalls on the other; all beautifully timbered. "What a shame it's so empty," she said.

"What a shame there's no hay," he echoed.

She looked up at him. "Why, Mr Mason, what could you possibly want with hay?"

His face creased into a smile. "I haven't rolled a woman in the hay in a very long time."

She stood on tip toe and kissed him on the mouth. "You've been feeling horny all evening, haven't you, darling?"

He'd never known a woman to be quite so direct. "Shall we find ourselves a car or something, or go back to the house?" he asked. As far as he was concerned there was no question of refusal.

She was out of her skirt and down on her knees in an instant. He produced a condom and lost control of his hips. She paused to look up, a mischievous smile on her face. "Easy boy, easy."

He lifted her to her feet, turning her body to face the wall. She twisted out of his grasp, exhaling heavily. "No, darling, I prefer to see what I'm getting."

Their mouths merged and his hands found her breasts. "Give it to me," she gasped. "Do it—oh, yes, make me—make me. Please—more—harder, harder—I— " She began to shudder uncontrollably and he was racked by orgasm himself.

"You certainly know how to please a girl," she said, taking deep breaths. She was clinging to him, her body continuing to move against his. "That was so good."

"Any time, Mrs Forrest. Any time at all."

She took another deep breath. "An entertaining evening, all things considered—Mademoiselle desperate for Laura and getting myself laid. Just think," she added. "The whole weekend ahead of us." She slid a hand down between them. "And have no fear, I can take all you can give—horizontally, that is."

"What about your husband?"

"It's your birthday, Geoff Mason; poor Peter's a queer—*gay* if you can stomach the word. I'm the token woman—retained to safeguard his image—free to do what I like as long as I'm discreet. Why don't we put ourselves back together and finish this in bed?"

He laughed. "Your place or mine?"

SEVEN

Mason loaded a tray and went to join Carlow on the terrace. It was five minutes to eight o'clock and the Saturday morning sun had cloaked the Manor in its early heat, offering the promise of another fine summer day. Laura had gone to find Mrs Williams to confirm the day's menus.

Mason was full of himself as he set about his breakfast. A willing woman, perfect weather and the weekend ahead.

Engrossed in his newspaper, Carlow failed to detect Mason's mood. "Did you have a good night?" he asked without looking up.

"Sorry—?" Mason mumbled, busily munching on a slice of generously buttered toast.

"I said did you have a good night?" Carlow repeated.

Mason swallowed a mouthful of coffee. "Didn't I just. The delectable Fiona made very sure of that."

Carlow lowered the newspaper, his voice held to a whisper. "Christ, Geoff, if Laura gets to know—"

"There won't be any comeback," Mason added calmly, looking around to make sure no one was listening. "Our precious Chancellor's a bender."

"You try telling that to her," Carlow said.

"It's true—as God is my judge."

"So why would he proposition an ugly bugger like you?" Carlow cursed himself as he said it for the unintended pun.

"He didn't, you *nerd*; Fiona told me."

"One of your crusades, is it? He's queer, so it's down to you to screw his wife?"

Mason continued to look around. "Look—are you going to listen to me or not?" Carlow waited. "Thank you," Mason grunted. "They have what's apparently known as an *open* marriage. He entertains his *friends*, and she's free to do what she likes."

"So they lead separate lives," Carlow added. He had the last word. "Morrison too pissed to get up, is he? Incidentally, why did you invite them?"

"Why did I invite who?"

"Them—Wilder and Morrison?"

Mason looked hard at him and then at his watch. "Oh, no—not guilty, M'lud. Right— Morrison after breakfast, you said, and that's what you get."

Carlow seemed not to hear. "Hold the fort."

Throwing his newspaper into a chair, he strode in through the dining room, ran up the back stairs and into the linen room at the end of the house, leaving the door ajar. Two minutes later he watched Templeton's bedroom door open and Forrest slip furtively away.

Mason and Tony Morrison were close behind Carlow when he eventually arrived in the library. Mason grinned. "We thought it best to catch you straight after breakfast."

Carlow ignored him. "Morrison," he said cheerfully. "And how do we find you on this beautiful new day?"

The Honourable Anthony began massaging his temples as vigorously as shaking fingers would allow. "Bit of a head, actually, old boy."

"Reference last night," Carlow went on. "Geoffrey and I would like you with us in this."

'Would we, indeed?' Mason thought.

Morrison frowned. "Doing one's bit, wasn't it—setting out one's stall?" His eyes lit up—surprised to find himself remembering anything at all. "Yes—Europe—that was it—mustn't let Johnny Foreigner get away with too much."

Carlow interrupted. "Receptions and seminars for all the

right people. You know the score."

"As you say," Morrison agreed.

"Ten thousand plus expenses?" Carlow added. "How does that sound? You scratch our backs we're bound to scratch yours."

Amazed and disinterested in equal measure, Mason joined the conversation. "Come on, Morrison, what do you say?"

"Good, that's settled, then," Carlow added. "We can finalize the details when Laura gets back from France."

"A small advance, perhaps—?" Morrison began. "Beggars, choosers and all that?" He shrugged his shoulders. "Frightfully sorry, m'dear fella—awf'ly bad form."

"Sunday morning, all right?" Carlow enquired. "Shall we say ten per cent?"

"Capital—*Capital*—" Morrison laughed, disappointed when they failed to appreciate the joke. He screwed up his face. "Leave it to you, Geoffrey, dear boy, to spell it out for the spouse. Best coming from you. The old-girl's rarely keen on what one chooses to do."

Carlow and Mason arrived back on the terrace in time to see Forrest come into the dining room with his wife, Templeton making an appearance a respectable few minutes later. Carlow couldn't think why they bothered. None of the guests were remotely interested in how or with whom they chose to spend their nights.

"Come on, Geoff," Carlow demanded, "why did you invite Morrison and his woman?"

Mason stared at him. "What's wrong with you this morning? I told you—I didn't."

Carlow helped himself to more coffee. "Then who the hell did?"

Mason shook his head. "If it was neither of us, it must have been Jane—or one of her girls."

Carlow joined Templeton at the dining room table. He would speak to Jane later. "I thought we'd meet in the library," he said quietly. "A quick chat before the PM arrives. Richard

Wells will be responsible for the management and distribution of funds, so I'd like you to talk him through what Yarwood has to offer."

The civil servant nodded. "Incidentally," Carlow asked. "Where did you learn to play snooker like that?"

"I've played since I was tall enough to reach the table," Templeton said, knowing Carlow had little interest in how well he played snooker. "One develops a cue action, I suppose, and a feel for the angles, after which, in common with most things, it's about application and hard work. May I be serious for a moment?"

"Of course," Carlow said.

"I just wanted to say how surprised I was by Forrest's response to your question about terrorism."

"I expect a number of honourable members are burying their heads in the sand—too many, no doubt, " Carlow added, posing a question as much as making a statement.

Templeton sighed. "I fear the modern politician is rarely first class."

Carlow shuddered. Other than in bed, apparently. He glanced at his watch. "Please—I do understand. Shall we say ten minutes?"

For all his seniority, Templeton clearly viewed much of what happened at Westminster with the utmost distaste. It was definitely no act.

Carlow left him to finish his breakfast and headed for the library.

Laura made her way back to the dining room to eat breakfast with Danielle. The French girl was eager to see Carlow Mason acquire Chateau Darrieux—largely motivated, it was clear, by her obvious ambition where Laura was concerned. The Chateau's contribution to the Bordeaux economy was insignificant, but employment on that side of the river was a regional priority, enabling her to claim it as part of her brief.

"Ca va?" she enquired of Laura in that sex laden voice.

"What fantastic weather," Richard said to Andre as they came in from the terrace, one glance at Laura ending all thought of weather.

Anxious to see the room cleared and the table reset for lunch, Laura reminded them of the Prime Minister's visit. He was scheduled soon to be arriving for drinks before lunch.

Serious as ever, Andre claimed important people never visited the Chateau; certainly not Prime Ministers. According to him nothing exciting ever happened at Blaye.

Richard thought Prime Ministerial visits were hardly exciting.

"When the sale of the Chateau is complete," Andre went on. "I hope to travel—London, New York and Rome if I can."

"Yes," Richard observed, "It's good to get away from the rat-race now and again."

"Rats?" Danielle exclaimed, her eyes burning with conviction. "Men are the rats. Always they think of themselves and make the world full of problems. My English is good, Laura?"

Laura nodded to her and smiled. Like so many young people, they were so sure of themselves—so certain. They'd discover —much later, of course—that youthful priorities tended to be largely superficial and altogether less significant than they'd imagined. Then they'd be looking for something new to aspire to; something real and fulfilling; harder for each of us with each year that passed. "Most of us discover the truth about our lives after it's too late," she added. "Few of us find what we're looking for." She paused. "Right—let's finish breakfast and go for a swim."

"I'm afraid you'll have to excuse me," Richard said, not wanting to leave. "I have to meet Mike."

Gordon Templeton picked up a morning newspaper from the selection on the table. The library was cooler than he'd expected, a consequence, he decided, of the absence of windows in the wall facing east. The shelves appeared to be filled with politics, modern history and economics, plus, as far as he could see at a glance, everything from the classics to the latest best seller.

Carlow came in behind him. "So what do you make of our little collection?"

"Archer appears to reside quite happily between Amis and Barnes," he said dryly.

Carlow smiled. So there was a sense of humour.

The civil servant turned to face him. "Which of you is the librarian?"

Carlow laughed. "You're talking to a man who thought Flaubert's Parrot was written by John Cleese—or was it James Herriot? No—no books and libraries are best left to my wife."

They settled in armchairs by the open French windows watching Mason, Wetherby and Fiona Forrest on their way down to the boathouse. Mason had mentioned in passing that he'd offered to row them upstream to the village for a quick beer before lunch.

Carlow looked at his watch as Richard came in, Templeton noticeably straight faced. "Now that Richard's here, Sir Gordon," he began, "Perhaps you'd be kind enough to fully acquaint him with Mr Yarwood. We haven't retained him, of course, and it's possible we won't, but as Richard will be responsible for the organization and distribution of funds, I'd like his input—and it makes sense to update him before we move on."

Templeton looked down his nose as if divulging state secrets to someone Carlow had dragged in off the street. Richard was quick to interpret the expression. "I believe collaboration and trust are the *operative* words, Sir Gordon," he said.

Carlow smiled. "Sir Gordon—?"

Templeton grunted, unused to being reprimanded. "My apologies, Mr Wells. One has to be so careful these days. A word in the wrong ear—I'm sure you understand?"

"Indeed, *one* does," Richard responded facetiously. "My welfare is as much bound up in this as yours."

Glancing at Carlow, Templeton went on. "I'm not sure how much Mr Carlow has told you, but influencing those with the power to change the way the nation's business is conducted is paramount. Without converting them to a different way of thinking, we can't hope to see the introduction of the single transferable vote or end the power of political parties to dictate how we live."

Richard laughed. "Ah—so Yarwood *converts* people to a different way of thinking, does he? I rather thought his speciality was *screwing* them?"

Templeton looked at him and sighed. "There's no place in government for confrontation for its own sake, Mr Wells. It invariably ends in the wastage of resources better allocated elsewhere."

"Allocated to bastards like Yarwood, you mean? So we should happily forgo what we've every right to expect in exchange for our taxes, should we?"

Carlow was quick to intervene. "I'm sure there are a multitude of opinions regarding what needs to be done, but I wouldn't want anyone to get the idea that we're here to do them —concealing some kind of desire to take over, as it were; because nothing could be further from the truth. Yes—of course we want our system of government to change—turn over a new leaf, so to speak—ridding us of the Yarwoods of this world— but it will be for the electorate to decide which route we take. I'm sorry, Sir Gordon," he went on, "but it's very important that we're united in this."

"I quite agree," Templeton said. "It's easy to get carried away by our personal priorities. Mr Carlow is right, Mr Wells, our aim is to see parliament reorganized, not to control it—to ensure it can no longer be manipulated for personal ends."

"So this man, Yarwood," Richard continued, "has sufficient influence along the corridors of power to persuade our MPs—"

"And civil servants," Templeton interjected.

"Indeed, yes," Richard added. "So he has sufficient influence in *all the right circles* to persuade MPs and civil servants to propose and support a comprehensive programme of constitutional reform?"

"He does."

"It seems improbable to me."

Templeton looked at Carlow.

"Sir Gordon intends to fully establish what he's capable of delivering," Carlow assured him.

"And what he'll cost?" Richard asked.

"Yes—and what he'll cost."

"And you've agreed to do that, have you Sir Gordon?"

"I have."

"Then perhaps you wouldn't mind clarifying something for me?"

The civil servant eyed him suspiciously. "If I can."

"Given that Yarwood's activities are *questionable* at best," Richard continued. "How is it possible for him to operate when *you*—the British Cabinet Secretary—are privy to both what he does and the methods he employs?"

Templeton answered a little too quickly. "A few years ago my position was compromised; not, I hasten to add, over state secrets, money or anything of that kind, but I'm sorry to say Yarwood found out. As I explained to Mr Carlow, for better or worse he happens to be a member of my Club and I found myself being blackmailed. An ugly word, Mr Wells, but it is what transpired.

In my considered opinion, however, should Mr Carlow avail himself of this man's services, as I firmly believe he should, his activities will cease. If that happens I'll be pleased to expand on what I've said. In the meantime, I hope you'll find it possible to bear with me."

Richard shook his head as Templeton left the room. The man was bent in more ways than one—unlikely to be lying about affairs of state and money, perhaps, but how could they check? "We seem to be left with rent boys or something equally distasteful," he suggested to Carlow.

Carlow nodded. "And that's probably as close to the truth as we'll get."

"Then there's his mate, Yarwood," Richard added. "What if we end up paying him a fortune for nothing?"

"Look," Carlow said. "let's get their meeting over and see

where we stand. It's clear he wants us to succeed."

"Indeed—but if we didn't know he was compromised, we certainly do now. It's very definitely a percentage up-front for *Mister Yarwood*—if we retain him. Ante-up too much and it could be the last we see of him—Templeton too, for that matter. There'd be nothing we could do."

EIGHT

The church clock was striking eleven when they arrived at the Manor; the Prime Minister and his wife driven in one car, his Special-Branch minders occupying the others. Having exchanged the usual pleasantries, Laura invited his wife on a tour of the house, leaving the men free to do as they chose.

Here—destined to eat at his table—a guest in his home, was the personification of everything Carlow was now committed to change. He suggested a walk in the grounds prior to a drink before lunch. The Prime Minister accepted, dutifully attended by Templeton and Forrest.

Carlow was surprised to find himself keen to discover who the man was; what made him tick; who lived his life behind this particular version of the political mask? There were a host of questions he was tempted to ask—hypothetical, of course—the last thing he wanted was to invite the language of evasion to trip off another politician's tongue as *mint fresh* and plausible as ever.

Sidestepping questions with conviction was a talent with which they were born—an art form; a means of lying that set the political virtuoso apart from the run-of-the-mill MP. Their ramblings were accepted as if they must be informed; intelligent—a largely unwarranted gesture of respect that flew in the face of logic; as if everything they had to say had to have merit—had to be relevant to people's everyday lives.

Brown-suede shoes, heavy-brogue; Cambridge-blue shirt; cotton, with party-coloured cravat; Bespoke, twill trousers; British-leather belt, (animal humanely killed, of course), or optional braces. He smiled to himself. It was probably both. In truth, he was doing his best to close his mind—to understand why the Prime Minister had opted for the clothes he was wearing. They'd agreed to dress casually, but he'd clearly immersed himself so deeply in the creation of a casual image, that the image itself had become the matter for debate.

The cavalry twill trousers and vee-knecked sweater, along with the dreadful suede brogues and awful cravat, might have been chosen for him by a Cabinet committee. There had to be an explanation. Perhaps, like Templeton and Forrest, here was a man anxious to be seen as *the right sort of chap.*

Did the Prime Minister not agree, Carlow said—that the industrial emergence of Taiwan, Indonesia, Korea and India, to say nothing of China and the Eastern-bloc countries—when added to the escalation of terrorism and the unparalleled rise in indebtedness here at home—personal and government—combined to threaten not only our short-term stability, but our entire way of life?

He went on to explain that, on the previous evening, he'd received an answer from Forrest regarding our strategy for dealing with the situation, that was patently meaningless. He'd taken this to indicate either that we had no strategy, or alternatively, no realistic conception of what lay ahead.

Forrest resented his comments but lacked the confidence to dispute them in front of the Prime Minister. They interrupted their stroll to sit on a bench by the river.

"Mr Carlow," the Prime Minister began. "We face a wide range of problems, not just within the community itself, but also in our dealings with the rest of the world. The situation in the East is one of those problems."

Carlow thought this a masterly understatement. If only it could have been described as, *one of those problems*.

"Relevant countries will eventually join us," the Prime Minister continued, "but the process takes time: often too much, I have to agree, but the Community will enlarge. Meanwhile, we have to deal with the world as we find it; encouraging the growth of democracy when and wherever we can, at the same time seeking to demonstrate the positive advantages of a market economy."

"Laudable, I'm sure," Carlow said. "Quite splendid, in fact; but it doesn't begin to answer my question. I submit that you simply have to begin spending less time and taxpayers' money on the machinations of government itself and the world at large. Indeed, it's imperative you begin to concentrate our limited resources on catering for the needs of the millions here at home."

Taking a deep breath, he began to go deeper. Multi-national companies, including those among them that were essentially British, could smell subservient workforces and cheap raw materials whole continents away. They saw the east as a shortcut to dividends and profits and had rushed to stake claims. Advantage to the British people was the last consideration—if and when, indeed, it was a consideration at all.

"*In practice,*" the Prime Minister insisted, "we're actively engaged in increasing the size and number of available markets; reducing the likelihood of international conflict; creating jobs for our people, and widening our sphere of influence with each step we take. But to succeed in those markets, we have to become more efficient, and it falls to my Government to make the fact clear."

Carlow abandoned any last attempt to conceal his exasperation. "I'm sorry, but I believe it to be criminally naive to suggest our interests can or ever will interface with those of the East. Multi-national companies and many like my own here at home, are casting people aside like so much confetti. *Downsizing* you call it—a fanciful term meaning to create unemployment; a fashionable, self-defeating lunacy which can only end in the destruction of Britain as we know it. Whole industries will transfer abroad or be forced to close down; downsizing the downsized.

He went on sarcastically. *'What's your trade, old chap?'*

'Works Manager.'

'Really? I've got the very thing. Here's your brush and shovel. Tidy the place up; keep Britain great.'

'But I'm an Engineer with thirty years experience.'

'Dime a dozen, dear boy, especially of your age.'

'But I'm only forty-five.'

'Exactly. Time for retraining and you've come to the right place.'

'But—'

'No buts—take it or leave it. And don't expect unemployment benefits if you refuse honest work.'

Cynical? Undoubtedly. Sarcastic? Definitely. Exaggerated? I don't think so. Foreign capital already controls too much of what ought still to be ours. *Inward* investment, you call it. And yet you're already propping-up foreign companies with taxpayers' cash. Is that investment? Is it the best we can do? And do we seriously expect them to stay here when the *funny money* runs out?"

Calmness became the politician's defensive priority. "A point of view, I suppose," he said guardedly, "but wildly inaccurate." He smiled condescendingly. "If only it were that simple."

Carlow was becoming annoyed. "I'm saying, Prime Minister —it's a very long way from simple. These organizations dictate our economic policy, our fiscal structure, our foreign exchange regulations, and even worse, were that possible, they control the lives of an ever increasing number of the British people. How much more can we take? Is this something to be proud of? Do we honestly need it? Will it keep us secure?

The answer on all counts has to be no. And yet our Government—*your* Government, seems incapable of recognizing what is undoubtedly fact."

The Prime Minister had neither expected nor enjoyed the attack. "Sir Gordon?" he said flatly, giving himself time to formulate an answer. "How do you see this?"

The civil servant blinked, the glint in his sharp, grey eyes like that of a predatory animal sighting its prey. He'd brought these matters to the attention of Cabinet before; the Foreign and Trade Secretaries in particular. His opinion had never wavered, not least for many of the reasons Carlow had outlined. The emphasis in world trade was shifting, the evidence suggesting the shift would be permanent. The process was going to hurt. He would go so far as to say he thought our way of life may not survive it. But in the final analysis what concerned him most was that in order to combat its effects—to compete with low wage economies anywhere in the world, incomes at home would have to be slashed.

How was that possible, he wondered—lower wages, salaries and fees in a Society strangled by debt and encouraged without check to borrow still more? Wasn't it nearer to the truth to say we were close to disaster? Swelling the ranks of the unemployed was no answer. Part time work resolved nothing. Our once mighty manufacturing base was all but defunct. And retraining was too slow. Indeed, as many people were asking, retraining for what? Cosmetic cuts in public expenditure might have the potential to mollify a few people, but it wouldn't scratch even the surface of the problem. "The practical hurdles are obvious," he continued, "But it's the structure and performance of Parliament which have to be changed."

"Yes—" Carlow added into the silence that followed, his voice rising in volume as he was consumed by his fears. "For the first time in our history the Western economies are experiencing a decline directly generated by industrial progress in the East. The British people have already witnessed our insane willingness to surrender to the bureaucrats of Europe; watched our assets and business go the same way, but they've yet to realize their hopes for the future have been transferred to the East. When they do, and make no mistake the day will very soon dawn, they'll accept nothing emanating from Westminster. And you, Prime Minister, will go down in history as the man who had the courage and intelligence to save us, or the man who sold us out trying to serve the interests of capital, too much of it foreign or invested elsewhere."

He stood up and began to pace up and down. "Our labour

force won't shrink to fit the lack of demand. And you can't blame them for embracing a property based, greed orientated way of living—a state of mind encouraged by successive Governments, sustained by obscene levels of taxation and escalating debt. Neither can they be despatched on some kind of theoretical slow boat to China. The crisis we face isn't the world reaching a new equilibrium. It's not even the reshuffling of industry from West to East. That's unavoidable. It's our *heads-in-the-sand* failure to prepare for it and the period of transition which are likely to destroy us."

He paused. "I'm sorry, Prime Minister, but by failing to preserve our international independence while subscribing to an idealistic, European illusion, you're systematically depriving us of the will and the means to stand on our own two feet.

Our future is bleak. Indeed, it may already be too late to head-off the disaster now on its way. Failed methods won't save us. And the electorate understandably trust none of you. How can they when the majority of MPs of every so-called, political *persuasion* think and behave more or less exactly as you do? Indeed, when did we last hear a politician offer an honest opinion about anything?"

He shook his head. "I realize objectivity is difficult not to say impossible when faced with outmoded Parliamentary procedure, but I agree with Sir Gordon—the structure and performance of Parliament have to be changed."

The silence in the shade of the trees along the river, until then punctuated only by their voices and the birds luxuriating in the warmth of an English summer morning, was broken by the sound of a cabin cruiser making its way upstream to the village in good time for lunch. The man at the wheel, oblivious to their presence, was smoking a pipe, the sweet smell of tobacco smoke wafting across to them as he navigated the bend in the river. The smell came to Carlow from another world—a world he was old enough to remember and had once enjoyed. He suggested they continue their walk; turning back towards the house.

The Prime Minister finally broke his silence. "What you're suggesting, if I've understood you correctly, is that the transition from where we are now as an industrialized nation to the new equilibrium which will be ultimately reached through the passage of time and the evolution of trade, given the emergence of industrial power in the east, will be so destructive of western society in both the short term and long, it will create vast unemployment and threaten our entire way of life. As you see it, this will result in civil unrest across Europe and an exponential escalation in the risk of global conflict. You believe, therefore, that we're duty bound to initiate a comprehensive programme of domestic restructuring. Only this can safeguard our people when the EC breaks down—which it must, of course, if your hypothesis is correct. That's the basis of your argument, is it not?"

"Broadly speaking," Carlow said.

"If I accept it, then—for the purposes of debate, how should my Government begin to proceed?"

The first shot stopped them in their tracks. As they heard the second, the third and the fourth, Geraldine Wilder fell to the ground almost before they realized she was there or that the Prime Minister had been hit by the first.

She'd come out from the house, her stroll down the lawn scarcely worthy of note, walked casually up to the approaching group, engrossed in their discussion, and shot the Prime Minister from close range.

It had seemed to happen in slow motion and yet was over in an instant, the only sounds in the world those echoing gunshots. The reaction of his minders had been swift and deadly. She'd been given no time to retreat or think of firing again. She was dead.

NINE

Two weeks had passed since guests at the Manor had witnessed ambulances speeding down the lawn; since the onset of an immeasurable silence into which twenty minutes later had come the news that Wilder's bullet had ended the Prime Minister's life.

The media had been visiting and re-visiting the same well-trodden ground: the enormity of our loss; how he'd devoted his life to the people of Britain; countless interviews with family, colleagues, political observers and personal friends each feeding the flow. There seemed no end to it.

The newspapers had even wanted to photograph the spot where he fell, where Wilder had lain after his minders had shot her, their persistence nauseating and disruptive.

What had possessed the woman? She'd had nothing to gain —at least nothing of which anyone claimed to be aware. There'd been an affair with a junior minister; a man with a wife and young children sacked by the Prime Minister on the threshold, it was said, of a brilliant career, but the significance of that was unclear. And how had she known he'd be at the Manor? None of the guests had been told in advance.

Carlow's memories of these events would always be the same—the stark disbelief that something so destructive and futile could happen, added to the man's blood in the grass and on those awful suede shoes.

Despite the shooting, Templeton had gone ahead with arranging his meeting with Yarwood, at the eleventh hour asking Carlow and Richard to attend. Yarwood, it seemed, had insisted on a fee of fifteen million pounds.

"So you had your niece arrange for Wilder to be invited to the Manor?" Carlow said when Templeton arrived. Jane had confirmed there was no other way it could have been done.

"I did," Templeton replied easily. "But I had nothing to do with the shooting."

"You'd be talking to the police if I thought you had," Carlow informed him. "So—tell me why. She was hardly your type?"

Templeton expected nobody to speak to him like this, and was tempted to say so, but then he hadn't risen to be Cabinet Secretary by granting himself the luxury of saying what he thought. "It was a favour to a friend."

Carlow frowned. "Which friend and why?"

"Is it necessary to go into that?"

"You arranged an invitation to my home that ended in murder—now which friend and why?"

A friend—a senior colleague in Whitehall who happened to be a friend—Templeton insisted—had a longstanding habit of paying for sex. Wilder had provided the women, trading complimentary liaisons for introductions to potential clients from the right social set.

Carlow decided to let the explanation pass without pressing further for a name. Templeton was unlikely to claim what could be easily disproved. The women in question, the civil servant went on to say, were carefully selected and available only to those previously vetted or who came with the recommendation of one or more of her clients.

"If their financial capacity matched their social status, no doubt?" Carlow added.

Richard interrupted. "But how does that explain why the man came to you?"

"We often talked about sex," Templeton replied. "More than once about his obsession with these women. We'd been close, you understand, since Eton and Cambridge."

Richard glanced at Carlow as he spoke. "But why Carlow Mason?" he asked.

Templeton laughed. "It entertained VIPs on a regular basis, and I had access to it. My niece was employed in Mrs Garside's office at the time, thanks to Mrs Carlow."

"Why thanks to Laura?" Carlow asked.

"She introduced her following a request from my brother."

Carlow caught Richard's eye.

"Mrs Carlow explained your unusual method for selecting guests to be invited to corporate functions," Templeton continued. "I confess to the mild deception that prompted her to do so—after which it was the simplest of matters to have the Morrisons invited to the Manor.

Wilder was inordinately keen on the idea. It seems she had prior knowledge of Mr Mason's *exploits*, and saw the company as a potential source of revenue, I suppose. So—with it promising to be advantageous to an old friend and colleague, I was happy to oblige. But I knew nothing of Wilder's hatred for the Prime Minister, if that's what it was. It was public knowledge, of course, that he'd dismissed one of her lovers from Office—but I knew nothing more."

"So it was you who told her he'd be at the Manor?"

"It was."

"And did her women operate at Westminster *and* in Whitehall?"

"Apparently."

"Leading Yarwood to believe you were in the habit of procuring sexual partners for friends and colleagues?" Richard added.

"Unfortunately—but I had no relationship with Wilder, nor was I acquainted with any of these people. As I said, it was simply a favour to a friend."

Yarwood arrived as the civil servant ended. He was in his late forties—about the same age as Carlow, Richard guessed, but that was where any similarity ended. Of barely medium height, he was thirty pounds overweight, with greased down hair and ring-bedecked fingers which served to indicate precisely what he was—a *wide boy* as people used to call them; a sophisticated wide boy in a Savile Row suit, maybe—but for all that a wide boy. He claimed to be capable of exerting irresistible pressure on those MPs and civil servants who'd served him in the past, in addition to having a virtually unlimited capacity to influence others when required.

Acting on Templeton's recommendation, Carlow offered him the full fifteen million—five million in advance.

Yarwood promptly turned it down, saying that he'd no intention of underwriting the four to six million he claimed was destined for third parties. He didn't see why he should; there being a greater risk in the deal than he was used to accepting.

Carlow refused to vary the offer.

"How do we know you won't take the money and run?" Richard asked him. "Either way, the ten-million pound balance won't be paid until the requisite Bill has passed the House of Commons."

Yarwood responded with a howl of derision. "And that's my guarantee, is it?"

He finally relented, but only following extensive prompting from the otherwise silent civil servant.

Richard had doubted the logic of dealing with the man, and his grovelling civility to Templeton did nothing to change his mind, particularly as he supposedly held the whip hand in the relationship. "Where would you like to receive payment?" he eventually asked him.

Yarwood gave him details of a Cayman Island bank account, plus a long list of names. There were effectively two lists: the first, a group of MPs and civil servants he'd reason to believe would do what they were told; the second, according to him at least, equally influential but yet to be *pressed into service*. "I suggest you delete anyone you wish to exclude," he continued, "after which we begin with the first group, moving on to the second as soon as those in the first have been recruited.

I'll set the wheels in motion when I receive five million pounds and the green light from Sir Gordon; subsequent phases to begin following further consultation—again via Sir Gordon.

Best we don't meet again."

Glancing at Richard, Carlow nodded his agreement, at which Yarwood abruptly shook his hand and left, Templeton walking him to the lift.

Running an eye through the list—resolved to scrutinize it in detail as soon as he could—Richard made a mental note to investigate Templeton's relationship with Yarwood. There had to be more to it than he'd admitted.

Laura finally set out for Bordeaux with Danielle, Andre and Richard. Had Carlow been less insistent she wouldn't have gone. "I need you to take a close look at the Darrieux business," was all he would say.

Landing at Bordeaux Merignac out of a clear midday sky, they were driven straight to the Chateau, by-passing the humidity and heat of the sweltering city. Laura explained to Richard on their air-conditioned journey, that she was ill qualified to judge whether or not the Chateau was a desirable acquisition, or what might represent a sensible offer for its goodwill. That was for him and Mike to decide. She knew virtually nothing about wine and even less about vineyards. Her only concerns were the profitability of the business—or lack of it, of course, and the condition of the buildings. "I enjoy a glass of wine," she added as if to reassure Andre, "especially champagne and claret, but I've no idea at all where either is best produced."

As the car turned into the vine-flanked driveway up to the Chateau, Richard imagined himself coming home. In this latest of his fantasies Laura was waiting for him on his return from Venice or Rome, or some other exotic location. It didn't really matter where; his imagination was as flexible as it was vivid since the morning in the penthouse.

Only two hours earlier he'd had them joining *the mile-high-club* on an explosively orgasmic flight out of Heathrow. They'd made their intentions clear before the wheels left the runway, consummated their membership on the flight deck at thirty thousand feet, and enjoyed each other a second time exactly to coincide with the moment of touch down. His timing had been perfect—simultaneous orgasm as the tyres hit the ground.

It was easy to see why he fantasized about her, but no matter how much he fought it—and he'd managed to convince himself he was fighting—she invariably did or said something to trigger another. This was the closest they'd ever been—her legs crossed; her warm thigh against his. He could see himself featuring in the Guinness Book of Records for the longest recorded maintenance of a full scale erection. A prisoner of his imagination and intoxicated by her perfume, he concentrated as hard as he could on anything but her and waited for his arousal to subside.

The Chateau seemed somehow smaller and less grandiose than he remembered it. It needed a face lift, that much was clear, but it stood like a proud sentinel watching over its vines, vigilant and unflinching; peering out beyond the river to where the weather came from. As their luggage was carried into the house by a family retainer who looked as old as the building, Andre's parents came out to meet them, reminding Richard of his first visit.

Somewhere in his mid-fifties, Monsieur Darrieux was a man weather-beaten of countenance and permanently unsmiling. He'd been courteous enough in that stiff, rather too formal French way, but as Richard had discovered later, he'd felt threatened by them—suspicious of people who came from a world he'd come to distrust. He was at ease with his vines, but remained aloof, abrasive even, intent on demonstrating that here in his birthplace he was in charge.

His wife, Andre's mother, was a gentle, petite woman, grey-haired and unassuming, insecure like her husband, but blessed with an extraordinary smile. She seemed to smile for them both. It cast its spell over everyone it touched, Richard no exception. She was exactly as he imagined his mother might have been, representing the Darrieux family well with that smile. But it had lost its magic spontaneity since his last visit, leaving him saddened to see it so speculative and anxious.

Free at last to escape from the car, he introduced them to Laura. She spoke to them in French, isolating him from them, leaving him to the building which once they were inside was exactly as he remembered it—nothing had changed; its rooms cavernous and silent—peaceful and cool in welcome contrast to the atmosphere outside. The brightness of the day streamed in through tall, once optimistic windows, illuminating the silence; finding too much of the house empty—cared for and clean, but so obviously redundant. These were proud people in a proud building; their lives echoing in their footsteps as they concentrated on Laura. He could almost taste their anxiety. Did she understand, he wondered, that the sun, the rain and the vines had always controlled their existence? Did she appreciate that their lives ebbed and flowed with the seasons and the needs of the wine, and that this building in this place was all they'd ever wanted; the home they loved but could no longer maintain?

The family history was etched on their faces; indelibly imprinted on the fabric of the house as they surrendered to the inevitability of the end of the line. Everything and yet nothing was left for them here. This day had been a long time coming, but now it was here they were anxious to avoid shrivelling up and dying like forgotten grapes on the vine.

He'd come to this place to consider its suitability for CME's purposes, only to find himself more concerned for the people who'd be leaving it behind. He'd been given licence to disrupt their lives knowing he could install a company anywhere given the latest technology. Why couldn't economics leave God's real people alone?

Abandoning them finally and with considerable reluctance, he climbed the stairs to look out over their vines, the clouds, now few in number, still crossing the sky on their inexorable journey.

After breakfast the following morning, Laura and Danielle were driven into Bordeaux, the temperature in the low thirties, the humidity intense. Even the breeze off the river offered no respite as they arrived at La Place de la Bourse and the Chamber of Commerce. Laura was surprised a building with such an imposing facade could be so basic and inhospitable on the inside. They met Danielle's superiors in a cramped room two hundred and something, which even with open windows was too hot for comfort, Laura soon to discover how little there is to choose between the bureaucracies of Europe.

They welcomed the prospect of Carlow Mason acquiring Chateau Darrieux and promised written answers to any queries regarding the business or the region she might care to raise. She raised a whole series, the answers to which, in French, were promised for delivery to the Chateau within twenty-four hours. Unfortunately, however, it would take rather longer if she preferred them in English. They seemed disappointed when she accepted them in French.

They offered to introduce her to a suitable lawyer—an offer she was quick to reject; to express the hope that Danielle was continuing to be of service; she confirmed that she was; and to offer her lunch. She refused the offer; relieved when the conversation ended, preferring the humidity outside the building to the oppressive atmosphere within.

"What's wrong with these people?" she asked Danielle. "Why do they have to be so officious? Why not simply answer my questions?"

Danielle shrugged her shoulders and smiled. She'd often asked herself the same question, tempted to suggest Laura visit the offices of the Conseille Generale if she wanted to see real French officialdom at work.

As they made their way back from the river in search of a quiet place to eat, there were builders at work everywhere. Hidden behind boarded up frontages and sheeted over scaffolding, their raised voices, drills and hammers echoed continuously as if specifically to add to the stress and discomfort caused by the humidity and heat.

They decided to eat at a restaurant spilling out under an

awning into a small square with an obscure monument at its centre. One bottle of wine led to a second, despite Danielle's warnings, and Laura smoked a cigarette, which she did only rarely, trying to put recent events behind her—to relax and forget. The square, an oasis in a desert of buildings, quickly filled with people eating and drinking and trying to stay cool. Chatter and laughter echoed around them as the French, lunch-time ritual fascinatingly unfolded, with its multi-coursed meal and seemingly endless flow of wine.

It was difficult to imagine these people working again before morning, but the ritual was no sooner complete than they were gone—swallowed up by the beckoning walls of the City. They too retraced their steps, Laura wishing she'd heeded Danielle's warnings as her head began to spin.

She woke, regretting the wine but surprisingly relaxed. The French girl's flat was much as she'd imagined it: one bedroom, a tiny bathroom, plus a kitchen/dining/living room, all on the first floor of a three-storey building, its green-shuttered windows overlooking a narrow, tree-lined street.

It was after six o'clock and Danielle was nowhere to be seen. She ran a bath and was luxuriating in a warm breeze from the half-open window, lazily drying herself when the French girl returned. Finding Laura asleep, she'd taken the car out to the Chateau to collect a change of clothes for her. It would enable her to dress less formally for the rest of the day. She sighed, relieving Laura of the towel. "You have such a beautiful body. I would like to be beautiful like you."

Laura turned to face her with a wide smile on her face. "But you are."

"No—everything it is wonderful. Everyone they look at you and want to make love."

The noise and bustle of the day went down with the sun; the air cool and inviting, the vast galaxy of stars appearing to creep closer. As they walked together through the quiet back streets of Bordeaux, a gentle breeze was tip-toeing off the river, exploring the old city under a cover of darkness which seemed to Laura to lack the atmosphere of menace she'd experienced in other cities by night.

They came at last to a short flight of steps down to a softly lit basement. Danielle signed her in as her guest, and they were shown to a table in a corner, in an alcove.

"I'd rather like to smoke," was the first thing Laura said. "Do they have English?"

Danielle was back with them in an instant.

As they examined the menu, smoking, listening to music while sipping champagne which had been chilled to perfection, the pressures in Laura's life began to recede. She was enjoying the champagne and soon the entrecote bordelaise. "When in Bordeaux," she said happily.

Danielle pulled a face.

"Something wrong?" Laura asked.

"Entrecote with champagne––?"

Laura tossed her head, laughing. "Oh, didn't you know? We Carlows take champagne with everything."

Danielle had come into her life when she needed a friend; someone she could talk to; someone other than Mike and his preoccupation with himself and his business; someone who would understand how she longed to be herself, without pressure, without responsibility to others or having to concern herself with what people thought.

They finished eating and, refilling her glass, Laura watched couples dancing to music so bewitchingly relaxing and softly seductive that at first she failed to notice. But as they moved to and from the tiny dance floor, she became suddenly aware that all of them were female. She turned to look at Danielle, who was looking at her. "So are you––?"

Danielle smiled. "Does it offend you?"

"No—no, of course not. No—so in your flat, when you talked about making love—w-were you—?"

"Yes––I am sorry."

Laura sipped her champagne and lit another cigarette, not

knowing what to do or what else she could say. Danielle rummaged in her purse before lighting one too.
"What's that?" Laura asked.
"Marijuana. I smoke it occasionally when I need to relax."
"It helps?"
"But yes—like a bottle of good claret. Here—"
Laura hesitated, studying the girl's face; seeking reassurance.

They left the club in the early hours of the morning, intoxicated by the marijuana and too much champagne. Refusing at first, Laura had finally accepted Danielle's invitation to dance. She'd had teenage crushes at school; joined in pubescent experiments in dormitories and that sort of thing, but this was quite different. That had been girlish and until now long forgotten. This was a woman desiring her body, and whatever she tried to tell herself, she found it exciting.

All her inhibitions had vanished when the car collected them, Danielle closing her arms around her, tentatively at first, expecting resistance, but Laura was experiencing the same wanton excitement she'd experienced in the penthouse with Mike. She hadn't wanted to make love—she'd wanted to fuck.

She wanted to fuck now.

TEN

Richard thought the Chateau would make a perfect European headquarters—although he doubted they'd ever need one. It was more or less self-contained, far enough off the beaten track to offer relative privacy, and as close to an international airport as he thought they'd want to be. Its buildings needed work, but he was ready to recommend it.

"I'm obviously no expert," he'd said to Andre, "and I do realize that wine—at least, some of it—gets better with age, but even I can see you're overloaded with stock."

Andre claimed their wines were inferior to most produced on the Bordeaux side of the river. His father refused to accept it, or the prices on offer. Having spawned an ally like Andre, it was easy to see why Monsieur Darrieux might have lost the ability to smile.

On the English side of the channel, Carlow couldn't leave the Manor without playing cat and mouse with the media. Working from there was the obvious answer, but Jane would have to move in for it to be a workable solution. Accommodating as ever, she'd no sooner arrived than they were bombarded with newspaper reports and photographs of Laura in the arms of Danielle Chappon at what was being described as a *well-known club* in Bordeaux.

She refused to come home when he telephoned; so adamant about it, it was hard to see why she'd taken his call.

The first person he met on his arrival at the Chateau was the unsmiling Darrieux. He brushed quickly past him with an abrupt nod of his head, Richard faring little better as he showed him up to her room.

She was smoking a cigarette and neither looked at him nor spoke. "We have to talk," he said firmly, throwing the window open as far as it would go, flooding the room with fresh air and light.

"We drank champagne, smoked marijuana and had sex," she said. "Is that what you wanted to hear? Well—it's true, and I can't wait for the next time." Knowing how much he hated her smoking, she lit another cigarette.

She was so clearly set against him that he began to feel ill. Hurrying downstairs, he left the building and began wandering between endlessly identical rows of vines like a mortally wounded animal searching for somewhere to die. The man who had everything suddenly had nothing.

Even as he realized reasoning with her was futile, his emotions were screaming for him to make her come home. She couldn't have forgotten what they'd been to each other. He was met by Richard who'd come out to find him. "It's true," he told him blankly. "Every word of it's true."

Richard could think of nothing to say. What did you say in circumstances like these? "She's confused," he said at last. "It's hardly surprising after everything that's happened."

Carlow waved his arms. "She's behaving as if it's given her life a new meaning." He paused. "Oh, fuck it—let's buy the place and get home. Apologize to Darrieux for me, I behaved like a pig. Say there was an emergency. Tell him anything you like. We'll keep the staff on and pay what he's asking if he agrees to complete by the first of next month and stay on for the harvest. I'll find an agent, or somebody, to put a figure on the stock."

"I'd like it," Richard said, surprising Carlow.

"You'd like what?"

"All of it," Richard said seriously, "Stock, buildings, business —the lot."

"Since when?"

"The first time I came here, I think."

"I see," Carlow said, studying Richard. "We'll talk about it later. Now—tell the French bitch I need a room at the Chamber of Commerce—a room, a telephone, and an English speaking secretary for a couple of hours this afternoon. I'm going there now. Let's see if she's capable of more than fucking my wife," he added bitterly. "I'll send the car back for you. I want us back at the Manor in good time for dinner."

He turned, rounded the corner of the building and was gone.

Richard was beginning to feel tired as he went indoors to Laura. It was Danielle Chappon who answered when he knocked at her door. He spoke to her first. "Mr Carlow has gone into Bordeaux and wants you to leave. He's decided to buy the Chateau and needs a room at the Chamber of Commerce with a telephone and an English speaking secretary. I suggest you organize that now. There's a lot left to settle," he added, looking at Laura, "and we'll be leaving tonight."

He'd informed Andre and his father of Carlow's decision, passing on his apologies and provisos, Monsieur no less expressionless than usual on receiving the news.

The French girl gave Richard a neatly typed list of answers to Laura's queries about the region, the Chateau and its business—along with copies of its audited accounts. The name of the family's lawyer was soon in his briefcase, and Andre had agreed to fax the schedule of stock.

He thanked them. He had to leave now, but he would be back as soon as he could to tie any loose ends.

The secretary was waiting for Carlow when he arrived. Not to be too unkind about it, she was sour-faced and unattractive, her dyed, auburn-red hair pulled to the back of her head in a bun, she peered at the world through ultra thick lenses perched on the end of a rather prominent nose.

She made no attempt to hide her belief that the exercise was beneath her. Working for an Englishman, multi-millionaire or not, was demeaning enough without reducing her status to that of a temp, but she spoke English well and was capable of shorthand at remarkable speeds.

They were interrupted by the telephone. Jane had called the Chateau and been redirected by Andre. Dismissing the French woman, Carlow told Jane about Laura before explaining that they were preparing to leave and he wanted her to make sure Mason would be at the Manor when they got back. If he could, he was to arrange for Fiona Forrest to be with him. Jane was also to let Templeton know he'd call him at seven. The car was to be at the airport, but if anyone asked, he was out of the Country on business and she didn't know when he was likely to be back.

Richard confirmed Monsieur's willingness to stay on for the harvest, adding for good measure that he'd also arrived at a ballpark figure for the stock. Carlow nodded, but Richard thought it unlikely he heard.

Nobody spoke after take-off, an air of gloom enveloping the cabin as Carlow slumped motionless in his seat and stared out of a window.

ELEVEN

Mason was sitting by the ingle-nook with Fiona Forrest, a cigarette in one hand, a large scotch in the other. Jane was up-dating them with what had happened between Carlow and Laura in France, Carlow upstairs on the telephone to Templeton, Mrs Williams making them tea.

"I think I'd prefer another *large* gin and tonic," Fiona Forrest said apprehensively.

It had been five minutes past seven when Carlow and Richard arrived back at the Manor, Carlow making a bee-line for the telephone in his bedroom; spoiling for a fight. "So his heart-broken supporters have forgotten him already, have they?" he said sarcastically. The statement was greeted by silence. "So who'll get the job?" he demanded. The silence continued. "I said who'll get the job?" he repeated, reminding the startled civil servant that he expected answers to questions, not silence. The one-sided conversation was doing nothing to improve the atmosphere between them.

"Forrest," Templeton eventually replied, too easily persuaded that he was being left with no choice. "But it has to remain confidential until after the vote."

Prior to returning to Bordeaux, Richard reminded Carlow of his offer to buy the Chateau. To his surprise, Carlow agreed to sell without a moment's hesitation or further debate. This off-hand way of dealing with things was becoming increasingly common since the break-up with Laura.

The weather was gloriously benign when he arrived back in

France; soft and mellow, less intense by far than it had been in July and August. The grapes having escaped disease and unforeseen circumstance, time itself appeared to be holding its breath waiting for them to arrive at the peak of perfection.

Spring had been wet, the summer long, warm and dry with occasional rain, and it was suitably settled in this space before autumn. A gentle rain now would be too much to ask; a deft, final touch to what some were saying had the potential to be an outstanding year. As always, the fate of the wine lay in the timing of the harvest.

Monsieur Darrieux greeted Richard without smiling—especially without smiling Andre might have said on this occasion, as everyone waited for him to give the order to begin. He'd lived with the decision all his life, making it personally for more than thirty years. Too early and the claret would be inferior— too late, risking hailstorm and frost—they might end the season with no crop at all. He watched and waited as he'd always done.

In contrast, Madame Darrieux was following her daily routine without an apparent care in the world. Her smile had regained its radiance since Carlow's decision to buy. She clasped Richard's hand in both of her own as if to include him in her happiness. He kissed her on the cheek—surprised when she blushed.

He'd decided which of the Chateau's rooms to use as offices before leaving England, despatching Servant's hardware ahead of him. Now he was free to choose his personal quarters, drawn first and last to the rooms he would always look upon as Laura's —their South facing windows overlooking the main acreage of vines. Finding it hard to concentrate knowing she was almost certainly close, Richard asked Andre if she was living with Danielle in Bordeaux. Andre said rumour had it she'd bought a house, but he knew nothing of the French girl. He telephoned the Chamber of Commerce on Richard's behalf in search of an answer.

Richard found them together when he arrived at the address Andre had been given. Shaking hands seemed too formal, so he opted for self-conscious hugs and kissing both on the cheek.

Laura seemed pleased to see him. "This is a pleasant surprise," she said at the door.

She looked tired. "I'm here to install a computer," he told her, aware of the obvious tension between the two women.

"Can I get you a drink?" she asked.

"A beer would be good," he said, studying her closely. "How are you both?"

She consulted Danielle. "We've been fine, haven't we?"

The French girl said nothing.

Following the sale of her business, Laura had acquired this house and another on the Lizard in Cornwall, planning to spend part of the year in each. The ratio would very much depend on the weather. "Are you here on your own?" she asked him.

"For two or three days."

"Let's have dinner one evening, then, shall we?" she said. "You can give me all the news then." She turned almost apologetically to Danielle. "You don't mind if Richard takes me to dinner, do you?"

Danielle shook her head, still saying nothing.

Noting the expression on her face, Richard decided to give the impression his schedule was pressing. "I ought to get back," he said firmly.

Laura was clearly disappointed. "Oh, must you?"

He swallowed the last of the beer, looked at his watch and stood up. "No choice, I'm afraid. I'll wait to hear from you about dinner, then, shall I?"

The Chateau was a hive of industry when Richard emerged the next morning. Attempting to assess individual performances now would be impossible, but he nonetheless wanted to see everyone at work before concentrating on Servant. "Is there anything you need?" he asked, after telling Andre that *he* personally was to become the Chateau's new owner.

Andre greeted the news with a look of sullen indifference. "Father would like new barriques."

"Barriques?"

"Oak casks."

Finding an early replacement for Monsieur was obviously going to be crucial. "Get them," Richard insisted. "Get whatever you need."

After an hour preparing for the arrival of electricians, he was called to the telephone. They were expected at midday and he wanted to be precise about the instructions he gave them. Laura was on her way over and had replaced the receiver before he could stress how busy he was. Telephone engineers were due tomorrow, and even she couldn't be allowed to disrupt his schedule.

The electricians were unloading their van when her taxi arrived. As might have been predicted, he was unable to hold their attention as she made her way into the building, but an amalgam of his morceaux de French, their English, his previously chalked crosses and some gesticulation eventually communicated what he wanted them to do. Monsieur Darrieux had used them before, so he was relatively confident about leaving them alone.

Up in his room, Laura sat down on the side of his bed. "How's Mike?"

"Busy, of course, and the media are a pain, but, yes, he seems fine."

"Everyone else?"

"All in good spirits." He waited. "Look, Laura," he said finally. "You didn't come here to discuss people's health."

"Sorry," she said. "I'm having a bad day. May I have a drink?"

"Coffee?"

"No—wine, champagne—anything."

"Forgive me, but I don't think you should. You've already been drinking, I can smell it on your breath."

She took a cigarette from her handbag, abandoned the idea of smoking it and burst into tears. "I'm supposed to ignore everyone but her," she said. "She'll make my life hell for coming here to you."

He sat down beside her. "Don't tell her, then. She's frightened she'll lose you, that's all this is. And she's not the only one," he muttered.

She stared at him.

"Well, surely you—?" He paused in mid-sentence, his longing more intense in that moment than he'd ever thought possible. "Everything about you excites me. I want you, and it's been this way since the morning in the penthouse.

He paused. Laura said nothing.

"Oh, you'll be mine if I wait; if I'm patient." He held her at arm's length. "You've simply been to bed with a woman and found it exciting."

She smiled, wiping her eyes.

"Meanwhile, you have to stop abusing your body with champagne and marijuana," he continued. "I can't bear the thought."

She began repairing her make-up, her eyes bright with tears.

As she climbed into the taxi he wound down the window and closed the door behind her. "I'm sorry to ask you this, especially now, but I promised Jane and Mike that I would.

Did Templeton quiz you about the Carlow Mason routine for selecting guests? You know—people to be invited to PR functions and the like?"

TWELVE

Carlow had gone from not expecting an answer from Templeton to getting one that very much surprised him. Jane met him at the bottom as he hurried downstairs. "Sorry, Mike," she said. "I appreciate this isn't a good time to ask, but how long do you think you'll be wanting me to stay?"

He looked at her blankly.

"Me—here at the Manor—how long?" she repeated. "The office ought to be told. We don't want my being here linked with Laura walking out."

"Oh I see—yes—yes, until Christmas, then, say—if it's all right with you?"

"No—that's fine. Incidentally, have you considered moving to a different bedroom? You might find it easier when you wake in the mornings."

He frowned and shook his head. "It's a case of grin and bear it, don't you think?"

She studied his face. "If you say so."

He was dreading the prospect, wrestling with his emotions, closer than was comfortable to losing the fight. "I'm sure you're right," he said after briefly pausing to think, "but I can do that anytime, can't I—if it seems to make sense?" He tried to bundle his feelings aside. "Now then," he added quickly, hoping to sound positive. "How would you feel about supervising the running of the house?"

"Why me?" she asked.

"Well, it won't supervise itself, will it?" He put an arm round her shoulders. "What would I do without you?"

They joined the others in time to hear Richard expounding a theory about Victorian, child-labour—standing in the inglenook with his head up the chimney. Winter would see a blazing log fire there. It was rarely allowed to go out once the weather turned; its huge chimney an essential part of the central-heating as it climbed to the roof through the heart of the building.

Memories of what was beginning to feel like another lifetime came flooding back as Carlow stood there—bottles of claret breathing on the hearth; music; Pavarotti; Streisand—for a long time Laura's favourite—the ring of crystal—guests refilling their glasses; shadows flickering across the ceiling and dancing down the walls. Had it really come to this?

An overwhelming sense of disbelief forced him back to the present where the open French windows and setting sun on the terrace confirmed that it had. "The newspapers got it right for once," he announced as Richard emerged from the fireplace. "Laura's taken to sleeping with—well, to the best of my knowledge, with one woman so far." He sounded close to exhaustion. "So ends any chance of them leaving me alone. Jane's agreed to supervise the running of the house, so I've decided to work from here for a while. Bit of a mess, really, but you're welcome to join us. They'll make less of Jane being here if you're staying here too."

He joined Fiona Forrest at the bar at the back of the room. "Oh, and you might like to know Templeton says Forrest is bound for Number Ten."

"He's taking the piss," Mason hissed. "Well—who in their right mind is going to pick Forrest? Sorry Fiona," he added, realizing what he'd said.

"No apology required," she said easily, handing her glass to Carlow.

He refilled it automatically, outlining what he and Richard had agreed at their meeting with Templeton and Yarwood.

She was the first to react. "You do realize they're in this together?"

Richard couldn't contain himself. "You think they're working against us and yet you say *nothing*? Why—for God's sake? Why would you do that?"

Mason came to her rescue. "Oh, come on, Richard, we've no idea *what* they might be doing. And suppose they discover she's been checking them out?"

"They have," Carlow said offhandedly. "Templeton added two and two to her comings and goings and worked out the rest."

"*And* he conned Laura into talking about invitations to corporate functions," Richard informed them. "He told her Whitehall likes to vet people recommended for honours where it can, and with Mike's name on one of their lists they wanted to observe him at close quarters without his knowing they were there. I'm sure it didn't occur to her to question him further."

"I confronted him with that," Carlow continued. "He tried to justify his lying by saying it was a favour to a friend. This *friend* had apparently been offered sex with one or more of her women if he managed to get Wilder invited to the Manor. But he's no threat to us, and I'm satisfied he wasn't involved in the shooting."

He told them everything he knew about Templeton and Lloyds; including the women and ending with Yarwood.

"Sailing a bit close to the wind, aren't we?" Mason muttered.

Carlow couldn't hide his annoyance.

"I'm only telling you how I feel," Mason pleaded.

"So that was supposed to be an intelligent remark, was it? Jesus, Geoff—whose idea was this? The risk comes with the territory or have you forgotten that too?"

Richard interrupted. "We succeed, he wins—we fail—he's up the proverbial creek with no sign of a paddle. He's bound to be with us."

"Until somebody offers him more," Mason argued.

"Think," Jane said. "He discovered what Fiona was doing but to the best of our knowledge told no one but Mike—well, other than Yarwood. And tell me this—why would anyone offer him anything, never mind more? I'm not trying to defend the man, but let's not belittle his efforts." She turned to Fiona. "Why do you hate him so much? He's arrogant and ruthless, yes—and screwing your husband or whatever it is they do—but how does that change anything? Surely we accept what's on offer and make sure we win?"

Fiona's smile was less than affectionate. "So—*darling*—that's how you've survived in this *nasty-man's* world." She screwed up her face. "You may be right, of course. I hope you are. But I want to state for the record that I don't see it being that simple."

Her almost instant surrender surprised Mason. "I haven't mentioned it before," he quickly added, "but is any of this quite what it seems? The French girl, for example. She came hotfoot from France and made a beeline for Laura, but we know nothing about her, do we?"

"At least she managed to survive the usual overtures from you," Jane mocked.

Undeterred, he went on. "Then, with the Prime Minister and Wilder both dead, she jets back to France and shacks up with Laura."

"What's that got to do with anything?" Fiona asked.

Mason shrugged. "Laura a lesbian? Questionable, I'd say. And we still don't know why Wilder shot the Prime Minister. The whole thing's bizarre."

"You can say that again," Richard added, "Especially with Templeton telling her the man was scheduled to be here and when."

"I've been over that weekend a hundred times," Carlow said wearily, "I understand none of it." One eye on Mason, he passed on his personal version of what had passed between them. "Geoff and I could think of no one capable of running the business for us, and to be honest I'm not sure it's what either of us wanted. Anyway—we decided we'd have to sell or go public, the downside of flotation our being tied to a timescale we'd rather not keep. In fact, other than deciding to do what we're trying to do now, nothing was settled and we'd discussed it with no one."

Fiona Forrest sighed heavily. "I expect you're right. And we'd be mad not to use people like Templeton and Yarwood where we can—dubious characters or not."

Photographers continued to congregate at the gates of the Manor. Carlow had expected Laura's well publicized departure to see an end to their vigil. Only somebody with a vested interest in the village shop or the pub would have had cause to regret it.

Meanwhile, Fiona Forrest came and went unrecognized. "An official car, darling," she said happily. "That's what you need."

Having highlighted individuals whom Yarwood had given them good reason to believe were particularly suited to lending weight to their cause, Carlow had armed her with his long list of names. She'd categorized them by age, sex—political affiliation and a couple of additional headings born of information obtained since moving to Downing Street. She'd at the same time indicated the order in which she thought it best to approach them.

Almost eighty percent of Yarwood's names were directly associated with Westminster and Whitehall, the balance split more or less equally between the City and the Media. Carlow had returned her handiwork to Yarwood via Templeton.

Meanwhile, Richard had installed the computer they referred to as Master, Carlow informing Templeton that they were ready to begin and that he was keen to give Yarwood the go ahead before the Party conferences.

"*Obviously*," Templeton replied, his tone heavily sarcastic.

Carlow ignored his reaction. "But first I'd like to know what he has to say about Mrs Forrest's contribution. I suggest we meet here on Monday evening to discuss it. Incidentally, are Wilder's women still available?"

"How would I know?" Templeton grunted.

"Do I take that to mean your *friend* has lost interest?"

"Er, no—well, that's to say, I wouldn't have thought so."

"Well, find out, will you? If they are, we'll take them to Portugal for a week—present him with some *freebies*."

Jane came into the room as he was ending the call. "I'm going into the village. Is there anything you want?"

Carlow shook his head and went looking for Mason, finding him drinking tea with Mrs Williams in the kitchen. He pulled him into the dining-room and closed the door. "Right—now tell me why?"

Mason shrugged his hand off his sleeve. "Why, what?"

"Why this obsession with Templeton?"

"He's a threat."

"How many more times? He isn't."

"Well, that's not what Fiona thinks," Mason insisted.

"And you're serious about this woman, are you?"

"Serious enough."

Carlow raised an eyebrow. Committed to one woman at last—or losing his touch? "And what did you make of what Jane had to say?"

"I've told you before, there's more to our Jane than you seem to think."

Carlow shrugged. "Maybe you're right."

"Of course I'm right. You must have asked yourself, for example, what she'd be like in bed?"

"Not really."

"Oh come on, you must have. I tried once, you know—as no doubt she told you."

Carlow frowned. "First I've heard of it."

Mason studied him. "Anyway—she's only ever had eyes for one guy around here."

"Who's that?"

"Yeah, yeah—pull the other one. So is the bachelor life beginning to appeal?"

"Definitely not."

"Well, try your luck with Jane, anyway. You may be surprised."

THIRTEEN

Jane abandoned her walk into the village—a spur of the moment decision to take the day off. With Carlow taking her for granted and not exactly happy with her treatment at the hands of Mason and Richard, she couldn't wait to escape. She'd drive into Cambridge; buy some new clothes or something; enjoy a manicure and massage and decide what to do with the rest of her life. It couldn't be allowed to go on as it was.

Her hair was fair, if you ignored the encroaching grey. She'd found her Cambridge hairdresser only since arriving at the Manor, but he'd been no less specific for that about styles to suit her face and the shape of her head, claiming to be capable of all kinds of miracles with a whole range of colours. She'd refused to listen until now.

He *fitted her in.* It was the kind of consideration she'd come to expect from the fussy Italian. She'd wear it short; become a true blonde. Why not? She'd denied herself too much for quite long enough. *'Do this; do that; please Jane; now Jane—as soon as you've finished that, Jane.'* Supervising the running of the house was the latest imposition. She'd been with him for years, half the nation knew that. Laura had walked out the front door and she'd walked in the back.

No one would have believed for a second it was out of the goodness of her heart. Added to which she'd nothing to look forward to but his finding a new woman. What would he do without her? He was about to find out.

Then there was Richard—new cars, fancy clothes and money in his pocket. A few weeks earlier she'd been urging him to take the job that had since changed his life. No—enough was enough. She was too predictable, that was her trouble—too predictable by far.

Richard came downstairs from his morning session with Master. "I need to clarify a few things," he said to Carlow.

"Ten minutes," Carlow grunted.

"Have you seen Jane?" Richard added, heading for the kitchen.

Carlow shook his head, picked up the telephone and punched in a number. "Oh, hello. Mr Wetherby please––Mike Carlow." He waited. "Harry. How are you? Good—Good. Look, do you fancy a couple of days in France—a bit of a break before the Party Conference? There are a couple of things I'd like to run by you. Middle of next week—the Chateau for dinner on Wednesday—back midday Saturday. The aeroplane's at Stansted. You will? Good man. I'll expect you, then, mid-afternoon Wednesday."

He rang off and buzzed Mason. "We're flying to Bordeaux on Wednesday afternoon."

"Why—what's up?"

"Nothing's up. The two of us and Richard—plus Harry Wetherby. I'm still trying to recruit him."

Richard came in carrying a mug of coffee. "Mrs Williams doesn't know. Did Jane tell you where she was going?" he asked Mason.

Mason shook his head.

"Mmm—has to be Cambridge, then. She wouldn't take the car to go into the village." He frowned. "Still—unusual for her to go out without saying."

Carlow informed Richard that Harry Wetherby would be flying to Bordeaux with them. Richard couldn't have cared less "Look, this won't take long. Three things—transferring the Chateau to me, moving Forestry in, and what you want me to do about staff?"

"The Chateau could be awkward," Carlow said.

"Why's that?"

"Laura's a Pension fund trustee."

"You think she's likely to object?"

Carlow shook his head. "No reason she should."

"I'll talk to her, then," Richard heard himself say, despite it being the one course of action he wanted to avoid.

Mason sensed his concern. "What you need is a willing woman." *Obliging* women were his answer to everything. "There's nothing worse to deal with than a frustrated male—" Mason continued, "other than a frustrated woman, of course," he added as an afterthought.

"Okay—you sort out the Chateau with Laura," Carlow said. "Move Forestry in when you're ready and, well—you know the staff situation better than I do, so whatever makes sense."

Mason lit a cigarette, watching the smoke spiral up to the ceiling. "By the way," he said to Richard, "I was thinking of knocking off a few bottles while we're out there—if it's all right with you?"

Richard nodded, thinking about Laura.

Mason grinned. "Mustn't upset our new landlord—must we?"

Her skirt was tighter and that important bit shorter, her heels two inches higher to make her legs appear longer, and her fingernails and matching lipstick now flashed scarlet red. Not a grey hair to be seen, she had a new hairstyle, a new wardrobe, and had been waxed, manicured and massaged and outrageously pampered. Jane's long afternoon in Cambridge was over.

Having taken the plunge and transformed her appearance, she arrived back at the Manor laden with parcels, wondering how many women went to so much trouble with nothing to look forward to but nights on their own. Shouldering the door firmly closed, she turned and met Richard, her heart pounding so violently when she saw him that she was convinced he would hear it. What if she'd done nothing but make herself look cheap?

His face was a study of concentration as he looked her up and down. "What have you *done* to yourself?" he asked. Her heart missed a beat. "You look stunning."

Close to collapsing with relief, she managed to speak. "Like an old packhorse, more like, weighed down by this lot."

He took a step forward. "I'm sorry. Let me—"

"There are more in the car. Could you? Would you mind?"

Her elation was tempered by embarrassment. No one had commented on her appearance in a very long time—with the exception of her hairdresser, of course, who complimented everyone on everything and so didn't count.

Richard dropped the parcels and packages on her bed.

Still trying to contain her delight, she thanked him, glanced at her watch and ushered him out. "Sorry to hurry you, but I have a date for dinner and I don't want to be late." Closing the door, she pouted and posed in front of a full-length mirror. Not bad. Not bad at all.

Richard rejoined Carlow by the inglenook. "Jane's back. I was right; she's been shopping in Cambridge."

Carlow looked at his watch. "Ah—then she can—"

"If you value your life you won't even ask," Richard said quickly. *'I have a date for dinner and I don't want to be late'*—her words, not mine."

Carlow went back to his newspaper.

"What time are we eating?" Mason growled. When he was in one of his *moods* he tended to slouch and to growl, and Fiona Forrest was once again playing the dutiful wife at a Downing Street reception.

"Eight o'clockish, I think," Richard mumbled.

Carlow followed suit. "Yes—eightish—ask Mrs Williams."

If Mason heard what they said he didn't show it, noisily pouring himself a very large scotch. "Anyone want a drink?"

They refused him in unison as Jane came into the room wearing a figure-hugging black dress, shorter by several inches than she usually wore, together with spike-heeled sandals. Her hair was blond and cut short, accentuating the shape of her head and the arch of her neck. They had to like what they were seeing.

The years had created curves where she was once considered thin.

"I need to speak to Mrs Williams before I go," she informed them. "and I'm expecting a taxi. Would you mind calling me if it comes?"

Throwing her wrap round her shoulders she turned and went out.

They were suddenly silent, suspended on the moment. Mason was the first to react. "Do you remember those old Hollywood chestnuts? You know—the mousy secretary would take off her glasses, let down her hair or something and look impossibly gorgeous? There you are Mike, what did I tell you? Tired of being treated like your maid-of-all-work—seething beneath the surface waiting to erupt."

Jane was back from the kitchen when her taxi arrived. She waved her purse in their direction and swept out the door.

"Where's she going?" Carlow asked.

"How the hell do we know?" Mason grunted.

Jane hurried out to the taxi. She hadn't been to a restaurant in what seemed like an age—not looking forward to another evening on her own, but they didn't know that.

Summer was drawing to a close, autumn creeping up the lawn from the river. There was a chill in the air, leaves soon to be shed in their thousands as the trees along the river prepared to watch it slide slowly seaward through another long winter.

Richard sat by the inglenook wondering how many times the Manor had witnessed this scene; anticipating the day when with windows and doors tightly closed, the old fireplace would be called to active service again. "Mike?" he asked. "When did Jane last have a holiday?"

"Can't remember," Carlow muttered, his nose in the Financial Times. "She'll soon let me know if she wants some time off."

"But you do know what she's entitled to?"

"No."

"Don't you think you should?"

Carlow put down the paper. "Why the sudden concern?"

Richard shook his head. "Well—er, nothing really; it just might be a good idea to give it some thought."

FOURTEEN

It was close to midnight when Jane's taxi arrived back at the Manor. She set her alarm for six-thirty and went straight to bed. It was now seven-thirty. She'd started the day as she was determined to go on.

She was wearing a knee-length, silver-grey skirt, a high-necked olive green blouse, sleeves buttoned to the wrist; legs in black nylon and stiletto-heeled shoes. She'd considered the combination carefully before dressing. According to Mason a woman's legs were at their most attractive when presented like this—Laura's for example.

She'd never attempted to compete with Laura—no sane woman would have—but she hoped he was right; at least she hoped he was in her case. *She* considered them attractive: well proportioned, shapely; slim, neatly turned ankles. Carlow might even agree if it ever occurred to him to look.

She was on the telephone to the office when he and Mason came in. They exchanged nodded good-mornings, no comment from either about the change in her appearance or her unscheduled absence the previous afternoon.

"Good morning," Mason said. "How was your evening?"

She smiled. "Pleasant, thank you. Most enjoyable, in fact."

"Anyone I know?"

She shook her head. "I doubt it. A friend of my ex, actually. He once asked me to marry him but I was already committed. You know how it is?"

"Do I?"

She laughed. "Ah—maybe I should follow your example and

start playing the field."

Mason decided the comment was for Carlow's benefit. "May I say how attractive you look, this morning?" he added.

Carlow was on the telephone and probably not listening. She blushed. "You certainly may."

Richard watched them briefly before disappearing upstairs for his morning meeting with Master.

Carlow and Jane were in the drawing room when Templeton arrived on Monday evening, Mason yet to appear. Richard put his head round the door.

"Ask Geoff to look after him, will you?" Carlow said, more interested in his conversation with Jane, Richard thought, than anything he might have to say about Templeton.

"Mr Carlow shouldn't be long," he said on his return to the lounge, once again the victim of an irrational urge to escape. "Your usual, Sir Gordon?"

Templeton nodded.

Carlow's mind was clearly elsewhere when he and Jane eventually emerged. "Sorry about that," he said, "A few things we couldn't leave until morning. Good evening, Sir Gordon. Good of you to come." Templeton nodded but said nothing.

Richard thought Jane and Carlow might have had some kind of disagreement. But Jane seemed relaxed enough, the dress she was wearing pleasantly distracting. The women in his life might be older than he was, but they were certainly capable of commanding his attention.

Mason came in. He nodded to Templeton and poured himself a drink.

Templeton had failed to acknowledge Jane until she spoke. "Good evening, Sir Gordon," she said firmly.

"Mrs Garside."

Richard gave the civil servant the benefit of the doubt. A middle-aged homosexual with a liking for good food and political intrigue couldn't be expected to look twice at a woman—attractive or not.

They sat down to eat, Fiona Forrest once again absent from their action committee. And Carlow was right; her commitment to Mason was long overdue.

Mrs Williams' creations tended to monopolize Templeton's attention, but Carlow preferred meeting over dinner. He welcomed all the company he could get in the evenings now that Laura was gone. Wasting no time with small talk, he informed Templeton that, generally speaking, they weren't comfortable with the idea of retaining Yarwood. They didn't trust him.

Neither did he, Templeton assured them. The man was a mercenary and should be treated as such. Significantly, however, he was a mercenary capable of influencing the behaviour of a body of MPs and civil servants. Trade and Industry, Health, Transport, the Foreign Office and Defence were the departments primarily concerned—meaning that as many as five senior ministers might be numbered among those who would do what they were told.

A sorry situation, he accepted, but according to Yarwood these people understood that failure to do his bidding might not only bring down the Government, but almost certainly land them in gaol. They'd propose or support just about anything to avoid that eventuality.

"Indeed," he went on to say, "I think we can look forward to what might be termed a bloodless coup if we retain him." He added it with relish; leaving them wondering if his enthusiasm stemmed as much from the arrival of Mrs Williams' Bœuf Wellington as Yarwood's ability to initiate a coup, *bloodless* or otherwise. "In fact, my concern isn't for Government at all," he continued—"or the Lords for that matter. I anticipate considerably greater resistance from Her Majesty's Opposition. Not having wielded power for years, I doubt they'll welcome the prospect of never doing so again."

Having informed them that Yarwood could *instruct* what amounted to nearly half the British Government to do his bidding, Templeton appeared to be transported to some kind of culinary heaven. They nonetheless succeeded in covering every aspect of retaining Yarwood, and by the time they finished eating were unanimously in favour.

Unconcerned, it seemed, by the man's demand for fifteen million pounds, Carlow pursued his enquiry about Wilder's women.

According to Templeton, they were still active, there were ten of them, and given sufficient notice they could and would provide their services en bloc— subject to their finding the group they were being asked to *entertain* acceptable to them. The conversation left little to the imagination, prompting Jane to ask why Carlow thought it necessary to involve Wilder's women.

Carlow was impassive. "I think you can safely leave that decision to us."

"If I was happy to do that I wouldn't have asked," she snapped. "I've nothing to gain from this, and now you expect me to accept its risks without question. That being so, I trust you'll excuse me?" She got to her feet and left the room.

Carlow came down the next morning to find a handwritten note. He was staring out across the terrace when Mason came into the dining-room. "Ah—good," Mason said. "I wanted to catch you on your own. Tell me—is there a problem between you and Jane?" Carlow handed him the note.

> *Dear Mike,*
> *I'm sorry it has to end like this. I've enjoyed so much of our time together. I didn't complain in the past when you were inconsiderate, and I hasten to point out that there were numerous occasions when you gave me good reason. I put it down to your having a lot on your mind. But it's more than that now.*
>
> *You were worried about Laura, about things going wrong. I understood that, but at one time or another you expressed concern for Geoff, for Richard and even Fiona Forrest, yet to the best of my knowledge never for me.*
>
> *You involved me in this exercise whether I wanted it or not, finally objecting to my questions as if I'd no right to ask them. I've been at risk too, remember, and much more than your secretary since Laura walked*

out. But I've been treated to the same attitude from you, the same salary and given nothing to look forward to but your bringing home a new woman and being asked to move out.

So I shall start a new life. Who knows—somebody might even stop now and then to consider what I want. I shall go to an hotel for the time being, before going home.

Good-bye, Mike, I hope you succeed and find what you're looking for.
Jane.

They were sitting in silence when Richard came in. "Anyone—?" He saw Mason's face. "What's wrong?"

Mason handed him the note. He read quickly through it. "Good God, Mike, are you totally fucking mad?"

Mason restrained a waving arm. "Sit down, man, effing and blinding isn't going to help."

Carlow interrupted. "No, Geoff—no, I'm everything he can think of and a few things beside."

He hurried out of the room and bounded upstairs. Her bedroom was empty. Richard threw him the keys to the Porsche when he came down; furious, but knowing the Rolls would be a liability in Cambridge.

Doors slamming in his wake, the car snarled up the drive in a shower of gravel, heading for his first port of call—the Garden House Hotel. Her car was nowhere to be seen in the car park. The traffic was impenetrable as usual or Regent Street and Park Terrace might have resembled Monte Carlo. He circled Parker's Piece and accelerated up the ramp in a full frontal assault on the University Arms. There was her car. Heaving a sigh of relief he turned off the engine, abandoned the Porsche and hurried into the hotel, the smart, middle-aged woman of the three at Reception, instantly recognizing him.

"May I help, Mr Carlow?"

"Thank you, yes. I believe you have a Mrs Garside staying in the hotel?"

"Indeed we have, sir," she said without consulting the register. "She arrived a few moments ago. I believe I saw her go into the dining room."

He held up the keys to Richard's car and a twenty pound note. "The sports car—" He pointed out through the door. "—the red Porsche. Could somebody park it for me?" He frowned. "I'm sorry—but I could be some time."

She smiled sympathetically before taking the keys and the money. "I quite understand, Mr Carlow; leave it with me."

He found Jane sitting on the far side of the dining room in one of the big windows overlooking Parker's Piece. The room was by no means busy, but he managed to arrive at her table before she realized he was there.

The September sun was slanting in at the window as if to spotlight their meeting, the Piece criss-crossed by people coming and going to and from the Queen Anne car park, into Newmarket or Hills Roads, or aimed at the Hotel on the way into town.

An engine wailed out of the fire station on the far corner, blazing its way in fits and starts through the heavy traffic—Cambridge at its most frantic—students on bikes and countless people on foot making it easy to imagine the entire population spending their days on the street. A waiter was beside him before he could sit down. "Coffee and toast," he said automatically, looking at Jane.

The waiter nodded and left.

"I've come to apologize," he began.

"You seem to think a salary and a mortgage are enough for someone like me," she said angrily. "You've paid me well down the years and I'm grateful, but I'm a single woman in case you hadn't noticed—an intelligent one, I hope—and I'd like to indulge myself occasionally before it's too late. Laura and Fiona Forrest have what they want. Why shouldn't I? I've earned it."

Becoming increasingly upset, she hurried out of the room and up the stairs. He was close behind her as she fumbled with the key to her room. She crossed to the window and stood looking out. He put his arms around her.

"No, Mike."

He tried to turn her round.

"Mike, I said, no."

"We should have done this a long time ago," he said breathlessly.

She was incapable of resisting, and when he was uncharacteristically clumsy, she responded by helping him to undress her. They fell across the bed and she felt the hurt melt away.

"What's wrong?" she asked as she lay watching him.

He shook his head. "I'm an even bigger bastard than I thought."

"Why?"

"This, I suppose."

She laughed. "Forget it. If I hadn't wanted it, it wouldn't have happened."

"No, but there's no point either of us making promises we can't keep."

"So do I get the respect I deserve—*and* the financial reward?"

He was slow to respond.

"Well, make up your mind."

He nodded. "Of course you do."

She smiled and snuggled close. "Right—but I wouldn't say no to a *detailed* apology."

FIFTEEN

Everything about owning an aeroplane appealed to Harry Wetherby. He aspired to something less ostentatious perhaps than Carlow's thirty million pound jet, but like many an avowed socialist he found the trappings of wealth overwhelmingly seductive.

Jane flew out with them. Mason had gathered her up in his arms as if she'd been missing for months when she arrived back at the Manor. He knew instinctively what had happened—a sexual sixth sense honed to a sharp edge by his predatory lifestyle.

The grape harvest was complete. Andre said he'd never seen his father so close to smiling—once again failing to explain how it was possible to measure degrees of unsmiling.

Madame Darrieux prepared an evening meal to which they sat down together; English and French. It was in celebration of the harvest, she said through Andre; the combination of her pea soup, confit de canard, cheese, coffee and cognac cause for celebration in itself.

After they'd eaten, Carlow asked Andre to thank his mother for a meal he described as fit for a king—for her outstanding hospitality—before he and Wetherby, armed with a bottle of claret, made their excuses and adjourned to the sitting-room—or rather what passed for a sitting-room. The Darrieux family rarely sat down anywhere outside the kitchen.

Unable to think about anything but Laura, Richard asked if he could join them.

It was Wetherby who replied. "Aye, lad, and welcome." He said it without consulting Carlow, his yorkshire accent more apparent than ever. He slapped Richard on the back. "Food w'marvellous, weren't it? Worth t'bloody trip on its own."

Carlow slumped in a chair. He'd eaten the meal but couldn't have said he'd enjoyed it. It was no reflection on Madame Darrieux, she was every inch Mrs Williams' equal in the kitchen, but like Richard, he was finding Laura's absence harder to contend with on the French side of the Channel.

"Right, then," Wetherby said, settling back in a chair. "A couple of things to run by me, y'said?"

Carlow began rubbing his eyes and gathering his thoughts. "Yes—I want to change the British system of government."

"Y'what?" the politician grunted.

"I said, I want to change our *system* of government," Carlow repeated firmly.

Wetherby poured himself a glass of wine and lit a cigar.

Carlow suddenly sat up. "Do you know, Harry, whenever I come into contact with an MP—minister or not—and I have to say this includes you—I get the distinct impression that you believe getting yourselves elected to Westminster endows you with intellectual powers denied to we *ordinary* mortals. And yet confronted by a parliamentary system which legislates against you thinking for yourselves, you do nothing to fight it— ready and willing at the drop of a hat to ridicule those who do think for themselves. This leads me to conclude that such smug, self satisfied arrogance demonstrated by individuals who supposedly represent the people, has to be responsible for most if not all the problems we face."

Wetherby frowned. "Such as?"

"The obscene waste of time and money occasioned by Party politics might be a good place to start, to say nothing of most of you reportedly having your snouts in the trough. And if that weren't enough, we're expected to stand meekly by while you —that's to say a few of you—casually make the decisions on which our future depends. Why would we do that? Why is a population of more than sixty million people—some of them presumably sane—prepared to do that when the whole bloody shooting match is so obviously corrupt?"

The politician continued to puff on his cigar. "Have y'never 'eard of t'ballot box?"

"Yes, yes," Carlow went on, "Control is occasionally shuffled from one side of the House to the other—but ask yourself this. What does it achieve? What do we gain? Because I'm sorry to say the answer is nothing. It's a meaningless charade—a cynical waste of time and taxpayers' money."

He went on to summarize what he hoped to bring about and how he'd decided to approach it.

Wetherby waited for him to finish. "Now you listen—"

"No—" Carlow cut in, "You listen. Don't you want to see an end to parliamentary corruption? Don't you want to see us force the occupants of Westminster and Whitehall to seriously dedicate themselves to pursuing the national interest rather than spending their time and our money pretending they do? Forget what you'd *like* to believe, Harry; accept the reality."

The labour party leader thought about it. "It'd be treason. And even supposin' it could be done—it simply wouldn't work. Parties'd be left with no power at all."

"Exactly—and are you seriously suggesting that a Cabinet of Ministers appointed individual by individual by two-thirds majorities of sitting members of the House, would be incapable of organizing itself and the civil services to manage our affairs? Come on—is that what you're suggesting?" He studied the politician's face. "If so, why should we bother to elect *any* of you? And what if I told you the Tories are in favour?"

"I'd say you were mad."

"Yes, Harry, but what if it were true?" He put down his glass and pressed forward in his chair. "What would you say then?"

The yorkshireman shook his head. "You're off y'trolley."

"And that's *all* you've got to say?"

"Christ, man. What else can I say—when y'want to scrap the very essence of our democracy."

"Oh, please!" Carlow groaned. "Think, man—think what you're saying. What democracy? We have a parliamentary *Sys-*

tem, yes—but it's an insult to the intelligence—an outrageously expensive, indefensible farce. And you know it is. I beg you, Harry—stop trying to pretend it's advantageous to the British people or presides over anything remotely resembling a democratic process."

In the kitchen, inhibitions were disappearing with each bottle uncorked. Andre, their alcohol fuelled interpreter, was adding his own brand of linguistic chaos to the general confusion. A dubious talent, but no less amusing for that.

Richard had had enough. The dispute between Carlow and Wetherby unresolved, he said his good nights and went up to bed.

"Ah, oui," Monsieur Darrieux said, light apparently dawning following Andre's explanation of something Mason had said.

"Non! Non, Non, non," Madame Darrieux responded, growing more animated non by non, prodding her husband's arm and shaking her head.

Monsieur shrugged in expressionless resignation as she erupted in triumph, chattering wildly and beaming at Mason. What the hell she or they were on about he hadn't the foggiest.

"Interpreter please," he shouted.

"A votre service, Monsieur," Andre replied, studiously pouring himself yet another glass of wine.

Jane had lost interest in anything Andre had to say. Far beyond her alcoholic limit, she'd taken to flirting with Mason—a dangerous undertaking unless despite what had happened between them over the years, she'd decided to deliver. Whatever her motivation, she swayed across to Carlow when she saw him come in.

"You're drunk," he said firmly.

She giggled, slurring her words. "My room in half an hour. We'll see who's drunk." Unsteady on her feet, she looked up at him knowingly and swayed back to Mason.

Carlow left Wetherby with the others and went up to his room. He took a cool shower, not relishing the prospect of another sleepless night. But then why the hell not? She was drunk but she was offering. He was a sad case without Laura, but it felt like an eternity since the University Arms.

Laughter was still echoing up through the house when he closed his bedroom door and crept down the landing. Her room was in semi-darkness, a single lamp illuminating her presence on the far side of the room as she grinned drunkenly at him from the back of a sofa by the half-open window.

Mason was getting what he'd been wanting for years—her skirt round her waist, her legs spread receptively round him.

"More, more," she demanded, her eyes fixed on Carlow, her hips responding wildly to Mason's driving need.

Carlow turned away and hurried back to his room.

SIXTEEN

His Uncle Morgan said his mother had chosen the name Jonathan for the all too obvious reason that she liked it. But he hadn't offered the same excuse for his father. He said the man was a waste of space with his holier-than-thou chapel on Sundays and down the pub half the week.

It was the second time the desk had connected *Jonathan* Thomas to the woman on the telephone. Coincidence, he chose to pretend—well aware that his recent promotion made him the obvious repository for the daily influx of dross. It was easier off-loading it on *Nobby* Thomas than trying to overcome resistance from a more seasoned member of the department.

The well-spoken female claimed that a man by the name of Desmond Yarwood was bribing and blackmailing MPs and civil servants into proposing and supporting constitutional change: in short, trying to bring down the Government. She said they should talk to Michael Carlow of Carlow Mason or Sir Gordon Templeton the Cabinet Secretary if they wanted to know more. He threw down his pen and shouted for his Sergeant.

Chas Chambers, a man in his early thirties came round the door looking more like a city gent than a copper. The Chief Constable had stated in a radio interview that as far as he was concerned, *tidy* on the outside in an officer usually meant tidy on the in. Chas had taken it as a guaranteed shortcut to promotion. Gullible was Chas. "What do we know about a guy called Yarwood?" Thomas asked him.

Chas screwed up his face. "Who?"

"Desmond Yarwood."

"Never heard of him."

"Well, get on to records, then," Thomas added.

Chambers looked back at him blankly.

"Today would make sense!" Thomas insisted, making a mental note to give him a much needed talking to. Less vanity and a bit more industry wouldn't come amiss. He reached for the telephone.

Thomas had worked with Detective Chief Superintendent Keen before. Keen by name and keen by nature it had been said of him in Special Branch—at least he was until it was his turn at the bar.

They shook hands—unobtrusively, Thomas thought, unaware that everyone in the pub had them sussed the instant they came through the door. Half the population south of the river relied on that instinct. But it wasn't, *'congratulations on your promotion, Nobby; how are things, Nobby; what are you having, Nobby?'* Oh no—just: "What couldn't be said on the telephone?"

"Pint, is it?" Thomas enquired, knowing there was no need to ask. "D'you want some crisps or something?" he added as the girl took his order.

"No thanks, I'm too fat already."

Thank God for that. At least he wasn't expecting a free lunch.

"Second thoughts, though, I will have some nuts."

Thomas handed him his pint. "Cheers," he offered in return. "So why the cloak and dagger?"

"A woman has called the nick twice saying a guy called Desmond Yarwood is dishing out back-handers and threats at Westminster and up and down Whitehall. She says he's out to overthrow the Government. Hard to believe, I know, but it is why I called you."

"Overthrowing's too good for most of 'em," Keen mumbled into his beer.

Thomas ignored the comment. "She didn't sound like a nutter."

"Huh! So how do they sound?"

Unperturbed, Thomas went on. "She said we should ask Sir

Gordon Templeton or Michael Carlow if we want to know more. We're checking Yarwood out now."

"Don't waste your time," Keen added. "An old acquaintance of mine is *Mister* Yarwood. Second nature to him, bribery and blackmail—even if I can't seem to prove it," he added grudgingly. "Your lady-friend give you any more?"

"No—that was it."

"Carlow and Templeton, eh?" Keen continued. "Interesting combination, wouldn't you say? Put a foot wrong there, mind, and your feet won't touch the ground." He scratched his chin thoughtfully. "Templeton's brother topped himself, didn't he, and wasn't the number-ten shooting up at Carlow's place?"

Thomas nodded. "I was there. Woman named Wilder pulled the trigger. He'd sacked the guy she'd been having it away with. Least, that's the only credible motive we managed to come up with."

Keen pocketed the nuts, downed what was left of his pint in a couple of well practised gulps and got to his feet. "Okay. Leave it with me. If I come up with anything, I'll give you a bell. Thanks, love," he called to the girl behind the bar.

"Think nothing of it, Chief Superintendent," Thomas muttered.

Laura's sitting room was lit by sliding French-windows opening on to a patio and a walled garden at the back of the house. The floor was polished pine with a Persian rug at its centre, on which were arranged a glass-topped coffee table, a sofa and four easy chairs. The fireplace, more ornamental than functional, looked essentially English like everything else in this too-tidy room.

There were pictures on each of the walls, including three oils and four good quality prints by minor artists, not that Richard was an authority, but he was impressed by the watercolour above the fireplace. It was a beautifully crafted view of the Manor from the trees by the river. He wondered if it was significant that she'd brought it here to Bordeaux.

She met him with a hug; everything about her as gloriously

desirable as ever. His heart was racing. "How are you?"

"Fine."

"And Danielle?"

"She's gone," she said, trying to sound indifferent. "And you?"

"Progressing." He was delighted by her news. "I'm buying the Chateau—the business from Mike, the real-estate from the Pension Fund. He says you're a Trustee."

"I am—if he hasn't retired me, that is."

"I think he's planning to—oh, I'm sorry."

"Forget it. It's right that he does."

"No, I really am sorry. I shouldn't have mentioned it. But I do need your signature on the conveyance."

Crossing to the fireplace, she lit a cigarette from the pack on the shelf and blew out the smoke. "So do you plan to live over here?"

Her maid came in with coffee.

"Beginning sometime next year," he said. Watching her light the cigarette had given him an erection. "With plenty of comings and goings in the meantime, I expect."

She returned to the sofa, aiding and abetting his inability to take his eyes off her legs by easing forward to pour the coffee —the hem of her skirt sliding enticingly up her thighs. She dismissed the maid with a nod, looked up at him and smiled. "Incidentally, you'll be pleased to know I stopped the champagne and marijuana—Sugar?"

"One, please—brown, if I may." She handed him the cup. "I'm glad," he added earnestly, finally managing to concentrate on what she was saying.

"I often think about that day," she continued, sitting back with her coffee.

Your move, Wells, a voice whispered in his head. "May I ask what happened with Danielle?" he heard himself say. *'Chicken,'* the disgusted voice added.

"Her jealousy was destroying me so I told her to go," she explained. "It was hard at first—living out here on my own. I considered returning to England. But I'm settled now; happy enough in my own quiet way. What about Mike? Has he found another woman?"

He shook his head. "I don't think so."

She studied him. "You wouldn't tell me if he had." She stubbed out her cigarette in an ashtray and reached for his hand. "Come on. Let me show you the rest of the house." She pointed to the door on the other side of the hall. "That's where we sat the last time you came—the drawing room."

She showed him the dining room, the kitchen and the breakfast room, before leading him up the wide staircase that swept round one side of the entrance hall to the gallery above. "There are five identical bedrooms," she told him, opening doors but inviting him to look in just one. He knew where they were heading. "And this one is mine." Leading him inside, she closed the door behind them, drawing back full length curtains to reveal sliding glass doors and a roof terrace beyond.

The room was airy and spacious, the bed designed to suit. Doing his best to ignore it, he opened the doors to be met by a blanket of hot air and a panoramic view over pine trees to the south and the east. She smiled, sliding her arms around his neck and gazing into his eyes. "It seems like forever since we stood like this."

He grinned, shaking his head. "Did I really turn down an opportunity to take you to bed?"

She led him back into the bedroom, sitting him down before disappearing into her dressing room to emerge sixty seconds later wearing a red silk blouse unbuttoned to the waist, a short, white skirt and spike-heeled sandals, the combination spectacular against the sun-tan of her body and the long stretch of her legs. She wore nothing underneath, her breasts hidden and revealed as she moved.

She unzipped him, prompting his sudden sharp intake of breath. "Aah," he gasped—I, you—"

She devoured him, her mouth doing it—making him. He was delirious. It was over as soon it began.

"I'm sorry," he said breathlessly. "I just couldn't—"

She looked up at him and smiled. He leaned down and exposed her breasts—slowly, savouring the moment, his desire rising to a crescendo, transporting them both.

Half an hour later, he rolled out of bed. "I have to go."

"Let me come with you."

"I thought you just did," he whispered mischievously. "No—I really do have to go." He kissed her. "I'll come back tonight. You are happy about the Chateau, aren't you?"

"Of course," she said softly, rediscovering his erection. "And I've made my diagnosis. The patient is urgently in need of more specialist treatment."

They landed at Heathrow late on Saturday morning. The car dropped Carlow at the penthouse before heading north out of London on its way back to the Manor. Richard had stayed on in France.

"My name is Penny Wise, Mr Carlow," the voice on the telephone informed him. "I represent the group I believe you call Wilder's women."

"And what can I do for you, Miss Wise?" Carlow asked, wondering if her looks matched her voice.

"My contact said to call you at this number."

"Ah—right. I'll be needing your full complement for a week out in Portugal. Did he tell you that too?"

"Oh dear," she said. "Now I'm intrigued. Shall we say six o'clock?"

SEVENTEEN

The woman calling herself Penny Wise arrived at the penthouse at six o'clock, accompanied by Sue and Veronica. These weren't their real names, of course, Carlow understood that. But he was suitably impressed. They were not only exquisite to look at, they were tantalizingly available; making it obvious why Templeton's so-called friend had become obsessed with free nights.

Carlow was amazed. "But why do you do this?" he found himself asking, "—why prostitution?"

Penny Wise smiled. "We enjoy having sex," she said easily. "It's as simple as that. Each of us is at least twenty-five years of age and widely experienced when we come into this business. I'm told Lady Morrison and her partner insisted on it from the outset. And we're highly selective—individually as well as collectively." She paused, gauging his reaction. "Sue here, for example, specializes in threesomes—a man with two women." Sue looked up at him and smiled. "It's the reason she's here. Veronica, on the other hand, likes to give oral satisfaction." Veronica studied him.

"And you—?" he asked, "what's your speciality?"

She ignored the question. "Between twenty five and fifty—blond, brunette, redhead, some of us submissive, others more dominant; more or less *versatile*, I suppose you might say. More than enough *variety* to satisfy demand. So what have you in mind?"

"As I told you, we plan to entertain delegates at a seminar out in Portugal. I'd like your ladies to share a villa, attend three or four cocktail parties—and be, how shall I put it—tastefully sympathetic to any advances they receive?

The delegates will be out of Westminster and Whitehall—no doubt some of them old friends." Her face betrayed nothing. "We'll fly you out on a Thursday and bring you back somewhere towards the end of the following week. Eight nights in all, say, travel by private aeroplane, all expenses paid."

"How many delegates?" she asked.

"Approximately a dozen."

"Subject as I've said to our finding them acceptable, that will be one hundred and twenty thousand payable in advance."

He took a sharp breath. "Wow—now I see why you're attracted to this way of life."

"So would you care to sample our wares?" she went on. Her face hadn't changed. "All three of us, perhaps—together or in turn, or would seeing us with each other put you in the mood? I can telephone for a man if you'd prefer to sit and watch?"

"Thank you, no," he said quickly. "That won't be necessary. What notice do you need?"

"A week," she said.

"Right, how do I reach you?" He went on to promise her the list of delegates as soon as it was complete—plus the names of two or three reserves should they wish to exclude anyone on the list.

She handed him a card. It read, *Penny Wise, Personal Secretarial Services*, listing a cell-phone number but giving no address. He walked them to the lift.

"Such a pity," she whispered, reaching up to stroke his cheek.

Richard relied on Jane—had pretty much since they met. Even as his father lay dying she'd added a smile to a few well chosen words and done her best to reassure him. She was an optimist. Life had to go on. "What's wrong?" he asked, knowing there was no point in asking.

She said the first thing that came into her head. "I'm behind with my accounts." He invariably confided in her, why she wondered couldn't she be honest with him?

"Which accounts?"

She wanted to end it there; before it could go any further. But she couldn't admit to surrendering to Carlow in Cambridge followed by Mason in France. And she certainly couldn't tell him that, hangover apart, she'd loved every minute. Alcohol and sex without counting the cost. Boozing and fucking for the first time in her life.

She enjoyed the sound of the words and everything they stood for—yes, *fucking*, like modern women *fucked*. Women who gave as good as they got: women who were beautiful like she'd never be beautiful; liberated women free to live their lives like she'd never been free.

And he knew about the money. How could she argue she'd no future with Carlow when he'd paid her a quarter of a million pounds and no payslip to go with it—no formal schedule showing the deduction of national insurance and tax? "Household," she mumbled.

"Fetch your papers," he ordered.

She hesitated.

"Go on. Do as you're told."

She went through to the library, collected the household ledger, the bills and her general paraphernalia, and meekly followed him upstairs. He introduced her to the computer. "Master—this is Jane Garside. She won't share her problems with us, but she's in need of our help."

"Why do you call it Master?" she asked.

"Not *it*, woman. He'll be mortally offended."

"So why call *him* Master?"

"Oh, it's too complicated for mere mortals. Right—let's have a look." He opened the ledger.

"You're only a couple of weeks behind," he said after a few minutes study. "And it's straightforward stuff." He turned the final page. "Nothing at all, really—general expenditure, a Bank reconciliation and a couple of months pay as you earn. Come on now—tell me what's wrong."

She shook her head, but said nothing. "In that case," he added, "Perhaps you'd like to know I'm sleeping with Laura?"

It was as if he'd physically hit her. "You're what?"

"I'm sleeping with Laura. She split up with the French girl and—well—it just sort of happened."

"For goodness sake," she said anxiously. "Surely you realize Mike's show of accepting her leaving is only an act?"

He heard the break in her voice and watched a tear escape down her cheek. She'd always been devoted to her work, he knew that—but it hadn't occurred to him she might have feelings for Carlow—not that kind at least. She couldn't have, could she? No—not Jane. Year after year watching him go home to Laura, her entire existence revolving around the few piddling moments he'd even noticed she was there? Shit, she was capable of a lot of things—surely not that?

"I know exactly how he feels," she said wistfully. "Oh, he'll have other women if the mood takes him, but if he lives to be a hundred he won't give her up."

"Laura says the marriage is over." He realized it changed nothing, but what else could he say?

Jane wiped her eyes. "She's an astonishingly beautiful woman. You don't need me to tell you that. She can have any man she wants; woman too if the French girl was anything to go by. One gesture, half-smile, one flicker of an eye, and a crowd would come running. And like it or not, that includes Mike and Geoff."

"I can take care of myself," he insisted.

"She's seven or eight years older than you for a start," she continued. "Not that anyone would guess. And if Mike Carlow can't keep her, what makes you think that *you* can? I shudder to think what he'll say when he finds out—never mind what he'll do. As for me," she added. "I'm feeling sorry for myself, that's all. I walked out and wouldn't have come back if he hadn't come after me. All that time—nothing—I resign and hey-presto we end up in bed."

"The bastard," Richard grunted.

"No. I'm trying to say nothing had changed and yet I behaved like an adolescent schoolgirl. Hope soared. Pitiful isn't it? So easy to delude yourself. Second nature for me I'm afraid, where Mike Carlow's concerned. Years of practise, I suppose," she added, sadly. "But I'd hate to see you make the same mistake with his wife."

Okay, he thought—so he lusted after her body. Who didn't? But did it follow there was more to it than that? "Shall I feed this stuff to Master?" he asked, a long way from coming to terms with his feelings for Laura.

"Show me how it works," she said, resting a hand on his arm. "You will be careful, though, won't you?"

He covered her hand with his own, patting it gently.

The household accounts were easily accommodated. It took less than five minutes. He introduced her to a programme that simplified everything. All she had to do was feed it the information and it did the rest.

"So why *this*?" she asked, indicating Master. "There's the third floor at the office and the computer in France; why do you need this?"

"*This* as you put it, and the computer in France are quite separate from the office. We call them Master and Servant."

"But what do they do?"

"Why?"

"Curiosity, I suppose."

"Mmm—Well—as you know, none of my files are for general consumption. Everything about CME that is, is available from the office or Servant. What's relevant to CME but generated by us, is transmitted to them both. Everything else stays here with me. In that way we keep records on both sides of the channel, but only Master is complete. Are you with me so far?"

"I think so."

"Master's payments folder," he continued, "details everything: finance, personnel, taxation or its absence, currency matters and so on—specific information; from where and to whom —your quarter of a million, for example. Later, when everything gets complicated, they'll be reallocated or disguised."

"Yes, but how would it be accessed and managed if you weren't here to do it?"

"Knowledge of the system and the passwords. Master for here, Servant for France." He demonstrated. "Now we're in. You raise a file; edit, print et cetera, in the usual way. The girl responsible for Servant controls everything in France, but only we have access to Master. It's straightforward enough and I've explained it to Mike."

"Show me again."

He ran quickly through it.

"And you can retrieve all that information as easily as that?"

"With the exception of *special* payments."

"So what's different about them?"

"They're confined to a CD—file name, Cumulus; password, cumuluswcg—using our initials; Wells, Carlow, Garside—easy to remember."

"Cumulus as in clouds?"

"Yes, but you won't find the folder anywhere but on the CD."

"So I can't delete something important by pressing the wrong key?"

He laughed, inserting the CD and entering the password. Cumulus opened and appeared on the screen. He pressed delete. Master responded: *Are you sure you want to delete Cumulus—yes/no?* He indicated no, and the illustration ended.

"So it's just like any other computer?" she said.

"Of course. What did you expect?"

"I don't know. Anyway—thank you. I'll certainly use it in future."

With what Jane had said about Laura fresh in his mind, Richard telephoned her. He wanted the Deeds to the Chateau. Nothing should go wrong, but he'd fly out with the conveyance to be on the safe side. Added to which, the more time he'd had to think about it, the more he realized he couldn't wait to see her. He hardly dared admit it—but he was in love with her—had been, it seemed to him now, since their meeting at the penthouse.

But Jane had worried him. What if she was right? Carlow couldn't keep her—what made him think that he could?

"I'll get over as soon as I can," he told her, knowing it couldn't happen without Carlow's consent. And to his surprise, Carlow talked freely about her when he steered the conversation round to obtaining her signature. Mainly about her trusteeship and the conveyance, it was true, but easily, confidently, in marked contrast to the stunned disbelief that had all but paralysed him when he was faced with her relationship with the French girl. But even then he'd gone about his business as if none of it had happened. Oh, yes, the man was capable all right; capable of anything to which he chose to put his mind.

Richard had Jane book him a seat on a British Airways flight out of Heathrow. He telephoned Laura from the car, asking her to collect him from Merignac, conscious of Jane watching him as he put the car in gear.

When he and Laura eventually arrived at her house, he threw his luggage into the hall and they hurried upstairs. They couldn't get enough of each other, but it hadn't stopped them trying. "Can't you telephone the Chateau?" she asked him at breakfast.

He shook his head. "Mike's certain to call." He delved into his briefcase, looking at his watch. "Can we get this thing signed?" He put his arms around her. "It is why I came."

"Beast," she said.

He laid it in front of her and handed her a pen. "Here—Here—Here—there—there, and finally—here," he said turning the last page. "And now the copy."

She studied him. "Does he know about us?"

He shook his head. "I very much doubt I'd be here if he did."

"Play the grand hostess if you must," Mason said angrily, "but don't expect me to wait around while you do it."

"Listen, *darling*," Fiona Forrest snapped. "Screwing isn't owning."

After so many nights on his own, he needed reassurance. He'd accepted the situation initially, but it was time for it to end. "Look—be reasonable," he grunted. "I need to know where I stand."

"I accept Downing Street wasn't part of the original equation," she said. "But I promised to honour my agreement for as long as he's in Government."

EIGHTEEN

Carlow and Mason were discussing the forthcoming seminar over breakfast at the Manor. Mason seemed puzzled. "Is it going to be real?" he asked.

"How do you mean, real?" Carlow said.

"I *mean*—will it be a genuine seminar?"

"Of course it will. We'll be debating our economic and social prospects in Europe—or out of it, of course: sessions with Wetherby, three off Yarwood's list of MPs plus me and Fiona—each session followed by questions, answers and wine, women and song for the rest of each day—nothing on Saturday and Sunday."

Mason thought about it.

"You need to square it with your lady-friend," Carlow continued. "The female angle ought to go down pretty well from the Prime Minister's wife."

He finished eating before crossing the dining-room to the telephone. Harry Wetherby was down at Westminster—in touch with his constituency office by telephone. After leaving a message with his secretary, Carlow called Penny Wise. "Good morning. I trust I find you well?"

"I'm fine," she said brightly.

"It's on for next week," he continued. "There are a couple of things left to settle, but we plan to fly out there on Thursday."

"I'll call you this evening to confirm," she added.

He ended the call to be informed by Mason that they needed more space. He'd reserved rooms in the hotel, but they needed a second villa as close as possible to their own—plus two or three cars to ferry people around.

Carlow nodded. "I'll leave all that to you."

They were interrupted by Wetherby returning his call. "Harry—thanks for calling back. I'd like you to deliver a couple of lectures for me if you would—at a seminar in Portugal. Your take on our political, social and economic future in or out of Europe. Four half-hour sessions and, you know, the usual questions and answers."

Wetherby's response was instant. "Oh no, I'm having nowt t'do wi—"

Carlow laughed. "Yes—yes, you made that perfectly clear. Come on, you'll enjoy yourself. We fly out there next Thursday. Come to dinner at the penthouse on Wednesday, we can talk it through then. I've got somebody coming I'd like you to meet. I'll send the car for six-thirty."

Wetherby considered it, not entirely convinced.

"Harry—?"

"I'm here. Wednesday, six-thirty, y'say?"

"Yes."

"Make it seven."

"Seven it is. Where are you staying?"

"T'Grosvenor."

Carlow ended the call and re-dialled. "Miss Wise? Sorry to be a pain, but are you free for dinner on Wednesday evening? There are a couple of points I'd like to discuss."

"I'd be delighted."

"Splendid. My car will collect you from the Grosvenor at seven. Plan to stay the night at the penthouse. Oh, and bring a *diversion* for Harold Wetherby the Labour Party Chairman."

The Penina Hotel was less formal under the Trust House banner than it had been in Portuguese ownership. Mason made the reservations by telephone and emailed confirmation, stressing that the suite and as many of the rooms as possible were to overlook the golf course.

Citing security, and emphasizing that the suite was for

Michael Carlow and the rooms for British VIPs, he had the presence of mind to check the nationalities of other hotel guests for the period. If Carlow played the course, as there was little doubt he would, he'd want to have an idea what to expect.

High handicappers hadn't been allowed on the championship course in the old days. Since tournament professionals from emergent golfing nations had achieved success in America and Europe, however, hordes of their compatriots were taking up the game. Good for the industry, no doubt, not to mention the hotel which now accepted them, but disruptive to say the very least to the serious golfer, the course demanding enough without having to wait an age between shots.

Mason had long since decided that golf wasn't for him. He'd never understood what Carlow saw in it—a game took hours to complete and you had to walk for miles with a heavy bag on your back or spend your time jumping on and off or dragging one or other of those annoying buggy things. He telephoned Fiona.

"Mike wants you to speak at a seminar in Portugal," he told her. "We'll be flying out there on Thursday next week."

"Wants me to speak about what?"

"The future for women in the European Community, I think —give him a call."

"Is this the thing he's been discussing with Penny Wise?"

"It is."

"I'll think about it," she added offhandedly.

"Well, be quick about it, will you?" he growled, and put down the phone. There were times when women could be intensely annoying.

Carlow and Templeton had produced a shortlist of invitees from Yarwood's list of names, retaining three of them to speak. The fees they'd asked for an all expenses paid, luxury speaking engagement on the Algarve, were preposterous. Carlow asked himself why that hadn't surprised him?

He'd added Fiona Forrest's name to their number, more as an

afterthought than anything. Mason might have been tempted to fraternize with the Wilder contingent if she'd stayed at home.

Jane booked the usual caterers for the penthouse, arranging for Wetherby, Penny Wise and Wetherby's *diversion* to be collected from the Grosvenor. As she confirmed it and he telephoned Mason, Carlow wondered how Wetherby would react to being *presented* with a woman.

"She hasn't made up her mind," Mason informed him.

"What's the problem?"

"She seems less than keen to mix with Wilder's women."

"Shit, Geoff! Did you have to tell her about them?"

"I didn't say a word. She asked if this was what you've been discussing with Penny Wise. I could hardly deny it."

"Kick her arse, then," Carlow muttered as he rang off. Then, wham—it hit him like a fist in the face. He couldn't get back to Mason fast enough. "Run that past me again."

"What?"

"When did I tell you about Penny Wise?"

"Why?"

"No, not why—think, man."

"I don't remember."

"Well, did you mention her or Wilder's women when you talked to Fiona?"

"Why, for Christ's sake?"

"Stop saying, why. Did you?"

"No."

"You're positive?"

"Absolutely."

"You're absolutely sure you didn't mention Penny Wise?"

"How many more times? She did."

"Then ask yourself this. How does she know about Penny Wise—not to mention my discussions with her?"

NINETEEN

The fast fading light seemed strangely tangible. Surrounded by scaffolding and draped in what gave the impression of being rows of ill-fitting curtains, the Chateau was being sandblasted as if to proclaim its rebirth. It was something Richard had felt from the outset he had to have done.

Overnight accommodation had been added to his schedule of improvements, the spacious new dining-room, now virtually complete, soon to be serviced by an equally new, state-of-the-art kitchen. Good food and a bed for the night at a reasonable charge was the plan, even if providing them was proving increasingly costly with each day that passed.

His ongoing problem with the language had seen him using an English/French pocket dictionary to string words together. Watching him frantically turning pages had amused Madame Darrieux, initially—but they were soon communicating in this way as if they'd been doing it for years.

Richard was aware that she was a priceless asset at this stage in the Chateau's redevelopment. Everyone appreciated good food, and exploiting her culinary expertise had already injected new life into the day to day running of the place. Introducing her grandmother's recipes for meat and fruit pies had been a masterstroke, a timely response to their need for quick meals, but the day was fast approaching when demand would outrun her ability to supply, especially with Carlow Mason forestry personnel soon to arrive.

She was a remarkable woman, he was coming to realize that more every day; tireless, innovative, anxious to please, and he was still looking for an excuse to invite her and Monsieur to stay on. Andre had watched the situation develop, reminding her it was time for them to leave; sharply; accusingly; even jealously, Richard thought. She was doing her best to hide it, but she was clearly upset.

"So leaving's your number one priority, is it?" he growled at Andre the following morning. "It had nothing to do with you, then, that the Chateau nearly died?" He was growing more annoyed by the second, Monsieur enjoying his lunch oblivious to the developing argument. "So who do you blame?" he continued. "Antoinette?"

Antoinette was the diminutive lady who helped Madame Darrieux in the kitchen and with cleaning. Still Andre said nothing. "Let's see what your father thinks, shall we?" Richard was adding when Laura came in.

"He's been having a go at his mother," Richard grunted.

Andre shifted uncomfortably. The last thing he wanted was to fall out with Richard—not to mention his parents and especially now.

"Okay," Richard said. "This is what I'll do. I'll give you some new products to sell while I work with your father to increase our acreage of vines. And while we're doing that—your father, mother *and* yourself—will be salaried and given an opportunity to buy back into the business."

Andre hesitated.

"Well—go on," Richard growled. "Put it to your father—unless you'd rather I tell him how you've been treating your mother?"

Andre knew Richard well enough to know he meant what he said.

"Is he telling him?" Richard whispered to Laura as Andre spoke to his father.

She nodded.

"All of it?"

She nodded again, still listening to Andre. "You do realize how much all this will cost, don't you?" she whispered. "It'll be hard enough to design, manufacture and market a range of new products, never mind supporting the family while you do it."

"Jesus, Laura." He reached into his briefcase and threw a file of papers on to the table in front of her.

She found cost and profit estimates, cash flow forecasts, capital expenditure projections; everything in detail. He did nothing by half; the file also containing costings associated with the commercial launch of *Madame Darrieux's Original Meat and Fruit Pies*, as he'd chosen to call them.

It was Sunday evening. Their discussion had lasted the entire afternoon. The business would be divided three ways; Richard, the family, and at the eleventh hour, Laura herself. Eighty per cent Richard, the family collectively and Laura ten per cent each.

Richard would retain the freehold, of course, endeavouring at the first opportunity to increase the size of the vineyard. It would be a question of balance, really: quality at the Chateau, volume elsewhere. The cold-store would be financed by local grants and a loan from Credit Lyonnais or a similar organization, guaranteed by himself. They would inject half a million euros by way of working capital; half now, the balance when the cold-store was commissioned.

Having double-checked Richard's figures, Laura had agreed to oversee the launch of Madame's pies. "I'll use Giles Morton," she told him.

"Who?" Richard asked.

"Giles Morton. You remember Giles? He was a guest at the Manor that awful weekend."

The name eluded Richard. But then everything about the weekend of the murder had become pretty vague, excluding the shooting itself and how gorgeous Laura had looked the previous evening.

"Geoff's never liked him," she continued. "He can come across as a bit of a bumbler, I suppose, but the major retailers rate him which is good enough for me." She paused. "An interesting day, all things considered. This morning the family were leaving; now they've not only agreed to stay on, they're scheduled to hand back a significant slice of the cash they were paid to move out—Monsieur in exchange for the prospect of more vines; Andre with the chance to visit cities he's been dying to see, so busy when he does he'll have no time to explore them, and Madame with the catering to supervise—*plus*, as if she won't have enough to contend with, a pie manufacturing plant to keep an eye on.

"An amazing coincidence, don't you think?" she added, "all this just happening to coincide with Andre being unkind to his mother. They won't listen to a word he says, I told myself; then, *abracadabra* it's done and I still can't believe it."

Giles Morton was surprised and delighted to receive Laura's call. When his secretary announced she was on the telephone asking to speak to him, he ran his fingers through what was left of his hair and straightened his tie before taking the call.

In his mid-forties, this irredeemable victim of rich food and drink looked as if he'd been dragged half asleep out of bed and bundled up in a blanket. He always wore well-tailored clothes, but his body appeared to have the capacity to vary in size and shape from one hour to the next, ruining the appearance of whatever he chose to wear.

"Laura," he said, searching for the cuff of his shirt up the sleeve of his jacket. "This is a pleasant surprise."

"Giles, dear," she purred. "I have some new products to bring to the marketplace. Would you be an angel and show me what to do?"

He loved it, especially from her. "What kind of products?"

"We'll discuss that when we meet, shall we? I have my diary in front of me."

He consulted his schedule. "I have a window on—er—Wednesday. Shall we say lunch?" He was excited, looking forward to what had to come next. "Now—" he added eagerly. "Where shall we meet?"

"Bordeaux, I think." She said it quickly, followed by the telephone number of the Chateau. "Ring me with your ETA at Merignac and I'll have a car there to meet you."

Giles Morton was Managing Director of the public relations, marketing arm of Carlow Mason under the Chairmanship of Robert Barker. Mason had said more than once that much as he disliked Morton and his kind, Barker couldn't have done it without him. He viewed public-relations/marketing executives as parasites; parasites a sane thinking democracy didn't need. Indeed, we hadn't needed them to build the British Empire, but we'd been quick to lose it once we decided we did. Carlow must have viewed Morton as an asset or he'd have long since disappeared.

Giles claimed haughtily that he was one of the *Sussex* Mortons—whatever that was supposed to mean. According to him this supposedly aristocratic heritage—to which he frequently referred—afforded him entry into some very high places. And if you forgave him his looks, his performance in that regard was undeniably impressive.

Laura ushered him into the Chateau's big kitchen. "Sorry about the dust," she said, "We're having a spring clean." She introduced him to Richard. "You remember Richard Wells?" His reaction suggested otherwise. "Well, perhaps not," she continued. "We none of us care to remember too much about that awful week-end. You met at the Manor."

"Ah—yes," Morton said. "Hello, Richard—dreadful business." They shook hands. "Did the police manage to establish what possessed the wretched creature?"

Laura had replied before Richard could speak. "We thought we'd have something to eat before we get down to business."

Richard handed Morton a glass of the '82. "So, Giles, how's the world using you?"

"Moderately well, I suppose," Morton replied, not quite managing to tear his eyes off Laura. "My work's predominantly in-house at the moment."

"Well, cheers, anyway," Richard said brightly. "Thank you

for coming."

Madame Darrieux served their food.

Morton took a tentative mouthful. He'd never associated the French with meat pies and was agreeably surprised. "This is exceptional."

"Yes—it's the '82. We think it's our best."

"I meant the pie, actually," Morton added.

Richard laughed. "Oh, I see. Yes—they are good, aren't they?"

Morton dissected the pie with his knife. "The pastry melts in your mouth. What's in the filling?"

"Meat, grapes and red wine, among other things," Laura said. "Madame says it's a secret, family recipe over a hundred years old."

Morton took a second mouthful. "Remarkable—nothing close to it at home."

The room fell silent, Richard eventually suggesting he open a second bottle.

"Not for me," Morton said quickly. "Best if I keep a clear head."

Madame Darrieux delivered more dishes. "Sorry about this," Richard whispered. "There's nothing she likes better than impressing our guests. I'm sure you understand. We don't want to lose her."

Morton took a deep breath before sampling the second pie. "My word."

"Something wrong?"

He shook his head and laughed. "So when do we launch Madame's meat and fruit pies?"

Laura put a hand on his arm. "I'm sorry, Giles. I couldn't resist testing them on you. They're incredible, aren't they?"

He smiled. "Indeed, they are. Quite the best I've ever tasted."

Laura introduced Madame Darrieux and passed on his comments. Her smile lit up the kitchen and launched their campaign.

"Giles Morton for you," Jane whispered, handing the telephone to Carlow.

He frowned. "Giles—how are you?"

"Fine, thank you, Mike. Just back from Bordeaux, actually—Chateau Darrieux. I take it you've no objection to our running the campaign?"

Carlow thought quickly. "I've been up to my eyes. Which campaign is this?"

"The pies."

"Oh, the pies. Who did you speak to?"

"Laura and Richard Wells."

"Right," Carlow said. "What are they suggesting?"

Jane left the room and hurried up to Master. She'd hardly sat down when Carlow came in behind her. "What do you know about Laura and Richard?"

She was dreading the thought of having to give a direct answer. "How do you mean?"

"I can't believe what Morton has just told me."

She busied herself with the computer, holding her breath. "And what was that?"

"They've asked him to run a campaign to sell meat and fruit pies."

Carlow confronted Richard as soon as he got back. "Giles Morton rang—something about a campaign to sell pies?"

"Yes—Laura suggested I use him," Richard said easily. "I'm converting an outhouse to a bakery and cold-store and starting mass production."

"So you've seen a lot of her, then?"

"Who?"

"Laura, of course."

"Oh, I see—well, yes—I suppose I must have what with this and the conveyance. And she's invested some cash," he added quickly.

"Has she indeed?"

"Sorry I was gone a bit longer than planned," Richard went on, "Refurbishing the damned place is costing me the earth."

TWENTY

Chas Chambers ran into DI Thomas's office to answer the telephone. He'd earned his disfavour once and had no intention of doing so again. "DI Thomas's phone," he announced.

It was Keen on the line. "It's DCS Keen, Guv'" he called round the door, "—DCS Keen on line two—"

Thomas hurried in and waved him away. "DI Thomas."

"Nobby—it's Keen. I mentioned Westminster and our suspicions about Yarwood and my sources clammed up."

"Did they, indeed? So where does that leave us?"

"You tell me. This *lady-friend* of yours—any idea who she might be?"

"None at all."

"But you'd recognize her voice if you heard it again?"

"I think so. Have you thought any more about Templeton and Carlow?"

"Oh, yes," Keen groaned. "Whatever Yarwood's up to it won't be his cash on the line."

"Which puts Carlow in the frame," Thomas added.

"It does—but I seem to be plagued by Templetons at the moment."

October had abducted a mist-shrouded afternoon from the run up to Christmas and seen it weep softly in protest for the rest of the day. Carlow's mood matched the weather. He nudged up the thermostat on the central heating and peered into the gloom through the big penthouse windows, the lights of the city spread out below like a post-wedding carpet of luminous confetti.

It was five o'clock—dark before it had any right to be. He turned on all the lights and ran a hot bath. For years, when he'd been confronted by problems which appeared to be insoluble, there'd always been something or someone to turn to—a meeting to plan; a report he had to read; a letter to dictate: things sufficiently immediate and demanding to divert his attention. If he'd ever needed his old self-confidence, he needed it now.

Penny Wise arrived with her colleague and the clearly disgruntled politician. "Harry—" Carlow said, expecting and getting what his mother had described as an *old fashioned look*.

"Bastard," Wetherby whispered. The women had introduced themselves in the hotel foyer, in full public view. He blamed Carlow for not warning him.

Penny Wise introduced her colleague. *Amanda* was an elegant woman with naturally blond hair and turquoise blue eyes —mid to late forties Carlow guessed, although he'd have hesitated to say so if asked. Penny Wise, the business end of the duo, was dark skinned and curvaceous, probably of Indian origin and in her mid thirties.

They opted for champagne.

"I've got a decent bottle for us, Harry," Carlow said. "There— take a look for yourself."

Ignoring Carlow's *bottle*, Wetherby helped himself to a very large scotch and retired to the sofa, surprised when Amanda settled alongside him.

Carlow sat down. "So are we all set for Portugal?"

Wetherby said nothing.

"I thought we'd ask Amanda to act as your personal assistant, Harry, while we're out there," Carlow continued.

Wetherby grunted something unintelligible and sought reassurance in his scotch, recalling everything he'd ever said about middle-aged politicians and their *female* assistants.

"Why, thank you," Amanda said in a voice light-years removed from anything the yorkshireman had been to bed with.

"I shall look forward to that." Her eyes sparkled mischievously as she smoothed the lapels of his jacket, the gesture so unselfconsciously intimate she must have practised it for hours for it to be so effective. One small sweep of her hand and Wetherby was lost. "Perhaps we can rehearse your lectures together, Mr Wetherby?" she said quietly.

He hesitated, his eyes finally meeting hers, "Why not—and y'might as well call me Harry, lass; everyone does."

"Thank you, Harry," she replied softly, a perfectly manicured hand *accidentally* coming to rest on the back of his own.

He hadn't allowed himself to think about it; the idea inconceivable—out of the question until the touch of her hand had set his mind free. As Mason had once observed on a similar occasion, there was little doubt he'd *sample the full menu before his next bowl of cornflakes.* Wetherby was free to say no, of course, but who in their right mind would have chosen to say no to a woman like Amanda?

They sat down to a meal that lacked the home-cooked appeal of a Mrs Williams creation. Wetherby picked at his food, telling himself that *Amanda* couldn't possibly be interested in someone like him—a man who hadn't thought about women in that way pretty much since his wife died. Anyway, he hadn't the heart for it anymore—and certainly not the body.

In contrast, Amanda was clearly enjoying herself, laughing at Carlow's well-used stories and responding with her own, intent on encouraging Wetherby by allowing the hem of her skirt to ride subtly higher as the evening wore on. Finally, in the absence of discernible progress, she took him by the hand and got to her feet.

Carlow was impressed by her perseverance.

"It's time for my beauty sleep, isn't it Harry?" she said. "A girl has to look after herself."

Carlow grinned. "The far bedroom is yours. You'll find your bag on the bed."

She nodded, keeping a firm grip on Wetherby.

Carlow threw off his shoes and tie as the couple disappeared.

"Now—Miss Wise," he said, settling back in his chair. "I want the names of Wilder's partners."

"Who said there were other people involved?"

"You did. Sit down."

Surprised by his tone, she did as she was told. "Whoa now," he added, "other *people—plural*?"

She looked him in the eye. "There's nothing more to be said."

"Not less than twenty five years of age and sexually experienced—Wilder and her partner insisted on it; remember? Look, I'm not concerned with the morality or legality of what you do, but let's not forget who shot the Prime Minister."

Her eyes opened wide. "I had nothing to do with that."

"Fine—so you won't mind talking to the police?"

She glared at him. "I'll deny every word of this if anyone asks."

Carlow waited.

"Geraldine started the group with Fiona Forrest about ten years ago."

"And what part did Mrs Forrest play? Carlow asked."

"She vetted potential clients—*obliged* more than one of them, too, or so I've been told. But I'm sure there were others. I may even have met one."

"Man or woman?" Carlow asked eagerly.

"Man."

"Describe him."

"Tall—"

"Wearing glasses?"

"Yes."

"With a habit of tipping his head forward to look over them?"

"Not that I noticed."

"Slim and grey-haired—a fussy, cold sort of fish?"

She shook her head. "No, nothing like that. An evil looking man with the blackest eyes I've ever seen."

"But you don't know his name?"

"Sorry, no. Fiona said he was a very good friend. That's how we describe them—good or very good, depending on how often they use us—regulars or otherwise, you understand? I assumed he was a source of introductions rather than a client."

"I see."

"But he kept staring at me, his eyes promising what he'd do to me if he ever got the chance. I thought it might be the colour of my skin, and was terrified he'd try to book me."

"But he didn't—try to *book you,* I mean?"

"No—thank God."

"And what makes you think there were other people involved?"

"Little things that were said."

"Anything else you can tell me? It's important."

She shook her head.

He stood up and, pulling off his shirt, changed the subject. "Amanda seemed surprisingly keen to bed dear old Harry?"

"Her speciality."

"What, old blokes like Harry?"

"She doesn't go to bed with geriatrics if that's what you're thinking. *Old* Harry's going to feel twenty years younger by morning—lucky man."

"Really?"

"Yes, really."

He chuckled. "Right—time for your *speciality*."

"What about the police?"

"Forget them. Come on—surprise me. I've been looking forward to this for days."

"This way," she said, leading him into the shower and closing the door behind them.

Carlow's mind was racing. An objective analysis was required. He'd been doing his damnest but with little success. What he'd received from Penny Wise—including her *speciality*—had done nothing to assist.

So Fiona Forrest knew everything at first hand; not just the sketchy stuff they all knew or something she might have gleaned from a Downing Street grapevine. She knew these people by name—might even have recruited some of them. And where did Templeton fit into all this? Who else was involved? Were they party to the murder? Concentrate, he kept telling himself. Forget the supposition and stick to the facts. The tense face in the bathroom mirror stared back at him. He went back to bed.

"I was beginning to think you'd got a woman in there," Penny Wise said.

"Just the one?" he said offhandedly. Yarwood was doing what he'd been paid for, Templeton everything asked of him and more, as Jane had been quick to point out. But if this was a conspiracy, who were the conspirators and what were they hoping to achieve?

The women were available to the occupants of only the wealthiest of bedrooms. The reasoning there was clear. What was difficult to understand, almost impossible in fact, was why, having been told about a partner—Geraldine and *her partner*, for Christ's sake—he'd done nothing to give the partner a name.

Penny Wise had risen early, left a note for him and gone. She'd been right about Wetherby. He looked like the cat that got the cream as they sat down to eat. "Sleep well?" Carlow asked him.

The politician looked at him in disbelief. "I didn't get to close m'bloody eyes until it w'time to get up."

Carlow smiled as Wetherby helped himself to a second bowl of cornflakes.

"What's s'funny?" he demanded.

"Oh—just something Mason once said. So you're happy about Portugal?"

"Is the lass coming?"

"Of course."

"When do we leave?"

"That's the spirit. And now I'll have to hurry you." He crossed the room to the telephone and called Mason."

"He's gone into the village for cigarettes," Jane informed

him.

"Ah." He looked at his watch. "It'll be twelve before I get there, and we have to talk. Get him to call the car if there's a problem."

Wetherby was ready to leave when he ended the call. "I won't live to regret this, will I?" he asked as the lift began its descent.

"Nothing's certain, old son, in this mad bloody world."

"Thanks a bundle," the politician grunted. "I've already witnessed enough double dealing at Westminster to last me a lifetime."

Carlow laughed. "I promise you, Harry, we're on the same side."

Carlow explained to Mason and Jane how Fiona Forrest had teamed up with Wilder ten years earlier. It had come straight from the horse's mouth, he told them—direct from Penny Wise. She was sure there'd been more people involved—partners, that is—including one she'd met.

For once in his life Mason could think of nothing to say.

"That was *definitely* why she married Forrest, then?" Jane said.

Carlow nodded. "These women are available to only the wealthiest of punters, and what better way to meet them than marrying a queer at the centre of Government? Read alcoholic for homosexual and it was a similar story with Wilder."

"So what now?" Jane asked.

He shrugged. "The good Mrs Forrest has clearly been lying from the start. She knew about Templeton's niece all right. We'd be downright stupid not to wonder what else she knows."

"So how have we managed to come this far?" Jane continued.

"Perhaps they're too busy with the women to bother with us?" Carlow suggested.

Jane thought about it. "Possible, I suppose—particularly if Yarwood forced them to gather information as well as having sex."

"What kind of information?" Mason asked.

"I've no idea. But these women spend their time in some very exclusive bedrooms, don't they—and Templeton has access to information about some very up-market people."

"So—?"

"So what he's passed on to us could have come from either or both of these sources."

Mason looked confused.

"For heaven's sake think, Geoff," she grumbled. "Even with the Iron Curtain gone, markets are certain to still exist for intelligence gathered from politicians and civil servants. Improbable, you may say, but if his principal aim has been to collect ammunition for blackmail—and the evidence suggests it probably has—the repercussions could be endless. And we can't ignore the fact that despite Yarwood's far reaching influence, your *lady-friend* failed to point him out."

TWENTY-ONE

Gordon Templeton arrived at his desk to find the telephone ringing, his secretary informing him that a Mister Carlow had been trying to reach him.

Seizing the first excuse to escape he'd had in a week, he arrived at the Manor as relaxed as Carlow had ever seen him. Mason and Jane would join their conversation later—if, given the circumstances, there was one left to join.

Carlow greeted him coldly. "You knew exactly what Fiona Forrest and Wilder were doing, didn't you—why didn't you tell me?"

"I didn't think it relevant."

"So was it relevant to something else you're involved in?"

Templeton frowned. "I'm sorry, but I don't understand."

"I think you do. These women are providing sexual favours to a growing circle of men, we know that; but it's not all they provide, is it?"

Templeton hesitated, eying him warily. "You're right, of course," he said finally, still studying Carlow's face. "Wilder approached the then Fiona Hamilton, arguing that providing sexual favours for men and the occasional woman, had the potential to make them rich—*very* rich, if they concentrated on serving the right people and weren't shy about charging exorbitant fees.

And but for being against the Law, the idea appealed to the ambitious Miss Hamilton. Not to be denied, Wilder insisted that as long as they confined themselves to catering for the wealthiest and best connected in society, and the women they retained to offer *the service* were without exception, mature, attractive to look at, well educated, sexually experienced and outstandingly well remunerated; in short, perfectly suited to the environment in which they'd be called upon to work —they'd be able to guarantee privacy with everything taking place behind securely closed doors.

This removed most if not all Miss Hamilton's concerns, and they set about establishing themselves by initially catering for a close-knit circle at Westminster and in Whitehall. Later, they hand-picked husbands for themselves whose social standing might be expected to assist them in achieving their goals. As you know, Wilder became Lady Morrison and Hamilton Mrs Forrest. The men having neither a sexual interest *in* nor capability *with* women, the one homosexual the other an impotent alcoholic, they were free to serve the clientele they'd set out to serve.

According to Mrs Forrest demand rapidly increased and they were soon able to add to their number, everything progressing smoothly for several years. But they hadn't foreseen what lay ahead. Approximately five years ago, shortly before Miss Hamilton became Mrs Forrest, none other than the resourceful Desmond Yarwood appeared on the scene."

Carlow screwed up his face. "Why doesn't that surprise me?"

"He undertook to keep his knowledge of their activities to himself," Templeton went on, "if they agreed to have their ladies put a series of questions to their clients—questions, of course, that were designed to provide him with information he could subsequently use against them. Wilder and Hamilton had no choice, and after several months worrying what he might demand from them next, the newly married Mrs Forrest confided in one of my colleagues, who immediately referred the problem to me.

By this time Yarwood had a comprehensive list of their clients—fully aware, thanks to their questioning, of where and by whom most of those who weren't sitting MPs, Whitehall civil servants or members of the House of Lords, were employed, plus to whom each of them was related, with whom they had relationships, sexual and otherwise, and almost certainly more. The situation was potentially explosive. So—knowing he would have made himself known to most if not all of them, I did the only thing I could; I challenged him.

Unfortunately, my past being less than blemish free as I told you, I was able to relieve the pressure on them only by undertaking to provide him with information myself. I threatened to have third parties go to the police should he ever decide to expose them—or me, for that matter, but I'm not sure he believed me.

So you can see how the opportunity to involve myself in your project arrived like manna from heaven." His brow furrowed. "Nothing's guaranteed, I know, but I think his receipt of your fifteen million pounds will put an end to his activities, at which point I shall retire from public life. I've advised Mrs Forrest to consider something similar."

"So you succeeded in controlling Yarwood," Carlow said thoughtfully, "to some extent at least, but as far as she's concerned our opting to use him amounted to consorting with the enemy?"

"Indeed. She's convinced he'll eventually return to knocking at her door."

"As, of course, he might very well," Carlow added.

"Quite. But, as I said, I consider the possibility remote and have told her so. His influence will be all but destroyed by his involvement with you."

"But that's no consolation to her, is it? Neither she nor you can be certain of anything. Is there anything else I should know?"

"I don't think so."

"So you had no direct relationship with Wilder and her women, have no idea why she arrived at the Manor with a gun—or what prompted her to use it?"

"Precisely—except that, like Mrs Forrest, she no doubt lived in fear of Yarwood."

"I see that—yes. But you were never personally involved in their enterprise?"

"Good Lord, no."

Carlow stood up. "Right—I think that's all I needed to know, unless you've something to add?"

Templeton shook his head.

They were playing snooker when Jane and Mason returned. Jane noticed Carlow studying her legs as she straightened her skirt and settled by the fire. Mason joined her. He'd been a model escort all evening, worried about Fiona, but attentive and considerate.

"So—?" he said to Carlow.

Carlow poured them drinks before outlining his conversation with Templeton, asking Templeton himself to relay the questions he'd been asked and the answers he'd given.

TWENTY-TWO

Carlow liked to hit a soft draw off the first tee at Penina. On this occasion he'd pushed his ball too far out to the right. It was playable, but he'd have to fade a long iron or little wood to have any chance of finding the green with his second.

Jane drove the buggy.

"Blocked the bloody thing," he hissed irritably.

She thought it best to say nothing. The game had been equally confusing on television, with talk of *birdies and bogeys, cutting it up and running it in,* to say nothing of *borrows,* and *greens that were ten or eleven on the stimp meter,* whatever that meant?

They referred to some of their clubs as woods when clearly they were metal, and it had even been suggested that if they carried on the way they were going, some of them might not make the weekend. If their facial expressions were anything to go by, it might easily have been a life and death issue.

She'd given up watching in the end—wondering if the leading players were paid millions of pounds, or maybe it was dollars, to lead ordinary mortals to believe they could master the game—if, of course, they paid for lessons, bought the equipment, the clothing and all the other paraphernalia that apparently went with it. Convincing the incompetent they had talent was obviously big business.

She drew up alongside the ball and watched him select a club from his bag. He hit it perfectly, she thought, only to see his face contort with agony. "Down—DOWN!" he shouted. "Oh, go on—get in there."

"If you don't mind my asking?" she said as he apologized for his outburst and they headed for the green. "Exactly what sort of game is this? In all the years I've known you, you've made decisions that frightened me speechless with an air of almost total detachment, and yet an inanimate, inoffensive little white ball seems to be wreaking psychological havoc, and we haven't been out here for more than ten minutes?"

He laughed as much at himself and because she was right as at the way that she said it. "You have to hit balls every day if you want to play this game well. The golfing gods are fully aware that I've recently hit none. Perhaps we should sit down one evening with a bottle of wine and a video, and I can try to explain?"

She was all for the wine, but decided against telling him what he could do with his video.

Leaping off the buggy, he retrieved the ball from the dry ditch short right of the green, and abandoning the hole, directed her through the trees to the second tee. "Come over here," he said. She obeyed, leaving the buggy and doing her best to hide her disinterest.

"Right—" he said earnestly. "The object of the game is to get the ball into each hole in the fewest possible number of shots, making the *aggregate* for the full eighteen holes—the *round*—as low as you can make it. This hole is what's known as a par four, indicating that four shots are the maximum a player should take. A tee shot, a second to the green and two putts.

One shot less than par is known as a birdie; one more, a bogey. Not that it's relevant. Call them what you will, it won't change your score. The green's at the far end on the left." He pointed into the distance. "Can you see it?"

"No—oh yes I can. To the left of the gateway?"

"That's it—over the ditch, alongside the hedge. I can reach with two shots, so I want to hit my first down the right, leaving the widest possible angle for my second to the flag. You'll see what I mean when we get further down. Too far right, of course, and I'll find myself in the trees. If you stand behind me—" He waved her further back—"you should be able to follow the flight of the ball."

The tee shot he'd been looking for at the first, he now produced at the second. He hit it marginally too far right, but with the ball drawing it took a favourable bounce and came to rest in an ideal position on the right hand side of the fairway. "Did you see how it curved from right to left?" he asked her.

She nodded.

"Well that's a draw. If the curve's bigger and more violent, it's known as a hook. In the opposite direction, left to right, a little curve's a fade and a big one a slice. They're not difficult to achieve once you know what you're doing, but controlling the severity of the curve requires a great deal of practise—it's known as working the ball."

She wondered why he didn't save himself the trouble and hit the thing straight, at the same time deciding it might be wise not to ask.

They'd come out on the first flight with half the delegates. Harry Wetherby and the others, along with Mason and Fiona Forrest, would arrive on the second. With the aircraft to themselves, Wilder's women were scheduled to touch down at Faro in the late afternoon.

Mason and Fiona Forrest might have been expected to welcome this opportunity to get away from London together, but the atmosphere between them was noticeably strained. She continued to insist that had she added Yarwood's own to his long list of names, and he'd found out, he wouldn't have hesitated to expose them, no matter what Templeton said. When all was said and done, it had been his association with Yarwood which had led her to distrust him in the first place. And, yes, she had married Forrest to aid their expansion—as Geraldine had Morrison.

Mason left the aeroplane a long way from happy about anything she'd said.

Carlow settled for nine holes. Jane learned a lot about golf—too much perhaps. Indeed, long before they drew up at the bar by the pool, she'd made up her mind it wasn't for her.

The first drink was marvellously cold, inviting a second, but they decided to change and come back for a swim.

She parked the buggy, ran up to her room, showered, changed, and hurried up to his suite. He came to the door only half dressed. "Do you know?" she said breathlessly, "today's the longest we've ever been together without talking about work."

"If you say so."

She crossed to the window. "I keep thinking about France. Why didn't you sack me?"

He smiled. "Good question."

She turned back to face him. "Of course, I could always apologize now—?"

Night falls on the Algarve, fresh, clean and welcome. Faces glowing with the warmth of the day leave the sun to its rest, its task forgotten till morning. There's such certainty about it. Dressed for dinner, and more relaxed than she could remember, Jane stood on the balcony overlooking the swimming pool excited by the prospect of the weekend ahead. In their short time at Penina, her relationship with Carlow had mellowed. She was less anxious about it now; determined to enjoy every moment.

Albeit old fashioned in some respects by modern standards, the hotel itself was comfortable and spacious. It had been designed to accommodate wealthy golfers and made no apology for the fact. You arrived to discover that venturing further into the Portuguese countryside was unnecessary. Everything you were likely to need was here at the hotel. Bordered by villas flower bedecked and white, the Penina Estate was a place to rise early, ahead of the sun's heat—a place to relax to the sound of water sprinklers and motor mowers, to listen to running water filtering the swimming pool and the raucous revelry of the frogs in the watercourses, welcoming the new day.

But there was little but toil for the Portuguese in this affluent world apart. Friendly; unobtrusively providing the hotel's five-star service, they pandered to every whim of every guest, leaving them to eat, sleep, swim, play golf and make love—and in no stressful order of priority.

Jane took the lift to the ground floor and wandered through the brightly lit foyer. The Wilder contingent would be absent tonight, their activities scheduled to begin at their villa the following evening—at a party to which everyone had been invited. A dance-floor had been laid in the garden, the trees festooned with coloured lights and a spotlight for the fountain, the summer-house a temporary bar—caterers moving in.

According to Mason the fun would start when they let the dog see the rabbit. This evening, they were meeting for drinks and introductions before dinner. The main restaurant was at the other end of the hotel. This, the Fish Restaurant, smaller, a la carte and much the more intimate, was ideal for small groups to spend their evenings together.

He jumped to his feet and offered her the chair beside Fiona Forrest. The victims—Jane could only think of them as such—began to arrive in twos and threes. Eager to be seen in the company of their esteemed leader's wife, those from the Government benches made a beeline for her, while the Whitehall civil servants among them and those from the other side of the House, settled for nodding in her direction, avoiding what some might have seen as fraternizing with the *dark-forces of capitalism*.

"Are y'all right, lass?" Wetherby asked, crushing Fiona Forrest in a bear hug and pecking her on the cheek. He seemed not to care what anyone thought.

Jane thought her miscast as a Prime Minister's wife. She displayed the customary airs and graces, and it had to be improbable that she was the first Madam cum prostitute to reside at Number Ten, but it was difficult to ignore.

Drinks materialized as if by magic, the service excellent, the restaurant busy as they sat down to eat. Jane decided on smoked salmon followed by charcoal-grilled sole. She'd no knowledge of Portuguese wines, leaving the choice to Carlow. He opted for a white Joao Pires, offering to share the bottle with her. *Pickies*, as she instantly referred to them, suddenly appeared; pate, carrot, melba toast and butter, not forgetting the inevitable olives, and for one precious moment she experienced the heaven of pure joy, so deliriously happy was she to be there with Carlow.

The victims were predominantly male. Indeed, there were only two women at the table in addition to Fiona Forrest and herself. She'd seen one of them on television but couldn't place the other, wine soon flowing in quantities which perhaps demonstrated why the House of Commons cellar was a regular bone of budgetary contention. In contrast, the single, perfectly chilled bottle of Joao Pires was delightful.

They adjourned to their beds around midnight, the seminar scheduled to begin at nine-thirty the next morning. It had been organized that way; Saturday and Sunday free, leaving the victims the maximum possible time for *play*.

Jane was down early to finalize arrangements. Carlow would play the welcoming host, followed by sessions featuring Wetherby and himself as the first pair of speakers.

The morning surprised her. Both men were accomplished performers, their belief in what they were saying instantly communicating itself. Social change within the European Community, or the lack of it, was Wetherby's theme, while Carlow opened with the anti-social conduct of big business generally, and more specifically the Banks.

Given the diverse political beliefs of those present, Jane was enthralled, especially by the question and answer exchanges. The other speakers, including Fiona Forrest, of course, had yet to be heard, and the delegates had yet to experience the first of the Wilder parties, but by the time they adjourned for lunch and the day, she was convinced the formal proceedings would be beneficial to everyone. "Who's the woman with Harry?" she asked Carlow as the gathering broke up. "She's remarkably attractive as well as attentive."

"Yes, she is, isn't she? Her name's Amanda. She's his PA." He grinned. "At least she is while we're here."

Jane enjoyed a snack in the cool of the sandwich bar before strolling down the lawn to sit by the pool, settled under a parasol with a book when Carlow stopped at the top of the bank behind her.

"Ah—there you are," he said. He was dressed for golf, his bag on his back, heading for the practise ground. "I thought I'd hit a few balls before we take a spin up the coast. There's a little restaurant I know—" He hesitated. "If you'd like to, I mean?"

"I'd love to," she said eagerly.

She watched him stride purposefully away. "Remember," she called after him. "It's only a game."

He grinned and waved without turning round.

Someone dived clumsily from the springboard half way down the pool. The cascading water seemed to sparkle like a million Portuguese diamonds in the brilliant midday sunshine. The glow she was feeling was not all from the sun.

"Penny Wise seems efficient?" Mason said, for want of something to say.

Fiona Forrest's response was cold and impersonal. "She does what she's paid for."

He was silent for a moment. "Look, we can't go on like this."

Now she said nothing.

"So do you want to split up?" he eventually asked.

"If that's what you want."

"No, it's not what I want. I expected to be asking you to marry me once we'd sorted ourselves out. And marriage had never crossed my mind before I met you. Now I'm clear about nothing."

She'd listened to men talk like this before.

"Discovering what you do has hit me hard," he continued. "I'm doing my best not to be hypocritical, but to be frank I find it, well—I find it sordid and distasteful. I doubt very much if you've ever wanted for anything—a good home, education or the rest, so, I'm sorry, but I can't stop asking myself—why—why prostitution?"

"Money, what else?" she said instantly. "Daddy might be wealthy, but I've had to work for everything I've got. Yes, there were *perks* when I was younger; horses, cars and the like as soon as I was old enough, and I do understand that most people don't get even that, but I wanted the best—*my* things; my *own* things. I'd no desire to be replaced, as my mother was, by a two-faced bitch out to spend my husband's money and take my place in his bed. Those women are the whores. No—I'd no intention of contemplating my old age in that situation, and nothing has changed.

You can't imagine what it's like to be a woman. There's no question of *opting* to do this or that. There's no time—too many man-made conventions and prejudices eating up the years with no guarantees at the end of them. So I took a shortcut. Geraldine summed it up. She said servicing male lust was the quickest and most reliable highway to profit. *'They'll fuck anything that moves,'* she said—*'cheat on their wives, mistresses, girlfriends—yes, even their mothers, without batting an eye. And they'll pay good money—and plenty of it—if what's on offer is packaged the way they like it.'*

If we hadn't provided the service someone else would. We aimed for the top. Maximum gain for the minimum of effort was our motto, and it worked. At least it did until Yarwood came along. So I won't be apologizing. I won't be saying I'm sorry and pretending to regret it, because I'm not and I don't.

Anyway, what's so different about what you and Mike Carlow have been doing all these years? Don't you line *your* pockets for as little as possible in return? At least we make people happy —well, those who can afford us. How much happiness can you claim to have contributed to this sorry round? You're making the effort now, I see that—but take a good look at the people you've enlisted to help you. That ought to tell you something.

You get your head straight about me, and I'll let you know

how I feel about you—if you still want me to. But don't expect me to jump into your bed every time you feel horny. We sort this out now, or we call it a day."

"Fair enough," Mason said, thinking it was a long way from fair. He left her, drove round to the villa for a final check with Penny Wise and the caterers before making himself scarce. He wouldn't be good company, anyway. And seeing her with these women would only make him feel worse. He'd drive into Portimao—yes, that's what he'd do—have a meal and a few beers. Things might look different in the morning.

But marrying a homosexual to increase your turnover? Come on! And to then have the audacity to tell him to like it or lump it. Shit, no—it was a long way from fair.

Fiona Forrest arrived at the party expecting to find him. Half an hour later, when he'd failed to appear, she let Penny Wise know she was leaving and took a car back to the hotel. She looked in the bar and both restaurants. He was nowhere to be seen. Up in their room, she poured a large gin and tonic and lay down on the bed, while back from their drive up the coast, well fed and relaxed, Carlow and Jane called in at the villa.

The party was in full swing, the garden a fairy-lit scene of music and dancing. They weren't surprised by the absence of Mason and his lady friend, until they learned she'd left after half an hour and he hadn't been there at all.

They drove back to the hotel and were sitting drinking coffee when he came in. Carlow took one look at his face and offered him a cup. "We thought we'd relax for a few minutes before turning in," he told him.

"So you didn't go to the party?" Jane said.

Carlow poured their coffee and ordered large brandies.

Mason was in some kind of daze. "She gave me an ultimatum. I come to terms with her *profession* or basically, it's off. Can you believe that?"

Carlow shook his head. "More to the point, can *you*—and do you even want to?"

"I told her I was shocked, but it sounded ridiculous coming from me."

"Oh, come on," Jane said indignantly. "It is prostitution we're talking about. She didn't hop into bed with a couple of old friends. The motive was money. She even married Forrest to maximize her income. You've every right to be shocked."

"I agree," Carlow echoed. "But the problem's in your head. If you see her as a prostitute, it's over. Alternatively, if you see her as a woman with a past you can both put behind you, I'd say you have a chance."

"Any doubt at all," Jane stressed, "I suggest you forget her."

Carlow nodded. "I agree with that, too."

Thinking it was easier said than done, Mason swallowed the last of his brandy, wishing them an unenthusiastic good night, and having established at Reception that Fiona had the key, headed for their room.

She opened the door to his knock, but neither of them spoke as she went back to bed.

TWENTY-THREE

Chas Chambers put his head round DI Thomas's door hoping to find him. Thomas looked up. "Ah, good," Chambers said eagerly. "Can I have a word, Guv?"

Thomas was tempted to refuse—to say he was too busy—that he had a mountain of paperwork to get through. He wouldn't have been lying. But then Chas had responded well since they'd had words, his performance noticeably improved. He'd even begun to look like a copper.

Thomas dropped his pen and sat back in his chair. "Okay—get us some coffee."

Chambers disappeared to return with two mugs. "You said DCS Keen talked about being plagued by Templetons?"

"Yes."

Chas sipped his coffee. "Well, it set me to thinking."

"Thinking about what?"

"I believe I'm right in thinking that our informant suggested we contact Templeton and Carlow if we want to know what Yarwood's been up to—right?"

Thomas nodded. "I'm listening."

"Well—as I see it, the shooting had to be premeditated. Why else was *her ladyship* walking about with a gun? And how could Templeton's brother—a man with no visible means of support—live in a bloody great mansion weighed down by a mortgage big enough to make your hair curl?"

"And—?"

"Oh, I don't have any answers, but it stands to reason Templeton does. His brother's activities must have been dubious or why keep them to himself? I'd say that, they—that's to say him, and probably Carlow—definitely know a lot more about Yarwood and the rest of it than they'd have us believe."

Mr Williams couldn't have interrupted Richard at a more inopportune moment. He was enjoying a perfectly cooked piece of his favourite smoked haddock with a generous helping of potato mashed with butter and milk. Mrs Williams served the combination exactly as he liked it.

There were three men at the door, Mr Williams informed him—policemen, they said—demanding to be taken to Mr Carlow—refusing to accept that he wasn't at home.

Richard reluctantly abandoned his food and went out to meet them. "My name is Keen, sir, Detective Chief Superintendent Keen," the senior policeman said. "My colleagues are DI Thomas and DS Chambers." They thrust proof of identity under Richard's nose.

"I'm afraid Mr Carlow's at a seminar in Portugal," he told them, the ashen faced Mr Williams standing at what he clearly hoped was a safe distance behind him.

"You won't mind if we come in, sir?" Keen said. "We do have a warrant."

Richard managed to sound indignant. "Now wait a minute."

Keen simply ignored him. "Everyone in here," he barked at the DS. "Who else is in the house, sir? We don't like to cause more distress than we have to."

"Mrs Williams—she's the cook, and her maid—plus Mr Williams here."

"That's all?"

Richard nodded. "Other than me."

"Take DS Chambers to the others, Mr Williams—if you wouldn't mind?" Keen said. This was obviously a well practised routine. He and Thomas stayed close to Richard.

"And your name, sir?" Keen enquired.

"Wells—Richard Wells."

"And why are you here, Mr Wells?"

"I work for Mr Carlow." He told himself their presence was no real surprise. Intentionally or not, Yarwood could have let something slip. He wondered if Templeton had also been visited. Yarwood might have got the idea they were about to renege on their agreement.

His heart dived into the pit of his stomach. The Cumulus CD was lying on his desk—all the police would ever need to dot every I and cross every T of what they were engaged in. Names, addresses, account numbers, how much, from where and to whom—all of it was there.

He watched Keen thumb through the papers on Jane's desk before systematically searching the drawers, his sharp eyes alert, pausing only to lean back in her chair. "Mrs Garside?" he asked. "Mr Carlow's secretary, is she?"

Richard tried to appear calm. "Personal assistant, I think you could say."

"I see. Not in today?"

"I told you—they're at a seminar in Portugal."

Keen consulted his notebook. "Ah, yes—yes, I have a note of that here."

"So why ask for him at the door?" Richard growled.

"Habit, Mr Wells." He smiled. "The information we're given occasionally turns out to be less than reliable. I'm sure you understand."

Probably in his mid-fifties, above medium height but not tall, with a full head of fast greying hair, Keen wasn't Richard's idea of a Detective. A million miles from raincoats and trilbies, this one. Indeed, he gave the impression of having no other interest than getting answers to questions only he would have thought to ask. And who was it who said only the least virile of men keep all their hair? True or false, a man like Keen wouldn't give a dam.

He was watching Richard carefully, pausing only to scribble in his annoying little notebook. Yes—he'd done this a hundred times to judge by his attitude. "This the office, then?" he asked.

Mrs Williams and her maid were ushered into the room.

Richard tried to reassure them by smiling. "Temporarily. We've been working from here since the shooting. It happened out there." He nodded in the direction of the lawn beyond the terrace. "But I'm sure you know that already."

"Still," Keen added. "Seems like a nice place to work. Where's the computer, Mr Wells?" He consulted his notebook. "My officers dropped into the City this morning, and your former friends—their word not mine—*former*, that is, said Richard Wells is never far from his computer. Left, they said—made redundant earlier this year. Re-employed, though. And doing rather well if the evidence of their eyes was anything to go by —well enough in fact to be seen driving a new Porsche. Made a point of telling us about that, sir—you not going back to see them and driving a new Porsche.

It seems some of them rather resent your *good fortune*. And I'm also led to believe there's the little matter of a chateau in France. We are moving in exalted circles, aren't we, sir? Mortgage arrears and social security benefits distant memories, are they, Mr Wells? Who would have thought it—one day redundant, the next the owner of a chateau in France?"

The doorbell interrupted. "Splendid," Keen said enthusiastically. "That'll be DS Ford. Clever chap, our DS Ford, sir—he understands computers."

He was examining Richard's face for changes of expression; tell-tale twitches or involuntary frowns. He smiled his simple-man-doing-his-job smile, waving his notebook. "Good old pencil and paper are good enough for me. These new fangled gadgets, eh?" He shook his head. "Makes y'wonder, doesn't it? Where *will* it all end?"

Desperate for an opportunity to pocket Cumulus, Richard showed them upstairs to Master. "This is the nerve centre for our expansion into Europe," he explained, trying to behave like someone oblivious to what he knew had to come. "It's still in its infancy, of course; the European company wasn't formed until June." His eyes frantically scanned the desk. "You should have been here, Superintendent—they were all over us like ants. You couldn't turn round without falling over photographers and reporters. I swear none of them slept. But then it turned out to be a very good thing we did set it up here, Superintendent—what with Mrs Carlow walking out, and—"

Keen interrupted. "Yes, yes—thank you, Mr Wells—thank you."

After introducing the policemen to Master, avoiding the word itself while trying to locate the CD, Richard was escorted downstairs. Keen was right, DS Ford did know his stuff.

When he was eventually called back, he was amazed to find they didn't have Cumulus. He was called upon to witness the transfer of Master's files to disk and to paper, and was overjoyed to confirm that the data removed was indeed such a copy.

Penny Wise was reporting the previous night's events to Mason over breakfast. Most of the delegates had been quick to take advantage of their unexpected good fortune. Encouraged to do so, some of the women had also made arrangements for tonight. She did have a problem, though. One of the two female delegates had enjoyed a few drinks and left the party early, while the other had tried unsuccessfully to get herself laid.

Penny Wise wanted to fly in a man. He could be with them by evening and stay at the villa with the girls. She grinned mischievously. "She won't forget this guy in a hurry, I can tell you."

Her enthusiasm was lost on Mason, but he raised no objection. Their conversation over, he collected a newspaper from Reception together with a message to ring Richard.

"Bad news, I'm afraid," Richard told him. "The police have detained Yarwood."

"Oh, shit!"

"As you say. I imagine you'll find it in the morning papers, the English newspapers out there being a day behind."

"Hold on." Mason scanned through the Telegraph. It was there right enough. *European businessman Desmond Yarwood helping Scotland Yard with their enquiries.* "I've got it. Anything today?"

"Not that I've seen."

"Thank God for that. Speak to you later."

Richard stopped him. "Not so fast. The police have been out to the Manor. I answered their questions, but I'm pretty sure they'll be back. They were probing. Somebody must have linked Yarwood and Mike. I don't think it could have been detailed, but he ought to be told."

"Oh, thanks a lot," Mason groaned. "Got any more good news?"

TWENTY-FOUR

The remnants of an early mist were clinging to the tops of the trees across the golf-course when Penny Wise took leave of Mason. The majority of hotel guests were still in bed, a few of the rest at breakfast or hurrying to secure a favourite spot by the pool, looking forward to the first swim of the day; waiting for the sun to break through.

Four middle-aged, male golfers on the tenth tee below the pool, were making an early start—laughing, swinging clubs to loosen overnight bodies, trying to convince themselves that ageing limbs were no barrier to what they were undertaking, their body language heavy with the unspoken fear of physical inadequacy.

The news about Yarwood and the police visiting the Manor, exploded on to this unsuspecting scene like a scatter bomb parachuting into every corner of their lives. If Yarwood's activities became public knowledge, markets would plummet, currencies with them—Governments in disarray as the truth about the British Establishment flashed across the world.

Undecided whether or not to return to England early, Carlow was being brutally frank with the increasingly frightened Fiona Forrest. She might very soon be looked upon as a curiosity—a sideshow—the Downing Street whore it was fashionable to joke about. His voice sounded harsh and unreal. "Who are you to be issuing an ultimatum to Geoff Mason? Jesus! And I'm not saying this because of Wilder's women. Oh no, that would be far too simple."

Mason shifted in his chair, fighting the urge to interrupt.

They were arguing among themselves on the threshold of a disaster that would stun the civilized world. He could picture the headlines—British Cabinet ministers bribed. Fraud among Whitehall civil servants; widespread coercion, sexual blackmail and sleaze at Westminster—while here at Penina life went on as if nothing could be more important than the golf course, the restaurant and days in the sun. Carlow pointed at Mason. "He's the best thing that's ever happened to you—or can't you see that?"

She was searching for words—for credible answers. "I didn't want to lie," she said. "I was trapped. I hadn't pointed out Yarwood and you decided to retain him."

"So much for trusting a whore," Carlow snarled.

She looked at him dejectedly, fighting back tears. Mason finally intervened. "Please, Fiona, you have to tell us everything—Wilder, Yarwood—everything."

"Why?" she asked. "Geraldine had her partners and I had mine. We kept their names to ourselves in case things went wrong. I knew none of hers, so they effectively died with her. There's nothing else to tell."

"So what is it these *partners* actually do—if anything?" Carlow asked.

"They introduce potential clients in exchange for cash or sex; whichever they prefer."

"You mean they introduce punters?"

"I prefer to call them clients," she said indignantly.

"And, Yarwood?" Carlow added. "Where does he fit into all this?"

"He threatened to expose us, unless—oh, I don't know—unless we met his demands and promised him more."

"More what?"

"Names—occupations, where and with whom our clients worked, if they weren't MPs or Whitehall civil-servants—if we knew, that is, or were able to find out—their sexual preferences, friends, interests, weaknesses. He insisted the girls memorize a series of questions to put to them at opportune moments."

"What sort of questions?"

"Who was sleeping with whom in the various government departments; cheating on a wife or husband, perhaps—was homosexual, addicted to drugs, sex, gambling—that sort of thing, mostly, anyway—plus some specific to individuals where he considered they might be more productive."

"So he knows the names of your partners?"

"In my case, partner—singular. I never had more than one."

"Who are we talking about?"

"Andrew Templeton."

Mason buried his head in his hands.

She seemed surprised by his reaction—as if she thought he ought somehow to approve. "He introduced more clients than anyone," she added, "until he was murdered."

"There was a suicide note, woman."

"I think he had some kind of problem with the insurance people at Lloyds," she continued, "—but there was definitely no shortage of money. We were paying him a fortune. No, he didn't kill himself, he was murdered."

"You seem very sure?"

"I am. It was Geraldine who shot him."

"She killed them *both*," Mason gasped. "Him *and* the Prime Minister?"

"She did."

"Good, God. And you've known this all along?"

She frowned. "Drinking, Andrew Templeton was just about bearable. Drunk, he was a sadist. According to him we were good for nothing but fucking. Geraldine hated him for that. But then it's fair to say she hated all men."

"So is that why she shot him?"

She responded angrily. "Of course not. They raped us."

Disbelief flooded the room.

Her anger subsided, leaving her looking demoralized and alone—tears beginning to stream down her face. "Fiona, please don't," Mason said, aware that, like it or not, he was hopelessly in love with the woman.

"I paid for his introductions," she went on, "but I detested the man. It was Geraldine who went further. She loved to humiliate upper-class *clones* as she called them. She hated them with a vengeance. He asked us to *entertain* him and an anonymous friend at his house, so she demanded an enormous fee and accepted on the spot.

He simply grinned and gave her great handfuls of money.

But we didn't do this—the chance of exposure multiplied tenfold. We always vetted people—no matter who they were. I reminded her of this as forcefully as I could, but she ignored me. Imagine arriving at Templeton's house a couple of evenings later to discover that his *friend* was the Prime Minister. Even now, I find it hard to believe.

Geraldine immediately tried to escape—making a sudden dash for the door. They grabbed her, laughing at her resistance —Templeton beating and raping her while the Prime Minister brutalized me. Then they changed places.

I feared for our lives, but we were eventually released. Geraldine's eyes were blazing with hatred. The memory's so vivid. I was unaware, of course, that the Prime Minister was her father. And I'd no idea she'd decided there and then that she was going to kill them. Although, to be fair, I might have been willing to pull the trigger myself."

Carlow wanted to abandon the seminar and fly home, but Jane was quick to restrain him, pointing out that the police were aware of none of what Fiona Forrest had told them. As far as they were concerned Templeton's death was suicide. Yarwood's arrest and their visit to the Manor, on the other hand, was more serious by far.

Finding it virtually impossible to concentrate on anything but what they now knew, Carlow nonetheless completed the seminar. And Jane had been right to restrain him—the police were waiting on his eventual return.

Richard contacted Superintendent Keen to ask why Carlow was being questioned. He wouldn't be drawn. Helping with his enquiries was all he would say. He did add, however, that he expected Mrs Garside to be released that afternoon. Richard pressed, but Keen refused to commit himself further where Carlow was concerned.

The BBC's one o'clock news announcement that multi-millionaire entrepreneur, Michael Carlow, was being interviewed by Scotland Yard detectives, prompted interested parties at Westminster and in Whitehall to prepare to close ranks, especially when the newscaster went on to refresh the public memory regarding Carlow's wealth, his split with Laura, and that it had been in the grounds of his country manor-house that the Prime Minister had been murdered.

Jane updated Richard with what they'd learned from Fiona Forrest, as soon as she got back, Richard explaining in return that the police visit had taken him by surprise. They'd removed everything: papers, disks, CDs; everything—but they hadn't taken Master's hard drive or discovered Cumulus. He'd no idea how, but the CD had disappeared."

"I took it," Jane said.

"But why?" He breathed a sigh of relief.

"Instinct, I suppose. We were tempting providence by keeping it."

The telephone interrupted. It was Mason. He'd stayed with the aeroplane to fly the women back to England—redirecting the flight, deciding it might be best to give Heathrow and the waiting police a suitably wide berth. Jane informed him they'd been preparing to question Mike when she left.

He gave her a telephone number. "You want Ben. Have you got that—Ben? If he's not there, leave a message for him to call you. Tell him I want the Manor sealed-up round the clock. Mike's sure to think I'm mad, but I'd rather that than see somebody hurt.

Ben's to let nobody in unless he's cleared it with you first—right—nobody? I'll bring him up to speed as soon as I get back. And I stress—nobody goes anywhere without one of his lads—

understood? Yes, and you'd better tell Laura what's happening; she could be a target. Oh—and don't let Ben's voice put you off."

Jane rang off, watching Richard's face as she relayed Mason's message.

"She's at the Chateau," he said, dialling the number. "Andre? Richard. What? Yes, yes, I'm fine. Get Laura for me, will you? Yes —now." He waited.

"I'm with Jane at the Manor," he told her, doing his best to avoid sounding anxious. "The police are questioning Mike."

She didn't seem surprised. "Why's that?"

"Helping with their enquiries—but they always say that, don't they? Andre's driving to Paris in the morning, isn't he?"

"I believe so."

"Right—pack a bag and go with him. Dress inconspicuously, book into a back-street hotel using a false name and then call me here. Geoff says none of us is safe and you could be a target."

"Who am I supposed to be avoiding?"

"Please, Laura, just do it. It's probably nothing, so try not to worry."

He put down the telephone and turned back to Jane. "Yarwood and now Mike; Templeton's bound to be next."

"Geoff thinks this is all down to Yarwood," she added. "Penny Wise—she's one of the women—believes there were and perhaps still are, other people involved—Andrew Templeton for example."

"But he's dead?" Richard said.

"Yes—and discovering he was murdered only adds to our worries."

"But if that was Wilder's doing, surely it ends there?"

"If it *was* Wilder's doing."

"So you think Yarwood's one of the other people?"

"Geoff does."

"So who else might be involved?"

"That's just it—we don't know. Fiona Forrest introduced Andrew Templeton to Wilder, but Wilder failed to reciprocate with names of her own."

"I see. So Yarwood could have been one of them?"

"Could have been, yes."

"Then why threaten to expose them?"

"We can't be sure he did, added to which informing on Mike could cost him ten million. Can you see him risking that?"

He shook his head. "Not a chance."

"Incidentally," she added. "One of the policemen said a *Superintendent Keen* would be interviewing Mike."

"Yes—Detective Chief Superintendent Keen—one of those who came here. I'd like to be a fly on that wall."

Jane rang Ben, understanding what Mason had meant about his voice as a bronchitic chuckle rattled down the phone. "Ees a toff is Mista Mason."

Jane passed on Mason's instructions and gave him directions to the Manor.

"Lock y'doors'n windas, darlin," Ben rattled, "me'n d'boys is on d'way."

Keen had kept him waiting in a room Carlow thought better suited to gymnastics or squash than interviewing people. The walls were bare, the ceiling high; recording equipment on a cheap desk pushed up against the table around which they sat. And that was the only furniture, other than the four ancient, wooden chairs they were sitting on—plus a disconcerting echo.

Keen formalized proceedings by announcing the time, date, and the names of those present for the record, his words bouncing round the walls like Carlow's imaginary squash balls.

"Sorry to keep you waiting, Mr Carlow," he said. "All this messing about when crime waits for no man as my officers keep telling me."

Carlow saw DI Thomas raise a disbelieving eyebrow.

"Now let me see," Keen continued, consulting his notebook.

"Any chance of a cup of tea, Superintendent?" Carlow interrupted. "I'm parched. Haven't had a thing since we landed."

Keen announced for the record that the DC beside him was leaving the room. "Are you familiar with a gentleman named

Yarwood, sir?" he went on. "One, *Desmond* Yarwood?"

"I'd re-phrase that if I were you," Carlow said calmly. "I've met the man, yes, but I'm hardly *familiar* with him as you put it."

"Thank you, Mr Carlow; just establishing a few facts."

"I quite understand," Carlow added. "From the little I know about Yarwood, I can see how you might find yourself at something of a disadvantage."

"Really, sir? We're informed that he's been engaged in bribing and blackmailing people into proposing and supporting various resolutions at Westminster—and our informant further suggests that *you* can tell us more."

The DC's return was noted for the record.

Carlow sipped the tea. "Sorry, Superintendent, somebody's put sugar in this." He held out the cup. "Would you mind? Er—what did you say?"

Keen's echoing monotone announced the DC's departure. "I said, Mr Carlow—we're told Desmond Yarwood has been engaged in bribing and blackmailing—"

"No—no, after that."

"You mean: our informant further suggests that you can tell us more?"

"Yes—that's what I thought you said. Good lord—tell you more? More about what? But then I suppose my dissatisfaction with Westminster and Whitehall is hardly a state secret."

The DC returned yet again. Keen recorded the fact.

Carlow took a second sip of tea. "Ah, that's better. Thank you, Constable. In fact, Superintendent," he went on, "I've just returned from a seminar in Portugal at which I asked a number of politicians and Whitehall civil servants to consider my views. I'm not alone in expressing them, of course, and I can only guess at what they might choose to do about them—if anything. You do your best to convince these people, but you can never be sure they even listen to what you say."

He waited. Keen added nothing.

"No, I'm sorry. The more I think about it the more I'm sure

it's only Party hierarchies and their whips who can influence MPs. People like your Mr Yarwood most certainly can't. I can't imagine anyone listening to a greedy boy like him, anyway. I was told he'd be an asset to us where our European project was concerned. Influential, it was said. I have to say I was far from impressed. No—if you want my opinion, he's a man of dubious pedigree with an exaggerated view of his own ability and importance. We spent a lot of time and money—too much, in fact—deciding how best to approach Europe; some of it unfortunately wasted on individuals like him."

"You have a Richard Wells working for you, Mr Carlow?"

"What's he got to do with it?"

"I understand he was declared redundant, but has since been re-employed?"

"That's correct."

"And why was that, sir?"

"Why was what?"

"Why was he re-employed?"

"His department decided they didn't need him—I decided I did. I'd have thought that was obvious. Look, I don't mind discussing my company's activities, but would you mind telling me where all this is leading?"

Carlow was way ahead of Keen. The policeman had obviously visited the Manor and the office—collected everything he could think to lay his hands on and was clutching at straws. "It was most unfortunate," Carlow continued. "Embarrassing, in fact. He did an outstanding job for us last year in France, but it seems things didn't work out when he got back.

Our IT people are a competitive lot, Mrs Garside informs me. Petty jealousies abound. So when we recently cut back on staff it seems he was one of the first his department let go. I'd no idea he'd gone, and I won't repeat what I said when she told me. He's the most talented young man I've come across in years."

"I understand he recently purchased a chateau in France?" Keen added.

"You're quite right, he did. Bought it from us."

"So where did he get the money, sir?"

"His problem. To be frank, I asked myself the same question when he offered to buy it. There was no way he could fund it himself, so I gave him first refusal; a strong hand to play with whoever was scheduled to come up with the cash—a *leg up*, I suppose you might call it. They get so little encouragement these days, don't you find?"

The hand-set crackled. "Geezer 'ere in a bloody great Roller says 'ees name's Carlow, Ben. A right sort'a toff. Shall we led 'im in?"

"Yeah, led 'im froo."

Carlow arrived at the door.

"Evenin', Guv'. Name's Ben. Boys is only bein' careful. Missa Mason said t'seal d'place up tight."

"Pleased to meet you, Ben," Carlow said guardedly—"Mike Carlow. Glad to have you with us." He shook Ben's huge hand, relieved to find his fingers intact as he went into the house. He was met by Jane and Richard. "What a day," he said, looking over his shoulder. "So what's with this, *Ben?*"

TWENTY-FIVE

Young Chambers was on to something. Keen couldn't quite put his finger on it, but Wells held the key—of that he was sure. Why had Carlow re-employed him? Yes—and why was he suddenly to be seen driving around in a fancy foreign sports car, to say nothing of his highly improbable purchase of a chateau in France? It was the real thing, too, down to the very last vine.

At eight the following morning he paid a second visit to the Manor.

"Oh, yes—didn't I tell you?" Richard said easily, "the pater left one a fortune."

"Do you mind, Mr Wells?" Keen responded dryly.

Richard grinned. "Sorry, Superintendent, it's my warped sense of humour. If you don't laugh you cry, I sometimes think. Look, any chance of keeping this to ourselves?"

Keen offered no reply.

"Well, what did you expect?" Richard whispered, nodding at the door. "I had to ask. His wife walked out—even you ought to know that. And he's far from happy about it, I can tell you. God, is that woman gorgeous—"

Even you—the cheeky young sod.

"—face, body, the lot," Richard continued, his voice barely audible. "Photographs don't do her justice. We've reached, how shall I put it, Mr Keen—an *understanding*? She's older than me, yes, I realize that, but I don't think it matters, do you? And he doesn't know."

Keen found himself whispering and looking at the door. "I

really couldn't say, sir."

Nothing just sort of happened where he came from—especially where women like Laura Carlow were concerned. The poor bastard of a husband was more often than not the last to find out.

"He sent me to Bordeaux," Richard explained. "I designed the software the company uses out there, you understand—and there she was shacked-up with a tasty *demoiselle*." He chuckled. "Between you and me I wouldn't have said no to a cosy little threesome. You know how it is?"

Keen decided he didn't.

"She gets her kicks on both sides of the duvet—" Richard added "—if you follow my drift?"

"Yes, yes, thank you, Mr Wells. I think I follow your—er, get the picture." In his day it would have been both sides of several blankets by the sound of it, but in this as in everything the world had moved on.

He remembered the newspaper photographs. How could he forget—not that he was trying or she was by any stretch of the imagination, his type. But then what woman was his *type*, especially since the advent of all this liberation business? And liberated from what he'd like to know? It was poor sods like him who needed liberating. When had any self-respecting woman wanted to share her life with a run-of-the-mill copper? Shit, half a chance along the way would have been nothing short of a miracle.

"It made no difference to me," Richard went on. "Cramped my style a bit, I suppose, but I couldn't complain, could I? She did lend me the cash to buy and refurbish the Chateau. No—my problems start when he finds out."

"So you bought the Chateau with the money she lent you?"

"Of course."

"But why did you buy it?"

"Food and drink. It's where the future's at, as they say."

Keen raised an eyebrow.

"Well, can you think of a better place to enjoy it than the

South-West of France?" Richard added.

"You've studied it, then?"

"That has to be obvious."

"Thank you, sir," Keen said quickly. "I think you've told me what I needed to know. You can prove all this, I suppose?"

"Oh, come on Mr Keen, you're not asking me to believe you haven't seen my records?"

What could Keen say? He'd been up half the night going through them.

"Seriously," Richard said. "Does he have to find out?"

"Thank you, Mr Wells. I'll let you know if there's anything else I need."

Richard congratulated himself on his portrayal of the over confident upstart. Keen appeared to have swallowed it. Extramarital fun and games were clearly not his cup of tea, and being ready for one of those he seemed happy to leave it.

Richard had been looking forward to this for weeks: heavy curtains drawn against the night, a long evening in front of the big, open hearth. Mr Williams had built the first fire of the season with logs from the dry stack in the yard. It was crackling and spitting, taking a firm hold. It reminded Richard of his father—one of the most predictable of men before the onset of the cancer that had ended his life.

They'd burned coal on the fire at home—most of the time, at least; a fuel created so far from the sun that there was nothing to sustain it; no expectation of renewal; no sap; no burning optimism with which to look forward. It seemed somehow appropriate for it to end its days on a cold morning hearth. Wishing he was with Laura, he was waiting for Jane and Carlow to come down for dinner. "Ashes to ashes," he muttered to himself.

Following his father's death, after Carlow had kicked him out and he was still trying to work out what he'd done to deserve it, Jane had telephoned to say he wanted him back. His return had enabled him to acquire Chateau Darrieux—and Laura, for that matter—but he wasn't fooling himself; he had no illusions. The opportunity wouldn't have come his way had the task been legal and straightforward.

Jane had taught him to look at the world rationally; objectively. Well, as rationally and objectively as anyone can. But now, as if to remind him of who he was and where he came from, he'd been taught another lesson. Superintendent Keen had talked about mortgage arrears and social security benefits as if they'd branded him an outcast. Was that supposed to mean it hadn't been the saddest, loneliest, most debilitating period in his life, he wondered? Didn't it matter that he'd sacrificed everything for his father and would have been willing to do so again? No —there was a stigma attached to having no money and no job. Regardless of the circumstances, you wouldn't find yourself in that situation if you weren't second-rate.

How many people really care about their fellow human beings, he asked himself? It seemed the reality didn't matter. It was creating the illusion of caring that was important. And Keen was right, it *was* unusual to be impoverished one day and of all things owning a chateau the next. Unusual too, to be classified redundant only to be reinstated and to all intents and purposes promoted. But it wasn't impossible. And to the best of his knowledge it wasn't a crime—not yet at least, even if only the naïve or mentally deficient expected to see justice and fair play.

Clawing your way back from the brink was only possible via one anti-social or illegal means or another. The price of success was a permanent first charge on your soul. The British *System* operated that way—condoned it—practically insisted on it. Conducting yourself *honourably* was an out-dated concept— an altruistic folly—no place for it in *the marketplace*; nothing to be *gained*. You learned to close your mind or you disappeared without trace, the stench of decaying conscience poisoning you irreversibly as you joined those around you in turning the collective blind eye.

He decided he was too much like Carlow for his own good. He'd compromised his principles, such as they were, in exchange for hard cash, and then relied on Jane to keep him psychologically afloat. That was the modern way. The only difference between Carlow and himself was that *he* was prepared to admit it. If you didn't have a Jane Garside in your life, you retained the services of a shrink—if you could afford the modern shrink's fees.

Jane startled him. "Penny for them."

"They're not worth it," he muttered.

Carlow had seemed distant when describing his encounter with the police. According to him it had been obvious they were clutching at straws. Richard was pleased something was obvious to someone. He took a deep breath. "Mike, I'd left Cumulus on my desk when the police came."

Carlow's face twisted in horror. "You'd done what?"

Jane tried to interrupt. "Richard, you don't have to—"

"Fortunately," Richard continued, "Jane had spotted it."

"Dreaming, were you—about fucking my wife?" Carlow grated, his voice colder than as ice.

"Mike! For goodness sake," Jane protested.

"It needed to be said."

"Not like that."

"No!" He held his hand up to Richard like a policeman halting traffic. "I don't want to hear it."

Following Mason's late afternoon return from Portugal accompanied by the noticeably subdued Fiona Forrest, they sat having tea by the inglenook waiting for Templeton to arrive. The wind had been fierce from the east for most of the day. Richard was adding logs to the fire, arranging and poking them to stimulate the blaze. Carlow was quizzing Mason about Ben.

"You don't know you're born," Mason mocked. "I've used him for years. There are too many fancy uniforms out there these days, *calling* themselves security. Something goes missing and they're the first you suspect. Ben's completely reliable—an unblemished record for us."

"How many men does he have?" Carlow asked.

"I've no idea, and I wouldn't dream of asking. It'll be as quiet as the grave unless somebody tries to get in. I hope for their sakes we don't get any poachers. And talking of poachers, has the car gone for Templeton?"

Carlow nodded.

Mason left him and went out to Ben. "The Roller's due back, Ben."

The handset crackled as Ben spoke to one of his men at the gate.

"Usual rates," Mason told him. "Bed and breakfast thrown in."

Ben nodded, the car drawing up as Mason spoke. Templeton was allowed to pass freely from tarmac to gravel through the big iron gates.

"I managed to contact one of Yarwood's people this afternoon," Templeton told them—"to ask if he might have said something to connect him with Mr Carlow and myself?

The man said the idea was laughable, informants of one kind or another being what he described as an occupational hazard with which they're quite capable of dealing."

"So," Mason said, "this informant referred to Yarwood only in the context of his work for us?"

"To the best of my knowledge," Templeton admitted.

"The idea of questioning you and Mike appears to have been thrown in for good measure."

"Indeed."

Mason screwed up his face. "That means the informant has to be one of us."

"Exactly," Carlow said.

"But all of us are at risk."

"The risk's very small," Richard added.

"Oh, really?" Carlow sneered. "Given your recent performance, I'd say that's debatable."

Five minutes later Richard left the room. Jane saw him go and followed. "I've had it with him," he told her. "I need time to think."

"Look, I ought to get back," Jane said anxiously. "Let's talk tonight."

He shrugged and set off upstairs. Less than half an hour later, she heard his car drive away.

"That about sums him up," Carlow said when she told him.

"Oh, come on. He no more expected the police than we did."

"You think so, do you?" Carlow snorted.

"Of course I do. This isn't about the police. It's about Laura. You told him it's over between you, and now you're getting your own back because he took you at your word. As for taking her to bed—put yourself in his place."

The following morning Jane discussed the situation between Richard and Carlow with Mason. They'd come down before the others and talked over breakfast. You could say what you liked about Mason, he always got up and got on with the day.

They discussed what had been learned from Fiona Forrest, Mason undertaking to talk to Carlow about his fall-out with Richard even though they both knew he wouldn't listen. "If memory serves me right," Mason said, "the last time we had a scene like this he made a prat of himself over you. Nobody's perfect, but I was there when he told Richard it was over with Laura."

"But the relationship isn't over," Jane added.

"As far as he's concerned—no. Good for Richard, I say. You wouldn't catch me refusing a night with Laura. Sorry," he mumbled. "Shit—did I say a night? Five minutes would be like winning the lottery."

Jane dismissed his reaction with a shake of her head. He couldn't stop himself exaggerating where women were concerned—especially on those occasions Laura Carlow happened to be involved. "To be fair, though," she continued. "It's not just his relationship with Laura, is it? He did leave Cumulus—well, if I hadn't spotted it—"

"You're right—" Mason groaned. "the dickhead. Still—if my aunt had balls she'd be my uncle, wouldn't she? The police have scrutinized his work and we've not been arrested—not so far, anyway."

"But he is overly preoccupied with Laura and France, isn't he?" Jane said.

"That doesn't excuse Mike's attitude towards him," Mason growled. "Incidentally, I gather his pies are selling like hot—well, pies—and he can't meet demand?"

"How he's managing at all is a mystery to me," Jane said earnestly.

Richard had left the room at the first opportunity, and by the time he dialled the Paris number Laura had given him he'd more or less resigned himself to the way Carlow was behaving. He rarely stopped to analyze personal relationships, which, he concluded, was why Carlow had been able to surprise him and why he'd taken so long to acknowledge his feelings for Laura.

But when the Air France Fokker took off for Bordeaux, he'd already decided to exercise restraint. He owed it to Laura, Jane, Madame Darrieux, and even to Carlow himself, allowing for his feelings for Laura.

Sales were better than Giles Morton had forecast, which was some consolation. And after such a successful campaign, he was unlikely to press for payment given Laura's involvement and more work to come. Even so, it would be months before demand increased sufficiently to reduce unit costs. And there was certainly no chance of that without access to his second million.

Easy come easy go was the only way to look at it. He emailed Carlow from Servant.

'Have returned to the Chateau. Thought it right to admit my mistake. Believe your attitude unreasonable. Want to see the job through. Let me know where we stand.'

Richard.

TWENTY-SIX

Jane telephoned Richard to say that Yarwood had been arrested and that DI Thomas had visited Templeton—going on to confirm that Carlow had received and read his email.

"What did he say?" he asked.

"Nothing really. He's not been himself."

"Hardly surprising," he added. "With Yarwood in custody and Templeton back in the Superintendent's notebook, he knows it's only a matter of time before they get round to him."

"So you think it's all over?" she groaned.

"Call Templeton, will you? Any light he can shed on the situation may tell us more." He didn't mention that this together with his fall-out with Carlow meant no second million and the end of his ownership of Chateau Darrieux.

"Jane—?"

"Yes, I'm still here."

"And fix a meeting with Harry Wetherby for me; where and when to suit him."

"You're not giving up, then?"

"No, I'm not giving up. I'll fly back in the morning. Speak to Wetherby now, if you can—oh, and get Geoff over to your place tomorrow evening. I assume you can put me up?" He didn't wait for a yes or a no. "Incidentally, did Wetherby mix with the women at Penina?"

"Oh, yes. She called herself Amanda—his temporary PA. Why?"

"Nothing specific. Right—I'll see you tomorrow."

He put down the telephone and settled down to write what

he'd been planning all day. He wouldn't be able to sleep, anyway, and with Laura due back he'd no desire to be working all night.

Jane telephoned Wetherby. "What's he want?" the politician asked.

"He didn't say. He's over in France—due back tomorrow."

Wetherby hesitated. "Mm—I'll be down at the House on Wednesday. I suppose I could see him then. Shall we say eleven?"

It was after three in the morning when Richard finally fell into bed, only to be disturbed by Laura fumbling around in the dark. "What time is it?" he asked, his face under attack from a succession of jaw-breaking yawns.

"Just after four," she whispered. "Go back to sleep."

He rubbed his eyes and turned on the light. "Good journey?"

She groaned. "Hardly. I'm going to have a shower."

"Do you mind if we talk?" he asked her.

She was too tired to argue. Andre wasn't the most engaging of travelling companions, but if she ever needed to travel from Paris to Bordeaux again, it wouldn't be by car—with or without Andre.

"You have your shower," Richard added. "I'll make us some coffee." He rolled out of bed, kissed her on the cheek and disappeared downstairs.

She threw off her clothes to slowly pirouette in the welcome gush of hot water; eyes closed, face upturned, breathing long and deep as she might have in sleep, inviting the miles to drain from her body. Emerging ten minutes later into the warmth of a bath robe, she felt unexpectedly revitalized as she went down to Richard.

"This won't take long," he assured her, pouring their coffee. He outlined what Fiona Forrest had disclosed along with the activities of the police relative to Yarwood and Templeton, and why he thought they'd soon be extending their investigations to Mike.

Laura continued towelling her hair. "So what happens now?"

He hesitated self-consciously. "Before we get on to that, I

need you to know that I love you. I've said nothing before—" He looked at her anxiously, taking a deep breath. "—well, you're married to Mike, and there was Danielle to consider."

She tried to interrupt, "Please, Richard—"

"Geoff was so sure you were in danger," he continued. "I panicked and couldn't stop reproaching myself for not having told you." She could see his hands trembling. "If something *had* happened—well—I eventually went back to accepting that I'd nothing to offer you even if you hadn't been another man's wife. Now—the way things are going I'll even lose the Chateau," he added despondently.

"You don't have to say anything," he added, fiddling with the handle of his coffee mug.

Her eyes were wide with concern, the only sound the measured tick of the big clock on the wall.

"Oh, Richard—" she said. His heart missed a beat. "It may seem an odd thing to say, but my looks are a curse." She discarded the towel and reached for his hand. "I've had a loving family, a comfortable home, money, fashionable clothes—everything I ever wanted; and yet I came down from Cambridge believing all men are the same—a single ambition common to them all."

Richard had no doubt what she thought that was.

"Then, one evening," she continued, "Geoff Mason, a man I then hardly knew, introduced me to Michael Carlow. He was good looking, charming, good company—making it easy to believe he was different. But once we were married he was quick to demonstrate that he was just like the rest." She paused—"Perhaps even worse. He *wanted* me—but it was the idea of possessing my body that he fell in love with. I was an *object*—an object he'd bought and paid for by marrying me; a decorative asset to be exhibited wherever and whenever he considered it strategically advantageous. I meant little to him as a person—and never have—so I set about building a life and career of my own.

I could see nothing to be gained from discussing it with him, even at the end—in fact, especially at the end. It had been obvious for a long time that our marriage couldn't last. Then he came home one day saying the Prime Minister had accepted his invitation to lunch at the Manor. And there *she* was—Lady Morrison—Geraldine Wilder—there on the guest list." She concentrated fiercely on what she had to say next. "Do you remember her affair with an MP? It was in all the papers?"

He nodded. "A junior minister, wasn't he—married with kids?"

"Yes—and it wasn't the first time it had happened in her family. More than thirty years earlier, her father, an ambitious Westminster MP, got her mother pregnant for a second time and ditched her. He was already married, and to cut a sorry story short, after the baby was born, her mother took her own life, Geraldine was fostered—and the baby was me."

"Hell's teeth," Richard gasped. "He was your father and Wilder your sister?"

"I'm sorry to say, yes." She sighed heavily. "I was put up for adoption—*given away*, according to Geraldine—my very existence a threat to his career. She never forgave him for disowning us—or for his callous disregard for our mother."

"He must have provided for you, though? Financially, I mean?"

"I've no idea. Anyway, having bankrupted more than one man with more money than sense, Geraldine snared a weak, ineffectual aristocrat. *Her Ladyship* or not, she made a point of retaining our mother's name and avenging her passing in any way she could—especially where upper-class *low-lives* like our father were involved—wealthy hypocrites whom, according to her, make a show of caring for others while using their social standing to abuse the victims of this world, most of them women.

It beggars belief that anyone could hate somebody for such a long time, the hatred ultimately so intense she had to confide in someone and so came to me?"

"She actually came to see you?"

"About eighteen months ago. As you can imagine, I didn't believe a word until my adoptive parents confirmed it." Her eyes were bright with tears. "They hadn't told me I was adopted. In the circumstances, they weren't sure they should." She tightened her grip on his hand. "And it didn't end there. A few months later she rang to tell me our father had raped her."

"Good God. It excuses nothing, I know, but he couldn't have known she was his daughter, could he?"

"She seemed neither to know nor to care. *'He has to die,'* was all she said. And she said it so calmly, almost casually, insisting that she was waiting for an opportunity and would need only one. I should have—oh, I don't know—reasoned with her or something; tried to change her mind."

"But you didn't?"

"No—I told myself she wouldn't do it when deep down inside I think I knew that she would. Her mind was made up. The proof was there to see in her eyes. But she said nothing about Fiona Forrest or Andrew Templeton."

"So when she *and* your father were invited to the Manor, you weren't surprised by what happened?"

She shrugged but said nothing.

"Did she talk about the women?" he asked.

"She'd decided we'd conduct some kind of sisterly *campaign* against men, refusing to accept that I'd no intention of selling my body to anyone."

"Did she tell you Yarwood had threatened to expose them?"

"Oh, yes."

"So you passed the information to Sir Gordon?"

She shook her head. "I think Fiona Forrest did that—via his brother."

"So does she know Wilder was your sister?"

"I don't think so. It didn't occur to me that Geraldine might have told her until our father had dismissed her junior minister and she'd begun falling apart. She was a remarkable woman."

"A point of view, I suppose," he added, "Go on."

"Well, the end came with Mike a week before the shooting; the day before you and I met in the penthouse. We'd been living like strangers for months and had arranged to spend the night there."

How could he forget?

"We'd argued that morning; even more heatedly than usual, and I'd had enough. He'd been at odds with everyone and everything; especially with me and the staff at Carlow Mason. It may have been knowing my sister was a prostitute and that our pervert of a father had raped his own daughter. I really don't know. But I desperately wanted to be free, and something inside me was suddenly released."

Doubt was written on his face. "I'm serious, Richard. I think it was one of the reasons I was attracted to Danielle. She was so confident and relaxed; so sure of who she was. I was determined to stop Mike treating me like some kind of decorative plaything, so I went in search of the most blatantly revealing dress I could find. There'd be no sexual intercourse for Laura Carlow that night—oh no—that night she would *fuck*.

It was an altogether new experience for me, fucking—a brazen assertion of unashamed lust and sexual independence. I pretended we'd just met, drank too much champagne, so aroused my whole body was shaking, taunting him; tempting him: playing with his emotions to say nothing of my own. I virtually raped him—did it to him, made him do it to me for most of the night. I'd made up my mind never to compromise again.

You were the first man to be honest with me, do you know that?—the first to admit to wanting my body for sex. By no stretch of the imagination did I play hard to get, but when we finally went to bed together there were no false compliments or endearments. I was neither the virgin of your dreams, nor a target for some kind of tawdry, no-strings-attached sex. You wanted me and when you considered the moment right you were going to have me. I couldn't wait for the day. And you were my friend. From the first moment I saw you, I knew that."

Her eyes flashed, her lips quivering on the edge of the resolve-melting smile he'd so grown to love. "So, you see, Richard Wells, you're not alone—you may find it hard to believe, but despite my recent confusion, I'm in love with you too."

He lay awake for a long time after they made love, Laura asleep in his arms. There was much to consider—too much, perhaps. He could ask her to lend him the money to secure the Chateau, but what kind of man told a woman he loved her and then raided her purse? No—what he needed was a final roll of the dice. But with Yarwood and Templeton out of the equation; soon to be followed, he imagined, by Carlow himself; what if she was right? What if what they'd set out to achieve was quite simply impossible?

He knew Mason and Jane would do everything they could to assist him, but he had somehow to recruit Wetherby and Forrest—a virtually impossible proposition even if he'd had all the time in the world.

He booked a seat on the first flight to London he could get, explaining to Laura over a hurried, late breakfast how and why Yarwood had been recruited and the tactics they'd employed before Templeton, Yarwood and Mike had been questioned by Superintendent Keen.

She was unimpressed; and even more so when he went on to outline his new strategy. There was no doubting its audacity, she said, but there were too many imponderables; the considerable machinery of the British Establishment lined up against him. Mike had employed Geraldine's women, and she could think of no better way to manipulate men—but their involvement did nothing to reduce the likelihood of failure; quite the opposite, in fact.

He didn't say as much to her, but he couldn't have been more meticulous in preparing for what lay ahead, giving himself what he considered to be the very best of fighting chances to hold things together. Anyway, there could be no turning back now. "Incidentally," he asked, changing the subject. "Were you aware of Andrew Templeton's connection with Fiona Forrest and the women—that they were his main source of income?"

"I think he told me everything at one time or another—

more often than not about the women he'd had—but, strangely enough, no reference to Geraldine and Fiona Forrest. He was half out of his mind when he was drinking, but he rarely stopped that—or gave up trying to add me to his list of conquests. I'd have refused even to talk to the man if he hadn't been Sir Gordon's brother."

"According to Fiona Forrest, they'd been paying him huge sums of money for introductions—more than enough to meet his needs," Richard told her.

"Had they?"

"You don't seem surprised."

She shook her head. "Quite honestly I'm not. Anything was possible where that creep was concerned. Alcohol and drugs alone must have cost him the earth."

"Alcohol *and* drugs?"

"Oh, yes. He tried to press them on me—among other people, no doubt; forever pouring me drinks he knew I didn't want, before offering me cocaine and drinking them himself."

"But you didn't—?"

"Richard—please!"

"I'm sorry. Let's change the subject."

"Why don't we? So is Mike paying you well?"

"A million up front, and there was to be another when it's over. A forlorn hope now, I'm afraid, but I need to collect."

"So who contacted the police?"

"My money's on Fiona Forrest. Their informant apparently referred to Templeton and Mike by name, so it could only have been her, Geoff, Jane or me—as far as Mike's concerned, definitely me."

"So he retained you to hide the financial truth, among other things, and now he doesn't trust you?"

"So it would seem. Although I'm pretty sure his attitude stems from my relationship with you. Fortunately, I was fireproof. I'd made very sure of that."

"But he's paid you a million?"

"He has."

"So how can you be *fireproof*?"

He took a deep breath. "I've got a confession to make I'm afraid you won't like."

"Try me."

"Mike agreed to pay a million pounds of personal funds into an account of my choosing. When you signed the papers conveying the Chateau to me you authorized me to operate an account in your name. I included the mandate among the papers you signed."

He waited.

"Ah—so his records show your million coming to me?"

He nodded, trying to gauge her reaction. "I paid for the Chateau and moved the rest of it later."

"I wondered when you'd get round to telling me."

"You knew?"

"Oh, come on, Richard—whatever their shortcomings, Banks do occasionally communicate with their customers. And, believe it or not, I do read what I sign. I thought you were acting on instructions from Mike. Incidentally, how much has he paid Sir Gordon and Jane?"

"Templeton two and a half million, tops—Jane a fixed two hundred and fifty thousand."

"So much for the Equal Pay Act," she added. "And what about Yarwood?"

"Fifteen million in total—*if* we succeed."

"In exchange for most of the dirty work, I expect?"

He frowned. "Look, he's been arrested and Templeton questioned by the police—not once, but twice. Jane's contacting Templeton for me now, but with Superintendent Keen watching and waiting and Yarwood in custody, we have to tread carefully and Mike's hands are tied. So—dirty work from Yarwood or not, if I don't come up with something, we may as well quit."

"Would that be so bad?"

"If I was happy to lose the Chateau—no. But I can't pay Giles without Mike paying me."

"No—but I can. Then you could keep it."

"Yes—and a few months down the line find yourself wondering if I said I love you to get my hands on your cash. No—I pay my way or the Chateau goes up for sale. Anyway, we've come this far —somebody has to finish what we've started for the benefit of us all."

She shook her head. "I'm not sure I agree, but—well, I'm here if you need me and the offer still stands."

He kissed her. "You're amazing, do you know that?" He glanced at his watch and kissed her again. "I've got to go. Will you run me to the airport?"

TWENTY-SEVEN

The atmosphere in the car was heavy with tension as Laura drove Richard to the airport. He kissed her goodbye, and acknowledging the greetings of the cabin staff, boarded the aeroplane. He had to stay focused if he was going to convince Wetherby he meant what he said; prepared to be ruthless, too, if and when the need arose.

He'd stayed overnight at Jane's house before. "I've put you in the same room as last time," she said at the door. "Geoff'll be here in time for dinner. Oh, and you're meeting with Harry Wetherby at the Commons at eleven o'clock on Wednesday." She automatically glanced at her watch. "I thought we'd eat about eight."

Hurrying up to the room, Richard hung up his suit, threw on a pair of jeans and a t-shirt and went down to the kitchen. Everything about Jane's cottage was homely—designed to put guests at their ease. She poured him a beer and returned to preparing their dinner.

Mason duly arrived a few minutes before eight. As far as he was concerned the Westminster project had ended with Yarwood's arrest—a welcome release, although he wasn't about to go public on the subject having proposed it himself.

Jane threw another log on the fire and they sat down to eat.

"So what do you think?" Mason asked.

Richard complimented Jane on the food. "About what?"

"The whole bloody shooting match," Mason said. "Yarwood, Templeton's brother, Wilder, the police."

Richard carried on eating. "I think we go ahead as we

planned."

Mason sat back in his chair. "How the hell can we?"

"Mike has to leave everything to me. I'm relying on you to make sure he does. Who knows, he might even acknowledge the necessity, coming from you. Superintendent Keen is watching and waiting, so it has to be me who runs with it now."

At eleven o'clock on Wednesday morning, Richard arrived at the House of Commons. The Labour Party leader didn't keep him waiting. "Right, young Wells," he said warmly, offering his hand and leading Richard into his office. "What's up?"

"It's this Yarwood thing, Mr Wetherby."

Wetherby waved him to a chair. "Have a seat, lad—sit y'self down."

"They've arrested him, haven't they?" Richard continued.

"So I believe."

"Then it'll definitely come out."

"Don't talk in riddles, lad, what'll come out?"

"That the Cabinet Secretary's brother supported himself financially by introducing men to Wilder's women—the women at Penina."

"So—?"

"So all bets are off, aren't they—if the newspapers find out?—which they will. They'll be into everything; Mr Carlow's involvement, Sir Gordon; the women—*you*—the seminar at Penina. Incidentally, please don't think I'm suggesting there was anything improper about your relationship with Amanda, but like Mason and Mrs Forrest, you did share a room—justified or not, unfortunate conclusions are almost certain to be reached."

Wetherby eyed him, lighting a cigar.

"Yarwood was blackmailing a Whitehall civil servant," Richard went on. "A woman. Might you be a target, I wonder? You won't have seen him and his cronies at work—but you must have been expecting this?"

"So Carlow really is attempting what he talked about in

France?"

Richard nodded. "Look, Mr Wetherby, I don't quite know how to put this."

"Out with it, lad. Say what you've come to say."

"Well, the tabloids are bound to have a field day, aren't they? Take Forrest, for example. His wife's activities and his relationship with Templeton are certain to destroy him—as, I'm sorry to say, yours with Amanda may well do to you. After all, she was one of the Wilder women, wasn't she?"

"Aye—but now't can be done about it now."

Richard went on. "Mr Carlow approached you because he saw you as a man as disenchanted with Westminster and Whitehall as we all are. I know you're one of *the few*, as it were—a politician the public respect—something of a rarity these days—but what can you claim to have achieved in your thirty years in the House?"

"I said no and I meant no."

Richard paused only for breath. "When he told me what he was planning and asked me to join him, I too thought he was mad—*off his trolley* as I remember you put it. The idea was unthinkable. What made him believe he could dictate terms to Westminster and Whitehall—multi-millionaire or not? But then I realized he was set on making an eleventh-hour attempt to stop the mindless destruction of this Country.

Nobody listens to politicians any more, Mr Wetherby—we both know that; and I'm sure you'd be the first to admit you brought it on yourselves—deceit by deceit, broken promise by promise. Added to which, you seem collectively determined to demonstrate that while the electorate does nothing to stop you, you'll continue to line your pockets at our very considerable expense. The arrogant, self-righteous posturing that too often goes with it might even be amusing if we weren't witnessing the criminal activities of people in positions of trust.

Yarwood's been arrested, likely as not soon to be followed by Messrs Templeton and Carlow, especially if we do nothing but sit on our backsides, meaning that to give ourselves even an outside chance of avoiding this, there are things to be done; and fast—some of them unpalatable but for all that, essential. But we're holed below the waterline if I can't convince you, and Forrest, of course, to speak with one voice. If either of you refuse—well—"

"You're trying to threaten me with that, are you?" the politician growled.

"Mr Wetherby, please. Forget *your* career; without your co-operation it'll be curtains for all of us. Surely you can see that?"

Wetherby heaved a sigh. "No—I've heard enough—I said no to y'boss and I meant it."

"And that's your final word—?"

"Aye—it is."

"Then, I'm sorry, but you leave me no choice. When we set out to do this, Yarwood provided us with what amounted to two groups of names to add to those we'd already listed; the first consisting of MPs and Whitehall civil servants with whom, to use his words, he'd previously *done business*; the second, people of influence in similar circles who had yet to be *pressed into service*."

The politician was becoming increasingly agitated. "I don't have time for this."

"Then I suggest you make some," Richard said firmly. "Among the second of the two groups, I found the name Wetherby—one Harold Wetherby; against which he'd written—and I quote: N.B. followed in brackets by a note to himself: '*You can't build it there but you can over here—and the land just happened to belong to his wife.*'"

Wetherby froze.

"And *Councillor* Harold Wetherby, *just happened* to be Chairman of the local Planning Committee." He paused to study the politician's face. "People have long memories, don't they, Mr Wetherby? I'd hate to see the gentlemen of the press add this to what they're bound to characterize as your *dubious* relationship with Amanda. And I'm sure I don't have to tell you that they'll already have taken careful note of your recent property acquisition."

Wetherby sat back in his chair clenching and unclenching his fists. The one action in his life he truly regretted was about to destroy him. He'd always suspected it might, but where was the justice? And the cottage—the ink on the conveyance was scarcely dry.

"It's all fine and good for Carlow," he grumbled, a look of desperation replacing his usually genial expression. "Taught you well, hasn't he? Christ, when I think of the sacrifices I've made."

"Having introduced the Single Transferable Vote," Richard continued, "Mr Carlow and Sir Gordon see the Lords becoming an elected assembly—the British Senate, as it were—or being disbanded. I know they favour the latter course of action in view of what they consider desirable—that's to say essential for the Commons."

"Let's have it, then," Wetherby grunted.

"After reducing the number of MPs by up to fifty per cent, clearing the way for their responsibilities and general accountability to be appropriately structured, they want to see the Lords abolished, first to speed the process of government and second to reduce its overall cost. After that you'll all be required to offer yourselves for election on Party tickets as usual, or as independent candidates, and once elected, collectively charged with appointing Prime Minister and Cabinet."

Wetherby laughed. "You've got to be joking."

"I assure you I'm not—each Minister to be the choice of a minimum of two thirds of the House."

The politician found that even more amusing.

"They suggest that everyone at Westminster knows which of you should be entrusted with Cabinet office—and by definition, therefore, which of you should not. So should you for any reason fail to complete the procedure within a fixed time period following a general election, Parliament will automatically dissolve, facilitating what they call a *supplementary* election at which no sitting MP will be permitted to stand."

Wetherby ceased to be amused.

"They further suggest," Richard added. "One, that every Cabinet proposal thereafter be submitted to the House for debate, amendment, approval or otherwise. Two: that the Parties, including their Whips, should they for some reason decide to retain them, have no standing in the House. Three: that constituency obligations become the day to day province of local government personnel. Four: that salaries are increased, subject to Members being present in the House on every day it sits. Five: that the ceremonial rituals of Parliament be discontinued, and, finally; that elections are held at fixed, four-yearly intervals.

But they fully expect to see the Parties trying to preserve some kind of future for themselves, hence the use they're making of Yarwood and the methods he employs."

Reaching into his briefcase, he placed a folder of papers on Wetherby's desk. "Two speeches for you to deliver; the first to your constituents; the second to your Party conference—plus a third I've drafted for a TV appearance by Forrest. Read them."

Wetherby grunted.

"You'll be pleased to know," he added, "that Yarwood's people won't be troubling you—providing you agree to cooperate, of course. In fact, improbable as it may seem, we're likely to see a significant improvement in your personal popularity."

Wetherby's reply was unintelligible.

"Now—" Richard concluded. "I'd like you to arrange for us to meet the Prime Minister. Somewhere private, I think. The taxpayer unknowingly provided the funds to acquire it—so why not your cottage?"

TWENTY-EIGHT

According to Fiona Forrest, Harry Wetherby had paid an inflated price for the mews cottage in Chelsea. It was where he shared a bed with Amanda when he stayed down in London. Not the most ethical of transactions, buying it from her—but the rules at Westminster did little to dissuade MPs from acquiring personal assets at the taxpayers' expense.

Richard had wanted the meeting sooner, but Forrest's schedule had made it impossible. He arrived, parked the Porsche and went into the house, Forrest's car scheduled to deliver him ten minutes later.

As far as Richard was concerned, the cottage was a cynical misappropriation of public funds, but it was no worse as misappropriations went, than others attributed by Yarwood to those on his list. Forrest's car arrived on time, dropped him and left.

After the cursory nods and grunts that passed for greetings, Richard handed him copies of the speeches he'd given to Wetherby, advising him to spend a few minutes reading them before they talked. It would have taken very little to prompt Forrest to turn tail and run.

Richard was drinking tea opposite Wetherby at the kitchen table, when, half an hour later, Forrest joined them. He immediately protested almost hysterically that Wetherby could do and say what he chose, but the British Prime Minister couldn't be expected to entertain the idea of delivering the speech Richard had written for him—especially on television—or, indeed, agree to be a party to such an obvious conspiracy.

Wetherby laughed, pointing out that he'd apparently failed

to notice that he was being given no choice—unless, of course, he *wasn't* in a homosexual relationship with the Cabinet Secretary, and his wife *hadn't* been involved with a group of prostitutes in partnership with the woman who'd cold-bloodedly gunned-down his predecessor.

Forrest slumped in a chair as the big yorkshireman stressed sarcastically that the *Right Honourable Gentleman* was obviously free to conduct himself in any way he chose. Personally, however, he'd worked too long and *fooking* hard to allow himself to be dragged in the mire by a thick, Tory queer—Prime *fooking* Minister or not.

After more large gins than were good for him and an ongoing verbal assault from Wetherby, Forrest changed his mind. Two hours later, their strategy agreed and choreographed in detail, Wetherby insisted Forrest wait for nightfall before leaving. '*Six to four on,*' as he put it, he'd otherwise end up being '*photographed at t'door by some fucking opportunist who just happened to be passing.*'

Eventually arriving back at Jane's house, Richard immediately called Mason, apologizing once again for repeatedly reminding him about Carlow's part in all this. Alerting Superintendent Keen had to be avoided at all costs, so he had to do and say *nothing*—and that, he stressed, meant nothing at all.

He did give him some good news, however; confidently predicting that a series of events was about to unfold which had every chance of producing the outcome they were seeking.

Matters outstanding between Carlow and himself would have to wait.

It might have been described as Wetherby Sunday; reports of his speech to his constituency party monopolizing the front page of every newspaper.

WETHERBY SLAMS PARLIAMENTARY CORRUPTION, was one of the headlines; WETHERBY QUESTIONS BRITISH DEMOCRACY, another. Richard liked: PARLIAMENT AN ARCHAIC SHAM, SAYS LABOUR PARTY CHAIRMAN.

Harold Wetherby, Chairman of the Labour Party and well respected by the House of Commons as a whole, recommended in his Sheffield constituency last night, that we undertake a wholesale reorganization of our parliamentary system before it's too late.

He said its antiquated methods and rituals were inappropriate for dealing with twenty first century problems, and to fail to acknowledge that was to invite self-destruction. We couldn't go on pretending that Westminster and Whitehall managed our affairs either efficiently or cost effectively when the entire population of these islands knew to their cost it was simply not true.

We claimed to have a responsible Parliament in a democratic society, but he saw no evidence to support either contention when economic and social platitudes, expressed more often than not for reasons of blatant self-interest, remained the principal passport to parliamentary power.

He appreciated that it was difficult to gauge public opinion on such matters; to differentiate between tolerance, apathy, and unspoken approval when there was so little public reaction to parliamentary performance, but we should nonetheless favour an electoral system based on the Single Transferable Vote, and reorganize procedure accordingly. Government could then be released from the shackles of Party politics, so eradicating the root-cause of parliamentary hypocrisy once and for all.

Asked what he meant by *'the shackles of party politics'*, he explained that no Government should assist capital to exploit labour, or vice versa, or set out to stimulate futile and costly confrontation between the various social and economic factions in our society. Parliament had to act positively but objectively on behalf of us all.

But this wasn't to suggest that government could ever be all things to all people; rather that it should be democratically constituted and rational in approach. What we had now—indeed, no adversarial, party-political system could be considered democratic, representative, or anything but divisive and anti-social if it empowered minorities lacking the support of more than half the electorate to legislate for our future.

And why, he went on to ask, did we tolerate Party Whips? Didn't a system designed to stop MP's voting as they saw fit not tell us everything about Westminster we needed to know?

Why were secretive minority groups permitted to exercise more control over our lives than Parliament itself? Didn't we care, or had we resigned ourselves to the probability that a British democracy would never exist? Indeed, was the current archaic sham, born of an age when the masses were looked upon as an inconvenient irrelevance, honestly considered to be acceptable today? Could anyone seriously argue it was the best we could do?

What motivated us to persist in playing meaningless, confrontational games when the very foundations of our economic structure were close to collapse—minority groups free to conduct themselves as if their arrogant likes, dislikes and personal preferences were the beginning and end of our existence? The future was a lottery for us all, and yet we still found ourselves listening to fatuous arguments as to whether this approach or that to given situations was good for *the Party*.

A Government spokesman was reported as saying:

'Mr Wetherby is well known for his radical views, but given the world in which we now find ourselves, we can none of us ignore the need for reform.'

Editorials set out to analyze his statement in depth as Wetherby challenged the Tories to disagree, announcing that he intended to expand on his ideas at the forthcoming Party conference, going on to argue that:

'Regardless of political persuasion or period in Office, no Government had demonstrated the inclination or necessary understanding of our situation to take steps to halt what many considered to be a Westminster sponsored decline in our fortunes which had been more or less continuous since the end of the second world war.

It came as no surprise that the nation had stopped listening to the superficial, not to say crass pronouncements of those in positions of power at Westminster. If they gave us no good reason to believe them; if we knew them to be habitual liars and considered them mercenary, bigoted and at best second rate, why would we bother to vote for them in meaningless general elections?

Those who cared one way or the other had given up believing common sense and logic would ever prevail. And to make matters worse, everyone with a grain of intelligence understood that there was no legitimate place in government for political regimentation, whatever its colour. Any that might manage to survive should find itself divested of power to dictate policy to the House or to seek to legislate for the conduct of our everyday lives.

Parliament had become an amazingly costly, juvenile squabble over who pulled the strings. Whether or not those strings should be pulled at all was of little concern to the people who pulled them. Indeed, the process of government rarely came near the House. It attended to priorities from a quite different agenda, and our elected representatives accepted the situation with their minds firmly closed—for the good of the Party but above all, themselves.

Crazy though it seemed, left to its own devices Westminster would never be motivated to change what was unceasingly manipulated for personal ends.

We had, therefore, to abolish the House of Lords; insist on the introduction of the Single Transferable Vote; demand that the body of the House, so elected, be required to appoint from their number, within a prescribed time period and by a two-thirds majority in every instance, those considered best qualified and suited to Cabinet Office, including that of Prime Minister. Failure to complete the exercise in the timescale allowed should then result in a supplementary general election at which no sitting member was permitted to stand.

Every sane person among us accepted that Government ought to include the full range of skills, training, general ability, political and social bias that made up the House, and that to accomplish it required the removal of even the remotest possibility of Party control.

The Labour Party Chairman insisted that in no sense did this mean coalition. It would result in representative government, however political and social vested interests might attempt to portray it. But we had at the same time, to stop surrendering parliamentary power to Europe, another basic nonsense to which we continued to subscribe. We had to stop touching the forelock to foreign enterprises in exchange for cosmetic injections of cash. These people weren't our partners. They were our competitors in every sense of the word. And the process was much more than demeaning; it guaranteed our eventual demise; yet another example of the self-serving naïveté of our elected representatives.

Despite the nature and obvious complexity of its problems, the East as we knew it, joined in due course by countries from behind the old iron-curtain, would collectively dominate the industrialized world—and we could do nothing to stop them. We had to make our own decisions and provide for ourselves.

He added that a significant number of the Shadow Cabinet shared his views, but declined to name them. Indeed, it was also true to say there was a great deal of cross-bench support for these ideas, even though many feared the retribution of the Parliamentary Parties. In openly declaring themselves now, individuals would be risking de-selection should there be a Party based election at some future date.'

'I've been a member of the Labour Party for close to forty years; repre-

sented you in Parliament for the best part of thirty, and you've always come first. I've never lied to you and I won't be starting now; Party or no Party.'

Richard thought some of it was a bit over the top, but it had been more or less accurately reported, especially given that Wetherby was a politician of more than thirty years standing and his was the erstwhile political way. But it had been an accomplished performance to date, and he'd congratulate him at the first opportunity.

Monday's headlines were very much as Richard had hoped. Timed to coincide with coverage of the Wetherby speech, his *anonymous* leak into Fleet Street was producing the desired response; newspapers claiming an internal memorandum from the Tory Party *think-tank* had been leaked; a revolutionary blueprint for the management of the United Kingdom finding its way into the hands of the Labour Party Chairman who was claiming its ideas as his own. The media were quickly in turmoil, claim and counter claim filling newspapers, television and radio news bulletins and hastily prepared current affairs programmes.

For their part, the Conservatives began by denying the leak —hardly surprising considering the memorandum didn't exist. But an official spokesman was quick to insist that the Party wouldn't dream of promoting such reactionary ideas.

Meanwhile, in direct and obvious contradiction to this, a growing number of Yarwood's Conservative Party *victims* were beginning to voice their support for what were being described as the *Wetherby* reforms—some in exchange for cash, some under threat of exposure for dubious activities or earlier collaborations—and a few who were actually in favour.

Westminster and Whitehall were in chaos, nobody wanting to be seen or heard supporting ideas that might be to their personal detriment. They nonetheless recognized that opposing Wetherby might in itself be the stance best avoided. And neither did they want to be thought spineless should they succumb to their political instinct and sit on the fence.

But there was nothing new about politicians being panicked by concern for themselves. Richard had forecast it—the first odds-on certainty he'd come across in years. Reputations were perceived to be at risk, a growing number on all sides of the House claiming to be weighing the arguments before making up their minds.

Having distanced themselves from Wetherby at the outset, the Labour Party leadership now began aligning themselves with him, while the Conservatives, continuing their policy of denial, were at the same time adamant his ideas weren't his own.

They wouldn't dream of advocating such a constitutional upheaval, they insisted, unless, of course, it was decided *in the fullness of time, in due course, and after due deliberation,* that it was in the nation's best interest.

It was stretching their powers of invention, but when had that ever deterred a political party from swearing black was white and expecting the electorate to take their word for it? At least they hadn't succumbed to the temptation to claim that these proposals were part of some kind of fiendish, socialist plot.

Wetherby himself, consistently denying knowledge of a memorandum, leaked or otherwise, had truth on his side and was beginning to enjoy it. He and senior colleagues had taken several years to construct these proposals, he now argued, and as they represented the culmination of a concentrated period of deliberation and planning, it was logical to have them debated at Conference and in the Country at large.

But the more he denied the existence of the memorandum, so the more the public believed it existed, especially as the Tories were also denying it. Dyed in the wool Party activists and so-called, constitutionalists on all sides of the House, were outraged, but it was entertaining to see so many biting their tongues as Yarwood's endeavours bit deep into Government, while the coercion of the opposition benches, due not only to Yarwood but to Wetherby himself, virtually silenced the champagne socialists on the Party's *trendy* left-wing.

Richard watched the arguments rage before deciding it was time for Forrest's television appearance, while Wetherby became an overnight celebrity after thirty years in the House.

Nobody knew how he'd single-handedly outplayed the Government, least of all his Labour Party colleagues or the Tories who were also amazed by the growing number of their own who were beginning to openly declare their support.

TWENTY-NINE

Superintendent Keen arrived early. He'd been out of bed since dawn, going through his notes. In addition to Yarwood's alleged subversive activities, his fingerprints on a wine glass found at the scene suggested that he'd also had something to do with the death of Andrew Templeton. Keen was a long way from convinced. He pulled up a chair to face DI Thomas at his desk. "Look, Nobby, he'll insist he was giving this woman information for the Cabinet Secretary, won't he?"

Thomas interrupted, "Good morning, Chief Superintendent —coffee?"

"No—" Keen grunted. "Er—well, yes—yes tea, if you're brewing?"

Thomas shouted for Chas. "My usual and a tea with two sugars," he ordered as Chambers hurried in. He turned to Keen. "I assume you're talking about Yarwood?"

Chas turned and went out.

"He'll say the woman's a nutter," Keen continued despondently. "And the evidence suggests she probably is. But nobody's gonna to take his word against that of a Whitehall civil servant, are they—Cabinet Office weirdo or not? Just my luck. He's guilty, all right, I'd stake my pension on it, but we'll never make it stick. Then there's Templeton's brother—blow his brains out; leave a champagne glass smothered in your fingerprints—the only glass in the room and no sign of the bottle? Naah—someone's taking the piss."

Chas returned with two mugs. Thomas thanked him. Keen grunted. "Sorry to butt in, Guv'," Chas said, "but if the champagne glass was a red-herring, it puts person or persons unknown in the frame—assuming suicide's a non-runner? And our informant said Yarwood was bribing and blackmailing *people*— *plural*; not a single individual. If we go public with alleged bribery and blackmail at Westminster and in Whitehall—saying that we see no reason at this stage to discount anything we're told, then, who knows—somebody might be tempted to come forward."

Keen couldn't have agreed more.

Yarwood had nobody to blame but himself. A mistake, albeit an easy one to make; separate sets of identical initials complete with the same surname—one in either section of his list—the one a senior civil servant, the other a lesbian security risk on Templeton's staff.

He sat staring at the wall as Keen came into the room followed by Thomas and Chambers. They sat down opposite him, Keen announcing the date, time and the names of those present for the tape. He planted his notebook on the table in front of him, smiling benignly. "So, *Mister* Yarwood—we meet again?" He sat back in his chair, his hands behind his head, the room falling silent until Yarwood spoke.

"Harassment," he grumbled sourly. "That's what this is. That pantomime last year and now twice in a month. What exactly am I supposed to have done?"

There was clearly no love lost between them. "We've received a very serious complaint—*Sir*," Keen emphasized. "The Cabinet Secretary's office say you're trying to blackmail their staff."

That evening, following his meeting with Richard and their confrontation with Forrest, Wetherby told Amanda that he could see no way to avoid what he described as the *second phase* of what he'd been pressed into doing.

"Yes—but is there nothing to be said for what Richard Wells and his friends are trying to achieve?" she asked. "If our system of government is failing us as you say, surely something has to be done?"

His instinctive reaction was to ridicule the idea. Instead, he took her hand and quietly admitted she was right, going on to explain that his father had been confronted by a similar problem—a problem which had also called for wholesale changes in the conduct of people in positions of authority. His approach had shown a certain naïveté, however. It was easy to claim this with the benefit of hindsight, but he'd no desire to make the same mistakes. Fighting battles you couldn't win made no sense, as he'd discovered later.

He accepted that his father had lived in a different time; almost another world, in fact, and with virtually nothing to work with in comparison with today, the factory owners ruthless in dealing with demands for higher wages and improved working conditions before his father came along, after which any failure on their part to offer suitable recompense for work carried out or to listen to legitimate demands, had seen the workforce threatening to withdraw their labour—to *strike*; although it had come to that only once.

He'd never forgotten his father's unconditional dedication to the welfare of the members of his Union, or that the factory owners had held him personally responsible for anything and everything that happened. How could he when the physical and mental pressures to which his father had been subjected had almost certainly contributed to ending his life? Perhaps his demands had been too ambitious? Who could say—better pay, working hours and conditions, holidays, sick-pay, pensions? But he'd never doubted for a moment that every one of his father's demands was justified. Indeed, that selfless dedication had motivated *him* to fight for workers' rights, too—first in local government, then down at Westminster where he'd been ever since.

Shortly before his untimely death, however, his father had called him at the House to say that most of the immigrants who'd found their way on to the company payroll since the war; predominantly Polish and Italian, were invariably quick to enrol and even quicker to pay their subs, while a growing number of British workers were beginning to refuse to join the Union at all.

Soon afterwards, a need for redundancies had arisen—a genuine need, there was no denying that—requiring him to recommend the dismissal of a number of English workers, in favour of *foreigners*. It had almost broken his heart, especially when he was accused of being a traitor—physically threatened, too, on a number of occasions; frequently enough, in fact, for the local GP to conclude that it was almost certainly the cause of his failing health: while, much to his own consternation, a disturbing number of MPs on all sides of the House of Commons had begun to exhibit concern more for their personal status and prospects than for the people they were supposed to represent.

The tendency had become so common that he'd been forced to conclude that his father's analysis of party politics and the average Westminster politician had been disturbingly accurate. And that was added to the fact that his insistence on a *fair day's pay for a fair day's work* was being dismissed out of hand by his own Trade Union. They preferred threatening to down tools if they didn't get something for nothing whenever they chose to demand it. The founding principles of the Labour movement were even then being actively ignored.

"I've never admitted this to anyone," he went on; "not even m'first wife." He hesitated. "Since Dad died I've avoided confrontation wherever and whenever I could. It frightens me *shitless*. I can't seem to forget that it was probably what killed him."

Amanda listened in silence before saying that from what he'd been telling her, he had nothing to fear. He should welcome what was now being asked of him in the sure and certain knowledge that were his father alive today, he'd not only approve, but support him every inch of the way—as indeed would she and every other straight thinking person. He should go ahead—make his father proud.

On the opening day of the Brighton conference, Amanda's words of reassurance ringing in his ears, Wetherby delighted in making the press corps as uncomfortable as he could. It was a cold morning made to feel even colder by an icy blast off the sea. Pursued by a dozen newspaper reporters, he went for a walk on the sea front. When he thought he'd dragged them far enough, each of them hoping for a quote for their trouble, he retraced his steps, his arrival at the conference greeted by a buzz of anticipation from the body of the hall.

Shaking a few hands on his way to the platform, he was quick to bring the meeting to order. *"Friends,"* he began, relishing the moment; scanning the faces of the delegates and the Westminster contingent seated on either side and behind him, *"What I have to say this morning may surprise many of you, particularly as it comes from an MP of some thirty-years standing."*

His sigh was clearly audible. *"I was reminded only yesterday that it's forty years almost to the day since I followed in my father's footsteps and joined the Party. However, as you will have gathered from my recent speech to my constituents, I consider the performance of Government and the behaviour of too many Members of the House to be a very long way from satisfactory. This has led me to conclude that were I not to further explain my concerns here today, I'd not only be failing in my duty to you, but also to the rest of the good people of the United Kingdom."*

He waited, firmly resolved; all thought of agenda forgotten.

"My father was a trade unionist—a shop steward, in fact—who laughed when it was suggested he should offer himself as a candidate for Westminster. Yes—somebody suggested it and his reaction was to laugh. But, why, you may ask—why would he laugh? What was so funny about the idea of his standing for Parliament?

The answer, my friends, is that it was not in the least amusing. And I have to make it clear he was far from amused, insisting that he didn't need to become part of it for party politics to make him sick to the stomach—going on to claim that the party grandees wouldn't want him around, anyway. They wouldn't offer someone like him the chance of a seat in the 'khazi at the end of our yard,' as I remember he put it, never mind the hallowed benches of the House of Commons. And, as I said, he wouldn't have accepted the opportunity even if they had.

But it did nothing to stop him encouraging me. Oh, no. As long as I realized and accepted that, Party or no Party, I'd be honour bound to faithfully represent my constituents and the wider population of this Country, all would be well. If I couldn't guarantee that—if there was a single doubt in my mind regarding my ability to dedicate myself to working on their behalf, so earning and deserving their trust, I should forget the idea.

All these years later I can say that if Westminster has taught me anything, it's that the only way to climb the political ladder is precisely the opposite. That's to say, each and every individual is expected to meekly toe the party line regardless of whether or not he or she considers it to be at odds with the needs of constituents and the population at large.

You see, my friends, in order to be admitted and to survive in the upper echelons of a political party—to acquire the power to influence policy decisions and have an outside chance of furthering the interests of those who vote to elect you—it's essential to avoid thinking or saying anything that might incur the wrath of the Party grandees, as my father consistently called them.

But I put it to you now. Is it likely that hundreds of dedicated men and women like him—people who, against all the odds, founded and built the labour movement—would have been prepared to do that? Would they have buried their heads in the sand? Would they have habitually said yes when every instinct they possessed was crying out to say no—or the opposite, of course? And do you think they would have kept their opinions to themselves?"

He paused, shaking his head and surveying the room. "Dear me, no. No, my friends, they most certainly would not. Had they at any stage been so inclined, you and I wouldn't be here today. Unfortunately, the modern expectation at Westminster is for Members to go along with the social niceties and hypocrisies that increasingly abound there, at the same time blindly accepting the often nauseating likes, dislikes and personal preferences of Party leaderships which belie the fact that genuine representatives of the people owe their allegiance to the people, not to political parties.

Ladies and gentlemen, this serves only to suggest that those of us who have achieved positions of power at Westminster, large or small, are no better than hypocrites—yes—hypocrites who have rarely, if ever, uttered a word contrary to party ideology or diktat, even on those occasions when we were fully aware that our constituents and the rest of the people of these islands needed us to speak out—and who, in so doing, have frequently demonstrated our concern for none but ourselves.

In reality, too many of us seem to regard ourselves as so superior to the people who elect us that it was recently suggested to me that we believe the masses were put on this earth for no better reason than to do our bidding. To describe this appalling arrogance as tragic may be the understatement of the century, but, sadly, it has become increasingly difficult to refute."

He paused, more to observe the faces of his fellow MPs than those of the delegates in the body of the hall.

"I've also to tell you that having seen this state of affairs grow steadily worse, I consider myself well qualified after thirty years, to say that my father was right—his jaundiced view of Party politics shown to be disturbingly accurate. And to be frank, I'd go even further: politicians gathered together under the auspices of political parties anywhere in the world are among the most financially and socially destructive forces mankind is capable of mustering."

He looked round the room.

"An exaggeration, you think? Well, what do you see when you look at and listen to the Government front bench?" Again he began shaking his head. "Yes—a row of self-serving hypocrites. And on our own side of the House?" He spread his arms wide in a gesture of resignation. "Sadly, the picture is equally depressing."

The hall remained silent.

"You see," he continued, "an MP's duty is so basic and straightforward it's impossible to misinterpret. To offer oneself for election in order to make one's way in the world is to declare oneself ill suited to the task. As my father argued, the majority of us are required to be nothing more than honest, hard working representatives of the British people.

So where are we to find our future public servants—men and women of the intelligence and integrity we so badly need?" He paused before answering his own question. "I fear they have always been few, my friends—rendered impotent for the most part —overwhelmed by the pressures imposed by tidal-waves of dogma, self-interest and greed. But I firmly believe they will re-emerge when we give them the tools they need and a mandate to use them—which we plan to do now."

There were mutterings in the body of the hall, but to his continuing surprise, not a single MP on the platform showed any inclination or desire to dispute what he was saying. He took a deep breath. "Ladies and gentlemen, you don't need me to tell you that Parliament is undeserving of our trust and failing us badly. Yes —the Labour Party has changed the course of history on more than one occasion in the past, and we've good reason to be proud of much of that record—but like each of the political Parties it was created in a world so different from that in which we now find ourselves, that, as is equally true of the others, it can play no legitimate part in a Government of the future."

He waited—still nobody intervened.

"But—" he continued, "we are at the same time presented with a once in a lifetime opportunity—an opportunity to make the most momentous and far reaching contribution to the lives and future prospects of the people of this Country a political party has ever been privileged to make.

How can that be? you may ask. Well, let me just say that when our current proposals for the wholesale restructuring of our system of government come before the House and are accepted. Oh, yes—I confidently forecast they will be accepted. Then the management of our great nation will no longer be entrusted to the smug, self-obsessed political class of which I speak. No—assuming they are then ratified by a national referendum, it will be placed in the hands of genuine representatives of the people for the very first time.

You see, my friends, we shall deliver what so many of our forebears dedicated their lives to. We shall finally create a parliamentary democracy."

A tentative smattering of applause gathered support in the hall.

"But we have to understand as we contemplate our future, that we are about to be subjected to the most sustained economic and social pressure we have ever experienced in peacetime or war; pressure in the final analysis so intense, so severe, that were we to fail to legislate for the changes I've done my best to outline—were we to neglect to squarely face the tasks we've no choice but to set for ourselves, then Britain as we know it cannot and will not survive."

He sipped from the glass on the lectern in front of him, allowing his audience to digest every word.

"And be warned—those who have long devoted their lives to maintaining control over ours," he went on, *"will object to these proposals—will actively campaign against them. Nothing new there, of course—nothing we haven't experienced before.*

But we have to understand that we cannot allow ourselves to be sidetracked into repeating the mistakes of the past. This time we have to ensure that every present and potential Member of Parliament is fully aware that he or she will be personally accountable not to a political Party; not to the British Establishment which has for so long held our lives in the palm of its hand, but to each and every one of us—to every man, woman and child in Great Britain."

The statement was greeted by a gathering wave of applause.

"Failure would exacerbate the current chaos and end in disaster. Never again must we allow the progress we make to be dismissed as outdated or irrelevant. Never again must we allow our infrastructure to begin falling apart. And never again must we allow greed and corruption in public life to go unpunished, aided and abetted by Parliament as we see it today.

But I need to impress upon you all that, even so, we won't enjoy what we face. There can be nothing comfortable or easy about it—no magic wand to be waved. Indeed, many of the steps we've no choice but to take will be hard to accept. But I give you my word—everyone and anyone elected to serve you when these proposals are enacted, will serve you honestly or serve not at all.

There'll be no Party smokescreens to cover their tracks; no whips' offices, no coercion, no dirty tricks campaigns to ensure they toe party lines. No—they'll know that they're directly accountable to every man, woman and child who can call themselves British.

My friends—the crisis we now face—a crisis visited upon us by people we trusted to safeguard our interests and which we underestimate at our peril—is as much an opportunity as a crisis; an opportunity, incidentally, which I've every confidence we have the capacity to grasp. And we must seize it with both hands. How? By concentrating our resources where they need to be concentrated—by not wasting time, energy and money meddling in the affairs of the rest of the world—by resolving here today to ensure that Britain as we know it is capable of surviving, making life as acceptable as we can for each other as we go through that process.

Ladies and gentlemen, I know we can do this—so let's show the world what the real people of Britain are made of—let's go to work for the benefit of us all."

He banged his fist on the lectern to emphasize his point, and as applause rushed through the hall, he again held up his hand.

"Before I sit down I have a message for those who'd like to believe they'll still find a way to get something for nothing. Hear me now, and remember my words—you will not succeed!!!

No—the energetic will prosper, the young, the old and the infirm will be properly cared for, but make no mistake; from the grasping millionaire, MP or Banker on the one hand, to the work-shy pauper on the other, the freeloader will perish. Our aims will never change, but our methods now must. We have to be equal to the challenges which face us, because—and believe me, my friends, these are not empty words—Britain is under siege!!! We have now to fight for our Country and the future of its people like we've never fought before.

So I ask you to honour the memory of men and women of principle like my father, and save it not only for ourselves and our immediate families, but for those who will come long after us all. My friends, they need us to stand together in support of these proposals."

He sat down to long faces on the platform, but a roar of approval and a standing ovation from the body of the hall.

THIRTY

The media frenzy which followed Wetherby's speeches came as no surprise to Gordon Templeton. In the wake of Carlow's earlier failure to enlist his support, however, the substance of them did.

That afternoon, Wetherby arrived half an hour late for their meeting, interrupting the Cabinet Secretary's customary break for earl-grey and biscuits. "This Yarwood character's working for Carlow, isn't he?" he said as he hurried through the door.

Templeton took his time over choosing a biscuit.

"Oh, come on, man," Wetherby growled.

The civil servant methodically un-cosied the teapot and stirred the tea. "I know he's been arrested. There's talk of little else at my Club." He leaned forward in his chair. "Are you sure I can't tempt you?"

Wetherby frowned. "I didn't come here to drink tea. Young Wells came to see me with a very clear message—co-operate or else. I won't go into detail. I know you're involved in this, so don't waste your breath trying to tell me you're not."

Templeton smiled. "Ah—an offer you couldn't refuse." He added a splash of milk to his cup before making an exaggerated show of selecting a second biscuit.

Wetherby hesitated. "So—am I missing something?"

On the eve of the Conservative Party conference, Big Ben chimed nine o'clock and Forrest was introduced; the programme captioned: A PRIME MINISTERIAL BROADCAST TO THE PEOPLE OF GREAT BRITAIN AND NORTHERN IRELAND.

Mason was still finding it hard to believe Fiona had married him.

'*Ladies and Gentlemen,*' Forrest began. '*After several of the most difficult weeks of my political life considering my position, I speak to you from Downing Street this evening, on the eve of my Party's annual conference, conscious that proposals of major constitutional significance have consistently been the subject of recent debate, not least at the Labour Party conference. I shall come to these shortly.*

First, I have to say that the cold-blooded murder which saw me assuming the Office of Prime Minister, deprived us not just of a public servant who dedicated his life to the service of his Country, but saw one of our great men cut down in his prime.

I suspect that, like me, most of you would have argued that regardless of how much we dislike or even hate an individual, or perhaps in this case their politics, it's not the British way to resort to physical violence. But we can't pretend it didn't happen, or that Britain can ever be the same place again.

Indeed, I confess to repeatedly asking myself if the selfishness, greed and overt preoccupation with the acquisition of wealth and status which has manifested itself in recent times not only within the British financial community but also sadly at the heart of our political establishment, in some way helped to motivate its perpetrator to commit this abominable crime?

That said, of course, it is also true to say that too many decent, hard-working people have been and indeed are being deprived of the basic necessities of life. Well intentioned or not, the policies my Government and I have pursued have not succeeded in changing this. Sections of the economy have responded favourably, it's true, but the outlook is bleak. This awful recession, perhaps the worst in our history, continues to wreak financial havoc with devastating consequences for lives and livelihoods up and down the Country.

So, with this in mind, I return to the recent newspaper reports, television and radio broadcasts, which have consistently argued that more draconian measures are urgently required if we're ever to overcome the difficulties we face. It has even been suggested that we change our System of government. And it may surprise you to learn that I share that opinion. Too long have we indulged in what have amounted to time consuming, costly and often juvenile Party political games.

I consequently find myself in agreement with the Chairman of the Labour Party—the Honourable Member for Sheffield—when he so eloquently argues that like so many aspects of life in Britain in these troubled times, the processes of government are largely ineffective and above all, too slow to take effect and too expensive to maintain. He is also correct in my view, when he says that our adversarial party political system is outmoded and counter-productive. Never again must those we elect to represent us be constrained by the ambitions of political Parties or pressurized by Whips or any other form of coercion into supporting legislation to which they do not subscribe. Furthermore, we cannot expect to find solutions to our problems by looking to Europe or the rest of the world.

Our difficulties, predominantly of our own making, can only be resolved if we utilize the training, expertise and experience of the best of our people regardless of political bias or social standing. And I submit that should we fail to acknowledge this, there will be much worse to come.

I thus consider it my duty to recommend to the House that we revise the manner in which we conduct the business of government; first, by introducing the Single Transferable Vote as the means by which we elect our MPs—and second, by disbanding the House of Lords; a wasteful and unnecessary use of resources in a properly constituted democracy; its members free thereafter to seek election to the Commons.

I shall further propose three things. One: that the number of MPs be reduced by as much as fifty percent. Two: that political Parties be divested of parliamentary status and power. And, three: that Members of Cabinet, including our Prime Minister, are appointed, individual by individual, by two-thirds majorities of sitting Members of the House. Following my Party conference, therefore—at which these matters will be at the top of our agenda—I shall lay them before the House as I've said, subsequently apprising Her Majesty of the outcome of that debate.

If these proposals are accepted and then ratified by the referendum that will follow, you will be asked to choose at a General Election those who will determine the future steps we must take.

I hasten to assure you that I believe it to be not only my duty to enable this—but my duty to enable it without delay. We have the ability and I hope the intelligence to overcome the obstacles we face. It remains only for us to rethink system and method before introducing the measures which can ensure our success.

I thank you for your attention and may God bless you all.'

Short and to the point as Richard had intended, he thought the speech had gone well. He called Wetherby to congratulate him and to ask what he thought of Forrest's contribution, only to find him surprisingly subdued. "Something wrong?" he asked.

"You tell me," the politician began. "I've delivered your speeches—added a few things that needed to be said, I think—but I've done what you asked. So what happens now?"

"How do you mean?"

"Well, you can't leave it there, can you? I've been at this game too long to expect a positive result from what I've witnessed so far."

"Yarwood's been active for weeks."

"Has he, indeed?" Wetherby continued, "No doubt paid a fortune to *magic* the outcome you're looking for? Answer me this. What if he took Carlow's money and sat on his arse, eh? What happens then? It's too late now to do anything about it—nobody you could tell."

"I don't think—"

"No, you obviously don't. And how do you propose to find out now that he's behind bars?"

"We've paid him five million pounds so far," Richard informed him. "He gets another ten—if and when he delivers."

"That's something, I suppose. But take it from me, I've seen too many majorities fail to materialize to sit back and hope. Check him out. And if you can't get to him, then Templeton's your man."

Cursing his failure to monitor Yarwood's progress, albeit unsure of how it might have been done, Richard could think of nothing to say. Wetherby was right. He rang off and turned to Jane. "I need to speak to Templeton—preferably tonight."

She looked at him quizzically. "Why?"

He buried his face in his hands. "Just call him, will you?" He shook his head. "I'm sorry; there was no call for that. Wetherby just pointed out that I'm not as clever as I thought I was; that's all." He screwed up his face. "And he's right—in more ways than one."

"We all have to face our shortcomings now and again," she said. Reacting to the expression on his face, she picked up the telephone and dialled. Two attempts later her dialling was rewarded. Following a brief conversation, she scribbled a note and put down the phone. "Did you hear that—his house at nine?" She handed him the note. "That's the address."

Following his television appearance, Forrest was being given a hard time at the Conservative Party conference, the delegates more antagonistic towards him than the Labour Party had ever been to Wetherby.

Several factors conspired against him. First: his obvious ineffectiveness as Prime Minister and Party leader. Second: the elitist clique within the Party had made no secret of considering his proposals outrageous, their interest in politics extending no further than enhancing their personal wealth, social standing or both. And if that weren't enough—his affected, Anthony Eden voice was perhaps the biggest turn-off for years to the rank and file of the Party and the electorate at large.

Richard arrived at Templeton's house even more anxious than usual. A middle-aged woman came to the door. She showed him into what she said was the drawing-room. Sir Gordon was on the telephone and shouldn't be long.

The room was tastefully furnished; the mahogany and leather façade not what Richard had expected. He was examining the water-colour above the fireplace when Templeton came in. "Mr Wells," he said, shaking Richard's hand. "Do have a seat. A drink, perhaps?"

Richard steeled himself. "No thank you, I'd prefer to come straight to the point."

Templeton nodded and sat down.

"I believe you originally expressed the view," Richard began, "that Yarwood would find it easier to convert the Conservative Party to our way of thinking than he would Her Majesty's Opposition."

"Indeed, I did."

"So may I ask if the Wetherby and Forrest speeches have changed that opinion?"

Templeton peered at him over his spectacles. "I don't know how you managed it, Mr Wells, and I don't want to, but I think it fair to say their efforts have allayed many of my fears."

"So you believe it's all systems go?"

"Well—we have to accept, I'm afraid, that Mr Yarwood's arrest has hindered our progress."

"You continue to have doubts, then?"

"I'm assured he's been largely successful on all sides of the House. Unfortunately, however, this comes not from him but from one of his staff. It may be accurate, of course, but—"

"So—as I said, you continue to have doubts?"

"Unfortunately—yes. Mr Carlow and myself are so to speak, *personae non grata* in some quarters these days, and have thus been unable to consult Yarwood in person."

"So what would you recommend?"

"I hesitate to suggest it, but I believe additional funds are required."

"Why?"

The civil servant produced a handkerchief and began polishing his glasses. "To allow more substantial incentives to be offered—to the Whips in particular, unless I'm very much mistaken."

"So are the opposition benches with us or not?"

"The proposed intention to reduce the number of MPs hasn't helped. These people are unlikely to welcome legislation that could make many of them redundant, but Yarwood is nothing if not persuasive. More funds, wisely applied, ought to secure what we want."

"Improved retirement incentives, you mean—bigger bribes?"

"Indeed."

"So how much should I allocate?" he asked, knowing he was in no position to *allocate* anything. "In total, I mean?"

Templeton hesitated. "Hard to say. You've a contingency fund, no doubt?"

Richard nodded. Templeton went on. "Much depends on Yarwood's reading of the situation, but I'd say, what—four or five million?"

Richard said nothing.

Templeton laughed. "Via me, perhaps? Best not deliver a cheque to Scotland Yard."

What was suddenly wrong with Yarwood's Cayman Island account? Richard wondered. Was this genuine concern, and how was he to judge? Templeton was watching him closely. "Do you have a problem with that?" he asked calmly—too calmly, Richard thought. "I presume you have the authority to release such a sum? I can approach Mr Carlow personally, if you'd prefer?"

"That won't be necessary," Richard assured him, conscious that the man was almost certainly aware of his fall-out with Carlow. No, he told himself; forget Carlow and what Yarwood may or may not have demanded, it had been Wetherby's comments that had prompted this visit, the question to be answered being whether or not he and Templeton were out to get their hands on four or five million? Out of character for Wetherby—but he couldn't forget that the yorkshireman *was* a politician, and it was unlikely that women like Amanda ever came cheap.

"I'll sleep on it," he said finally. "But not knowing what it will buy, I don't consider it an option."

Having considered the alternatives, Superintendent Keen suggested DI Thomas invite young Chambers to draft a press release. He wasn't optimistic about achieving a positive result, anyway, but it was worth a try—somebody might be tempted to come forward. Those close to government would keep their heads down, but that might not be true of people *indirectly* associated with Westminster, Whitehall and the City. It felt a bit like peeing into the wind, but he could think of nothing better.

He hated admitting, even to himself, that Yarwood looked like beating him again. He didn't doubt the slimy creep was guilty of the reported bribery and blackmail, but there was no evidence to support the view; nor anything concrete to connect him with Templeton's brother—alive *or* dead.

Chas thought the Labour Party Chairman was surprisingly keen to see what he'd presumably supported for most of his life consigned to the scrap heap. Might he have been got at? Thomas pointed out that if people with public profiles like Wetherby were *got at*, they'd be unlikely to admit it.

Forrest's television appearance and the widely discussed in depth analyses of Wetherby's speeches were continuing to dominate the news. Senior politicians from the two major Parties publicly agreeing with each other was a significant first, leaving Chas Chambers, if anything, more suspicious than before.

And they'd both been at Carlow's house at the time of the Prime Minister's murder. In fact, of all those associated with this, only Yarwood hadn't, and from what he'd been able to establish the man was looked upon as something of a social pariah —the *hired help*, as it were.

That said, the murder was always going to be followed by a leadership election. They couldn't have rigged that, could they —or for that matter anticipated what the trigger-happy Wilder had in mind?

And now Yarwood had succeeded in discrediting his latest

accuser. Chas and DI Thomas had questioned the woman, but they'd little to go on and had achieved even less. DCS Keen had called her a *weirdo* when she repeated the improbable story of Yarwood threatening to suggest that she was in a *relationship* with a secretary at the Russian Embassy.

Yarwood claimed to have done nothing more than ask her to inform the Cabinet Secretary of the activities of two of her colleagues—one involving a third party footing the bill for holiday accommodation in exchange for favours of some kind, the other following a compromising liaison with a foreign diplomat at a Caribbean hotel.

Asked why he hadn't personally delivered the information to Templeton, he claimed that given their membership of the same Club, he'd decided against. He'd then produced irrefutable evidence in both cases—copies of hotel bills, bank statements, emails, phone records—the lot. How he'd acquired any of it was a mystery, but it was enough to suggest he'd no case to answer.

Richard took a cab back to Jane's house, running to jump in as it came on to rain. He counted himself lucky to have found one at that time of night. He had still to establish whether or not Yarwood was party to all this. He couldn't see him risking ten million pounds as Wetherby had suggested, but the yorkshireman was right, he'd done nothing to check.

He rang Laura to ask her opinion of what he now planned, telling her he was missing her before giving her the gist of his conversation with Templeton, explaining that he now trusted the man even less than before.

She thought he was right to be cautious, especially given that he now intended to involve Superintendent Keen. He wasn't sure how best to play it, he told her, but it had somehow to end in a one to one with Yarwood.

THIRTY-ONE

Richard's telephone message for Superintendent Keen, said he'd read the Scotland Yard press release in the morning paper and had important information for him. In Keen's absence, the girl on the switchboard offered to connect him to another officer. He gave her Jane's telephone number, explaining that he was known to the Superintendent and would rather speak to him.

Keen rang an hour later. "Well," he said irritably, "what's this *important* information?"

"I'd rather not discuss it on the telephone, Mr Keen. Perhaps we could meet?"

"Where are you?"

"I'm staying with Mrs Garside." He gave him the address.

Keen was tempted to comment but resisted the urge. "I'll be there in half an hour. But I warn you now, I'll be very annoyed if you're wasting my time."

He arrived in twenty minutes. "So—?" he began, Richard's offer to shake his hand grudgingly accepted. "What's this information you can't discuss on the telephone?"

"Andrew Templeton was murdered," Richard told him.

Keen screwed up his face. "And you can tell me who killed him, I suppose?"

"I can. It was Lady Morrison—Geraldine Wilder."

"She shot Templeton *and* the Prime Minister?"

"Indeed, she did."

"And where, may I ask, did this *information* come from?"

"I'd rather not say—if you don't mind?"

"Of course I *mind*, Mr Wells. It's a country mile from admissible evidence if I can't quote its source."

"I'm sorry," Richard added. "I'm not trying to be difficult, but the lady in question would prefer to stay out of it."

"Ah—your Mrs Carlow?"

"No, *not* my Mrs Carlow." Richard shook his head. "Our dearly departed Prime Minister and Andrew Templeton raped the lady in question and Wilder at Templeton's house. And I thought you should know that Wilder was the Prime Minister's daughter."

"His *daughter*?"

"She was. My contact is married, Mr Keen, or I'd give you her name."

"Why tell me at all?" Keen growled. "These people are dead."

"I thought it my duty," Richard lied. "I understand you're holding Desmond Yarwood in connection with the shooting."

"You're very well informed?"

"It pays to be."

Keen consulted his notebook. "As it happens, Mr Wells, we're satisfied Mr Yarwood played no part in the Templeton affair. In fact, we've reason to believe he was never at the house. Somebody made a clumsy attempt to incriminate him, but I imagine that must have been Wilder, if what you're telling me is true."

"Yarwood could have introduced them," Richard added. "The man was Sir Gordon's brother, and they are members of the same club."

Keen scratched his chin, thoughtfully. "Yes—you are well informed. So do you know your employer gave his wife a million pounds at around about the time she lent money to you?"

Richard shook his head. "How would I know that?"

"You keep his records, don't you?"

"Corporate European, yes; personal, no."

"But doesn't it strike you as odd?"

"Odd—why?"

"She'd walked out on him, hadn't she? Why would he give her anything, never mind a million pounds? A *cynical* copper might think the money was *always* meant for you, Mr Wells—for services rendered."

Richard thought quickly and laughed. "I like it. Laura Carlow lending me money in gratitude for services rendered. But seriously, Superintendent—put yourself in his place. Imagine having a *bit on the side* at the University Arms in Cambridge and later in France, not to mention Portugal, and you're worth a whisker more than five hundred million—" He paused, gauging the policeman's reaction. "—Which do you think you'd prefer; the occasional million pound *gift* or open war in a divorce court?"

"Oh, come on now—she'd walked out on him."

"Indeed, she had. But which of them was the first to stray, I wonder? I repeat, Mr Keen; what would you do if you stood to lose a bloody great slice of five hundred million?"

The following day, with Yarwood about to be released, a back-bench MP came forward in response to Chas Chamber's press release. He claimed a man had threatened to tell his wife he was sleeping with his secretary if he failed to support the Wetherby/Forrest proposals when they came before the House.

He insisted the accusation was false, and after seeing a photograph of Yarwood, that he was the man. The threat, however, had supposedly been made while Yarwood was in custody. Shown the photograph again and asked if he was sure of the date and that this was the man, he insisted he was and was cautioned for wasting police time.

Twenty four hours later, nobody else had come forward, and warned by Keen not to leave the Country while his investigations were ongoing, Yarwood was finally released.

Richard immediately contacted Mason, saying he'd no time to explain, but he needed a telephone number for Yarwood. "You're as bad as Mike?" Mason grumbled. "Ask Templeton."

"Can't be done."

"Why not?"

"I think he's trying to rip us off to the tune of an extra five million."

"Ah—right." Ten minutes later, he rang back to say he'd spoken to Ben and would be surprised if he wasn't back with the information by morning.

Richard called Harry Wetherby. He expected to be meeting with Yarwood in the next couple of days and would he like to be there? Wetherby jumped at the chance, at the same time advising him to select the venue with care, there being every possibility that Yarwood was still being watched. It sounded melodramatic, but he could have been right, and why not, anyway—if it made him happy?

He settled on Jane's house. She'd agreed to his using it while she was up at the Manor. As Mason had predicted, Ben was back with a telephone number early the next day.

Yarwood was asked to say nothing to Templeton about the meeting. The reason would become clear to him later. He'd followed the speeches on TV and in the press and raised no objection to Wetherby being there. In response to Richard's warning about security, he claimed to have a taxi driver on the payroll who knew every trick in the book to avoid being followed.

Richard arranged for Mason to go to straight to Jane's house, while he collected Wetherby from Victoria Station. Predictably, the traffic was a nightmare, Mason and Yarwood reduced to drinking tea when he eventually arrived.

"Anyone want a proper drink?" he asked, explaining as he raided Jane's drinks cabinet, that the principal reason for his asking for this meeting, was that according to Templeton, Yarwood had asked for more money. He handed each of them the drink of their choice.

"Not once since I agreed a fee to do this have I raised the subject of money," Yarwood insisted, swilling the large scotch Richard had given him. He seemed genuinely annoyed at the suggestion. "As for sweetening the whips—where else would I start?"

Wetherby cut in. "Before we go any further, just in case anyone thinks I'm a target, I'd like to make my position perfectly clear. There'll be no blackmailing me. I know enough about everyone in this room to guarantee that, and in any case, after this comes before the House, I intend to resign—win or lose. No—no," he added as Yarwood tried to interrupt. "You may enjoy a certain *intimacy* with our esteemed Cabinet Secretary, but you're in over your head this time, my friend. Take my advice—listen and learn. You won't get a second chance."

Richard caught Mason's eye. Wetherby obviously knew something they didn't.

"Forget fancy Whitehall games," the big yorkshireman continued. "Forget that people like you scare the shit out of half the MPs in christendom, because just as the Law is more about furthering the careers of lawyers and judges than the pursuit of justice; just as our fiscal structure is more about satisfying the whims of the mandarins at the treasury than the collection of revenue; just as newspapers have less to do with reporting current events than promoting the opinions and interests of those who own and control them—so the average British MP is pampered, under worked, overpaid, and less involved in serving the people than perpetuating the myth that our system of government is *the envy of the world.*

In reality, *the world* for its sins, finds our tolerance laughable and our naïveté quaint. It used to be the Church on behalf of the Lord of the Manor which conned the masses into suffering squalor and degradation in exchange for the promise of life everlasting—now it's politicians who peddle unrealizable dreams in exchange for their votes.

The House may appear to decide how much tax we pay; whether rent, rates and the like go up down or sideways; the price of a dog-licence or a gallon of petrol; but believe me, it doesn't. Most MPs grew up believing they could make a difference—united we stand, divided we fall and all that malarkey. Now it's finally dawned that nothing we say or do changes a thing. The *System* to which we're taught to subscribe is designed to ensure that.

These days, so many of us have our snouts in't trough as somebody put it, that our duty to the nation and our constituents is a secondary consideration at best—where, that is, it's a consideration at all. That's why we're here. Mr Yarwood—why *you're* here. Now—how many names do you have on your list?"

"Five hundred—give or take."

"And of that five hundred—*give or take*—how many don't sit in the House?"

Yarwood hesitated. "Er—about twenty percent."

"Which, if my mathematics is correct," Wetherby replied, "leaves *four* hundred—give or take as you put it?"

Yarwood added nothing.

"Right," Wetherby went on. "Your list *excludes* two hundred and fifty of the six hundred and fifty eligible to vote, but *includes* a hundred who are not—is that right?"

Yarwood nodded.

"So for want of an accurate figure, you've approached four hundred MPs, when, to get what we want, we need to be able to count on the support of at least three-hundred and twenty-six?"

Yarwood glanced anxiously at each of them.

"So let me ask you this," Wetherby said quickly. "Did you successfully bribe, blackmail or otherwise influence *every one* of that four hundred?"

"Not all of them, no. Some were excluded, for example—you for one."

The big yorkshireman sighed. "So *how many* were excluded?"

Yarwood thought about it. "I'd say a maximum of fifty."

"Now we've finally established that—let's start this again. Have you met, interviewed, et cetera, all but that fifty?"

"Most of them, yes."

"*Most of them*, y'say?" The Labour Party leader was growing more irritated by the second. "So you've contacted most *but not all* of that three hundred and fifty?"

"Correct."

"What happens if those y'haven't contacted come out against us, others renege and the motions are defeated?"

"But they won't be, will they, if those we've approached do what they're told?"

Wetherby shook his head. "Quite so, but you do concede we need to be sure of an absolute minimum of three hundred and twenty six?"

Yarwood scowled at him. "Of course."

"So what do those you've approached expect to happen if *they* don't do what they're told?" Yarwood hesitated. "Well," Wetherby continued, "Do they expect you to expose one of them, some of them, all of them—or none?"

"But they've no idea how many and which of them we've approached." Yarwood added.

"*Exactly*. We've got there at last." They waited for him to go on. "We clearly have to re-engage with the *entire* three hundred and fifty—more if possible—in order to enlighten them."

"Why?" Yarwood demanded. "I know these people. I've had dealings with more than half of them for years."

"Really? And here was I thinking you were retained for your charm." Richard caught Mason's eye. "Right," the yorkshireman continued. "So how many of those you've approached were bribed?"

Yarwood thought about it. "One hundred and fifty."

"About half, then. And what have you promised *them* if they fail to deliver?"

"Nothing. We've bribed them, haven't we?"

Richard could feel Wetherby's frustration growing—failure staring them in the face.

"I assume none of these people are owed money?" The politician went on, studying Yarwood's face. "Y'do understand that this is no time for lies?"

Yarwood screwed up his face. "They were all paid in full."

"Right—so you revisit the *entire* three hundred and fifty—as I said, more if you possibly can—after which you schedule those you bribed—names only mind and no mention of cash—Party by Party—add those blackmailed, finalizing each list by sorting it alphabetically.

That done you deliver each list to the appropriate Chief Whip—*by hand*—stressing that *should even one of them fail to support our proposals*, then the list, will be released to the press, *in full*, along with a statement to the effect that each of them was financially induced to *oppose* them. Have y'got that—*OPPOSE*, them? No mistakes; no oversights—and each Whip gets only his own Party's list. And remember, no mention of money and no indication as to whether this individual or that was bribed, blackmailed or whatever. Have y'got that?"

"Of course I have."

Wetherby glared at him, adding vehemently, "It's not my fault you don't understand members' reliance on t'*System*. If y'did I wouldn't be preaching to you now. You're supposed to be the expert, remember.

What you don't seem to understand, and God knows you're not alone, is that the average MP is dependent on his Party. He doesn't pretend; it's not some kind of act. The reliance is total: so much so, in fact, that the majority are incapable of grasping that the mindless conformity expected of them, has systematically destroyed their credibility in the eyes of the electorate.

And, they—*we*, I suppose I ought t'say as I'm one of them—have routinely betrayed the British people by paying them/ourselves outrageous sums of money—so-called *expenses*, for some reason convinced it's not only *earned*, but an integral part of an *oh-so-grateful* nation's obligation to us. Yes—and as we're so obviously deluded—why would you expect any of us to think and behave like responsible adults? If Carlow, Mason and young Wells, here, hadn't taken steps to end it, we might be living with this lunacy for the rest of our days.

And we haven't won, yet—don't forget that. This is meat and drink to the media. They love it. They don't want it to end. So —get your people back to everyone on each Party list, warning them that if the motions *aren't* carried, their names and why they voted against them will be leaked to the press. No ifs, buts or maybes. Their names *will* be leaked."

Yarwood nodded.

"You've definitely got that, then?" Wetherby added, looking at each of them in turn. "In this way we present them with the collective responsibility for passing these proposals into Law, at the same time making them very much aware what they can expect if they don't." He paused once again. "Any questions?"

Mason was quick to respond. "Sounds good to me."

Yarwood was silent.

"Shit," Richard whispered to Mason, "we'd have had no chance without him."

"To say nothing of blowing several million quid," Mason added. "What do you think—give him half a million?" Richard nodded, watching him shepherd Yarwood to one side "The yorkshireman gets half a million, right? Comes off what we owe *you*—agreed?"

Yarwood hesitated before finally nodding his agreement.

Ten minutes later, having decided to exit via Jane's back door, he called his tame taxi driver, telling him to pick him up two streets away. He'd find him walking south. He made a point of shaking Wetherby's hand before leaving.

Wetherby shrugged. "That's it, then. No guarantees, I'm afraid, but I've done all I can."

Mason offered to ring for a taxi.

Richard spoke to Wetherby while Mason was making the call. "I'm sorry I had to drag you into this."

The politician shook his head. "Nay, lad, I was due a good kick in the arse. It's too easy at Westminster to go along for't'ride."

He didn't mention Amanda convincing him he was doing what his father would have wanted. "If Yarwood and his cohorts are half as influential as he seems to think they are," he went on. "If they dispel any doubt they mean what they say, I'd put the odds at fifty-fifty. Beat those and we'll carry the referendum with ease."

His taxi was at the door.

"Before you go," Richard added, "I'd like to say thank you. We—Mason and I, that is, believe a nest egg will be in order if we win—say half a million. So if you'd like to leave an account number?"

Wetherby consulted his diary, scribbled on a page and tore it out. "Incidentally, I trust the list with my name on no longer exists?"

"I saw to it myself," Richard told him.

Wetherby shook his hand. "I'm grateful."

"I'll let the dust settle before transferring the money—assuming we win, of course," Richard added. "Then if anything goes wrong—well, you know what I mean."

Wetherby went out to his taxi.

"Impressive," Mason said after showing him to the door. "Pity there aren't a few more like him."

Richard nodded. "Now to thrash it out with Mike."

"Good luck with that?" Mason said." He hesitated. "Look, I hardly know how to tell you this, but it was Fiona who contacted the police. She was desperate."

"Couldn't have been anyone else, could it?" Richard said calmly. "If not her, then who—you, me or Jane? I wouldn't suggest that to Mike, though, unless he asks—and that's highly improbable as he'd rather blame me."

Mason shrugged. "Yes—I'm sorry about that."

"It's not your fault. Right—it's the Manor for me in the morning. I want my cash—I've earned it."

"I can't argue with that," Mason said. "Fiona and I will be there about eleven. Oh, and you might like to know she's divorcing Forrest and we've decided to get married."

Richard grinned. "Thank God for that. I recall somebody saying there's nothing worse to deal with than a frustrated male."

He took ten minutes to mull over what Wetherby had said and all that had happened before calling Jane. It was Carlow who answered. "Mike?" he said quickly.

The line immediately went dead. He waited five minutes before calling again—relieved to get Jane. "Did you just call?" she asked.

"I did. He put down the phone."

"No surprise there. How was your meeting?"

"Harry Wetherby certainly put Yarwood in his place, but I'm

still not sure what to do about Templeton. Anyway, expect me in the morning."

"I'll tell Mike you're coming."

Richard grunted. "I'll be there about eleven. Geoff ought to be there by then. We're going to need a referee."

THIRTY-TWO

Laura explained that the office at Chateau Darrieux closed at six every evening; lines almost never left connected to extensions overnight. Only she and Andre made after hours calls, anyway. Andre was in Bordeaux for the evening and she'd been talking to Richard.

"Then you know about his meeting," Jane said, "that he's coming here tomorrow?"

"Indeed, I do. He insists he won't be leaving until he's paid what he's owed."

"Mike seems to be looking forward to it," Jane continued, "I've seen him angry, but never like this. What do you think I should do?"

"What *can* you do?"

"Then I'm afraid we're heading for disaster."

"It'll take something earth shattering to convince either of them of that," Laura said.

Jane took a deep breath. "You do realize that you're the common factor in all this, don't you?"

"Yes—Mike won't accept that our marriage is over, and no matter what I say to Richard, he can't bring himself to believe that I don't give a dam about Chateau Darrieux—any of this, to be honest."

"Will he have to sell the Chateau if Mike doesn't pay?"

"Oh, yes. He has some money in Switzerland, but it won't be enough."

"Couldn't you lend him some? You know—give him more time to think it through?"

Laura groaned. "Offered and refused."

"So," Jane added, "unless Mike accepts that your marriage is over and settles with Richard?" She was suddenly silent.

"Are you still there?" Laura asked.

"Yes—" Jane replied quietly. "I don't suppose you can lay your hands on Richard's Swiss Bank account—account number and address, I mean?"

"Hold on." Laura came back with the information. "But why do you want it?"

"God, I can't stop shaking," Jane said. "Why didn't I think of it before? I have to use Cumulus."

"*Cumulus*; what's that?"

"Tell me—" Jane said. "Do you mind if I tell Mike you'll divorce him if he doesn't play ball?"

"Well, no; I suppose not, but how will it help?"

"I'm not sure at the moment, but I'm beginning to think I can do this."

Richard had travelled the A1 so often since his move to the Manor that the car seemed to know every twist, turn and bump in the road. But there was no pleasure in the drive, no welcoming coffee in Mrs Williams' kitchen to look forward to, no relaxing seat by the inglenook at the end of his journey.

At least it wasn't raining, he told himself—there was no snow on the ground; the queue for the job centre wasn't round the next corner. But the East-Anglian landscape was bleak and inhospitable, making him feel like a stranger. He felt for his wallet, a few pounds in your pocket one of the *small mercies* to which his father had often referred.

He slowed the car to a crawl through the village. Nothing had changed—there hadn't been time. It was ten past eleven; the church clock its customary five minutes fast, the shop in the square open for business, the landlady of the pub busy at the door. She was forever cleaning and preparing. No—nothing had changed; the local farmer's cows making their disorganized way up the lane after milking.

He turned through the Manor gates and ran down the drive, the tyres of the Porsche chewing at gravel. The doorbell complained louder than he remembered it, announcing to the world that he was no longer welcome.

Jane beat Mr Williams to the door. "Good journey?" she asked, ushering him in, automatically throwing a log on the fire. "Mike shouldn't be long."

"Try not to worry," he whispered.

"I'll make us some coffee," she said.

Carlow pushed past her. Nobody had ever confronted him like this—so sure of himself, so smug. He'd almost pleaded with him to join him. Some joke. But he wouldn't get what he'd come for—oh no, there was no chance of that.

Richard spoke first. "I've done all I can so I'm here for a debriefing and my money."

"You tried to sabotage the project."

"That's ridiculous." Richard looked at Jane. "Why does he say that when he knows it's not true?"

"Take careful note," Jane replied, glaring at Carlow. "This is what jealousy can do."

Richard turned back to Carlow. "It was an oversight—I told you."

"Why don't you go?" Carlow snapped at Jane. "I don't want to end up fighting you as well."

"Well, you're going the right way about it," she said fiercely. "I stay."

Carlow shook his head. "Have it your own way. I've instructed Giles Morton to call in your debt—*in full*," he said to Richard. "Seven days from now I put in Receivers."

Richard laughed. "So you fancy a few years behind bars, do you?"

They were interrupted by the arrival of Mason and Fiona Forrest. Richard seized the opportunity. "Ah, Geoff, just in time—he's threatening me with Receivers."

Carlow stared coldly at Mason. "Stay out of this."

Mason's eyes blazed. "Who the hell do you think you're talking to? I'm in *this*, as you put it. We all are." He turned to Richard. "And I suppose you'll blow the whistle if he does?"

Richard shrugged. "That's about the size of it. What he doesn't seem to grasp is that I'm not and never have been directly involved in this. He thought he paid me a million, but he paid me nothing."

"Oh, I paid you, all right," Carlow sneered.

"Wrong—you paid my million to Laura—your personal funds, remember? And before you bang on about it, she knows —as you'll be pleased to hear does Superintendent Keen—well, most of it anyway. I told him Laura lent me the money to buy and refurbish the Chateau. And he's seen the proof. He's not interested in gifts you choose to give to your wife."

Mason interrupted. "Clever."

"Yes, it was, wasn't it? Don't you agree, *Mister* Carlow? I'm good at this sort of thing. It's why you retained me—or have you forgotten?"

Jane was praying that Carlow would relent, their bickering even more hurtful for being a fight over Laura. "So—?" she demanded. "What happens now?"

"I came for my money," Richard insisted, "and I don't leave without it."

Jane consulted her diary before reciting a number. "It's your Swiss bank account—isn't it Richard? Does Superintendent Keen know about that?"

Richard was visibly astonished. "And you?" she said to Carlow. "What are you going to do?"

"He can wave his fancy little business goodbye. He doesn't get a penny."

"You can do nothing to his *business*, you idiot. Fail to settle with him and you'll have Laura to contend with."

Carlow tried to interrupt. "Enough," she snapped angrily. "I warned him to expect trouble when you found out about Laura, but I didn't think you'd lose *all* sense of reason. And I examined his work. Did you? Did you bother?"

Carlow was still thinking about Laura.

"No—I thought not," she added. "You were so sure of him you offered him his money—win or lose. He had nothing to do with the police coming here, and nobody knows that better than you. So he mislaid a couple of CDs. Careless? Yes. But if it makes him a liar, what does it make you?

I'm sorry Fiona," she went on, "but this has to be said. When Wilder died, Fiona was so desperate to escape Yarwood's clutches that she telephoned the police."

"Is this true?" Carlow asked.

Mason slid a protective arm around her and nodded.

"It didn't concern me then," Jane continued, "and it doesn't now. Yarwood would obviously deny everything, and politicians bent on safeguarding their own interests are the best guarantee of secrecy on the planet. We've always known that. It was only a matter of time before the police came here, so I took Cumulus and its back-up to Portugal. But a public fight over Laura will destroy everything we've worked for. And that's all this is —no more, no less." She glanced from Carlow to Richard. "Go on, deny it." Neither of them answered. "So last night I called her."

Carlow seemed surprised. "You discussed it with her?"

"I explained the situation, and we agreed what I'd do. Right," she added. "Get it through your thick skull; she *won't* be coming back. Your marriage is over—and like it or not, you *will* settle with Richard.

Richard—you'll stop complimenting yourself on your good fortune with Laura and implement the plans you've been working on for weeks. You'd no intention of carrying out your stupid threat, anyway."

Mason couldn't help smiling.

"God—this is all so unnecessary," Jane grumbled. "Should either of you refuse, the police get an up to date copy of Cumulus, details of Richard's treasure chest in Switzerland and how he came by it, chapter and verse on Wilder's women and our *esteemed* Cabinet Secretary, plus a detailed account of *goings-on* at Penina. I shall then complete a tax return. Richard, tell them what that means."

He sighed. "She'll declare receipt of a quarter of a million pounds. CME's records, safe in the hands of DCS Keen, show no such payment. After that, only she and Laura will escape the Superintendent's notebook."

"Oh, and before I forget," Jane added. "Laura will sue for divorce citing Mike's adultery with me, I shall give evidence and we'll go halves on the proceeds." She looked at her watch. "That's all I have to say, now make up your minds." She turned and walked out; the room suddenly silent.

"Well—?" Mason asked, "What's it going to be?"

Richard spoke first. "Oh, come on, Mike."

They waited for Carlow to react.

He looked at them wearily. "Okay—I know when I'm beaten." His eyes lit up again. "You've managed well enough without me, so play it as you see it."

They shook hands, then both of them with Mason. Richard thanked him. "But we do need to talk about Templeton."

"I meant what I said," Carlow insisted. "Play it as you see it. I'll free up the account."

"Incidentally," Richard added, "you do realize we'll come out of this having spent less than twenty million; which means, if you're interested, CME doesn't have to go down?"

Carlow shook his head. "Richard, please. There'll be time for that later."

He found Jane in the dining room. She'd made a pot of tea and a sandwich, thinking it was probably the last time she'd be free to help herself from his kitchen.

"Ah—there you are," he said, sitting down opposite her at the table. "We surrender."

"What else could you do?"

He was studying her closely. "I'm forever apologizing to you lately, aren't I?"

"Don't say it—what would you do without me?"

He smiled. "Pretty close to the truth though, this time. And you were right, we could have blown everything."

"*Could* have?"

"Well—would have."

"Richard admires you, you know," she told him, "but he's brighter than you and has no desire to become some kind of Mike Carlow clone. He wouldn't do that to Laura. You did your best to make him quit, didn't you? And still he outsmarted you. What he's achieved with Harry Wetherby and Forrest, not to mention Yarwood—and with virtually nothing to work with, is extraordinary. Genius, I'd call it."

Carlow grinned. "You're right, he is brighter than me—it's why I recruited him."

She buried her face in her hands. "You're impossible."

"Laura's created a problem for herself now, though, hasn't she?" he said.

"Conspiring with me, you mean?" She shook her head. "You don't know them at all, do you? They're made for each other."

He smiled. "If I'm honest, I realized that some time ago. The Carlow ego's a peculiar chap."

"Tell me something I don't know."

He squeezed her hand. "What *would* I do without you?"

She laughed. "Oh, do shut up."

Laura was delighted as well as relieved to hear that Richard had secured his second million and was once again free to work from the Manor, especially given that, thanks to Jane, Carlow had also accepted that their marriage was over.

"So you fiendish women plotted against me, did you?" Richard said happily.

"We had to do something," Laura insisted. "Jane got it right, didn't she—anything less draconian and you'd have resisted—both of you? She knows you and Mike much better than I do—a determined woman is Jane."

"Isn't she just?"

There were loose ends to tie, not least the situation with Templeton, but once he'd attended to those, he'd be on the first available flight. He couldn't wait. He ended their call and rang Templeton, who offhandedly undertook to have his secretary get back with a convenient time and date for a meeting. "No," Richard snapped. "I want you here at the Manor tomorrow evening—dinner—seven o'clock sharp."

He ended the call and contacted Yarwood for a progress report, finding him unexpectedly enthusiastic. He'd been liaising with Wetherby, he said, and would have everything in place for the Commons debate.

After the best night's sleep he'd had in weeks, Richard updated Cumulus with Wetherby's Bank details, and breathing a sigh of relief, transferred his own second million. He then spoke to Mrs Williams. Templeton would be arriving for dinner at seven, but not staying the night. He'd leave the menu to her.

Any concerns he might have had about ordering Templeton to *get his arse to the Manor*, were dispelled by the doorbell at twenty minutes to seven. Mr Williams showed him in and Richard offered him a drink. "Dry sherry, isn't it, Sir Gordon?"

The civil servant nodded.

"I wanted to speak to you this evening," Richard began, "following what you said about money for Yarwood." He led the way to chairs in front of the fire.

"I don't think I—"

"If you'd let me finish," Richard continued. "I realized you were confident I couldn't ask him myself, so I provided Superintendent Keen with the information needed to secure his release. I've since spoken to him in person and confirmed that you were lying."

"So you're prepared to believe him?"

"I'm not prepared to believe either of you, Sir Gordon."

Templeton was flustered. "I think I'd prefer to discuss this with Mr Carlow."

"At this precise moment," Richard glanced at his watch, "Mr Carlow and Mrs Garside accompanied by Mr Mason and Mrs Forrest, are at something like thirty-thousand feet en route to Mr Carlow's villa in Antigua. They'll be back for the division in the House. Oh, and you might like to know Messrs Carlow and

Mason have offered me the Managing Directorship of the company."

Templeton couldn't hide his surprise. "So—so, er—congratulations are in order."

"And why would that be?"

"Your new position?"

"Shall we eat?" Richard said, leading the way through to the dining room.

Knowing how much they enjoyed her food, Mrs Williams announced her *creamy*, vegetable soup, followed by roast beef, apple crumble and home-made vanilla custard.

One eye on Templeton, Richard thanked her, noting with satisfaction that for the first time since the civil servant began coming to the Manor her food had failed to distract him. It was Templeton who restarted the conversation. "A misunderstanding would seem to have arisen, Mr Wells."

"And what's that?" Richard asked. "My word, this soup is delicious."

"Er—yes—quite so. I was about to say you appear to believe my reference to the need for additional funds was an attempt to obtain money for myself."

Richard was determined to make him squirm. "Do I?"

Templeton hesitated. "Am I wrong?"

"The first time you and I met," Richard said firmly, "you *appeared to believe* discussing our project with me—or should I say a person of *my standing*, was beneath your dignity—an undesirable imposition. And at our recent meeting you seized upon what you clearly saw as a golden opportunity to obtain a considerable sum for yourself by inventing a need for funds which, given Yarwood's situation, would be impossible to disprove. You clearly expected me to meekly comply in light of the imminent debate in the House. I have now to decide what to do about that."

The room fell silent, Templeton eventually adding: "None of this could be further from the truth, of course, but have you decided?"

"Yes." He waited for Mrs Williams to finish serving the beef. "Yes, Sir Gordon, I have." He waited for her to leave. "I believe Mr Carlow stressed that he wouldn't hesitate to destroy you if you were foolish enough to cross him?"

He helped himself to Mrs Williams' roast potatoes watching Templeton's appetite desert him.

"I can't say I recall—"

"Really?" Richard said. "Hardly a detail one would be likely to forget."

Templeton cleared his throat. "So have you decided—to destroy me, Mr Wells?" Richard noted the trepidation in the civil-servant's voice.

"What prompted me to join Mr Carlow's *crusade,*" he went on, "—other than the financial incentive, of course—was the hope that destruction of the status-quo at Westminster and in Whitehall, will rid this Country of people like you, Sir Gordon—people who too often enjoy their privileged status for no better reason than what or who *Daddy or Mummy* happen to be, and, above all, because they're able to call upon the necessary wealth and influence to attend a *socially acceptable* school and the Oxbridge college of their choosing.

However—destroying you would be counter-productive at this stage in our project. On the other hand, I can't allow the moment to pass without observing that were our situations reversed, I've no doubt at all my career would be over. Would you like some more of these carrots?"

Templeton said nothing, shaking his head.

"No—you can count yourself lucky," Richard went on. "You had no written agreement with Mr Carlow, but I shall honour it nonetheless."

Templeton abandoned his food.

Richard smiled. "Come now, Sir Gordon, we can't have you upsetting Mrs Williams, can we? But I do have one stipulation. When the House has divided following the up-coming debate, you will tender your resignation as Cabinet Secretary and retire from public life—regardless of the outcome. Is that understood and agreed?"

Templeton breathed a sigh of relief and returned to his food. "It is—er, yes—thank you."

Their plates were empty when Mrs Williams returned.

EPILOGUE

The Chamber of the House of Commons is notoriously inadequate at the best of times, and there was standing room only on the third day of the all important debate.

Wetherby was for the motions, of course; even so finding it disconcerting to be speaking in support of a Conservative Prime Minister. For his part, Forrest was being subjected to a concerted attack from one of his own backbenchers.

Did his Right Honourable friend the Prime Minister not think it reasonable to conclude from the recent Scotland Yard press statement, that an unknown number of Right Honourable and Honourable Members had been bribed or blackmailed into supporting the motions before them?

Forrest ridiculed the idea, insisting that rumours such as these were hardly grounds for questioning the motives of Right Honourable and Honourable Members. The motions before them had been put to the House, in good faith, by himself and the Honourable Member for Sheffield, and he assumed his Honourable Friend had no desire to impugn *their* integrity. If, however, he had proof of such events, he trusted Scotland Yard had been informed. Was this the case?

The Honourable Member confessed to having no such evidence and that he'd not been in touch with the police. He remained concerned, however, that such rumours had arisen.

Wetherby caught the Speaker's eye and was quick to support Forrest, causing general amusement by adding that were the House in the habit of discontinuing debate or failing to divide on the grounds that people were capable of spreading rumours about Right Honourable and Honourable Members, it would have ceased to function a long time ago. Tongue in cheek, he went on to add that rumour or no rumour, some said it had.

The atmosphere in the House was heavy with expectation. They were losing their terms of reference and most of them knew it. Even the Party die-hards were preparing for defeat.

If the vote went as was increasingly expected, it would take time to come to terms with the idea of becoming genuine representatives of the people, and many would never manage it, the loss of *their* services no loss to the electorate as far as Wetherby was concerned. He expected the Party based system of government which had so often bordered on farce, to be slowly squeezed from the national consciousness by the passage of time and the emergence of Britain as the independent home of its people.

Indeed, he hoped Parliament was at last presiding over the demolition of Party political power, and the hypocritical conventions which had for so long sustained it. *"Madam Speaker,"* he said in response to an interruption, finding himself surprisingly nervous as he looked up at the public gallery. Back from the Caribbean for the vote, Carlow, Jane, Mason and Fiona, looking bronzed and refreshed, were sitting with Laura and Richard. Yarwood was there too—sitting apart from the others.

"I must apologize to the House for the Honourable Gentleman's remarks. It seems he objects to hearing a spade called a spade, never having had occasion to use one."

There were loud guffaws from the Opposition benches.

"But, on reflection, Madam Speaker, perhaps I do the Honourable Gentleman an injustice. Of course he knows how to use a spade. We've all watched him dig the holes he so frequently falls into."

There were sounds of amusement from all sides of the House.

"No doubt he was born with a silver shovel in his mouth."

Even the miscreant thought that was amusing.

"Madam Speaker, we've heard the arguments for and against these proposals; we've listened to those whose sole aim in life is and

always has been to maintain the status-quo, and I've no desire to delay the House on what is after all a straightforward proposition.

Britain, like the rest of Western Europe and the so-called, developed world, has problems so fundamental, so serious, that we set about dealing with them now or ultimately perish. In essence, we're proposing here today, no more and no less than the reconstruction of Westminster and Whitehall the better to avoid that.

Indeed, I hope to see Honourable and Right Honourable Members on many another day, when hidden agendas are things of the past; when the only real issue before us is how we best serve the people.

Gone will be the fund-raising tea party, with its social-climbing snobbery daintily presented between slices of patronizing condescension.

Gone will be the bigoted Comrade, wedded to the distorted memory of how the faithful stood shoulder to shoulder in't bread lines.

Gone will be subservience to a social system which having consumed the best of people's lives, casts all but a privileged few aside without compassion or understanding.

Gone will be the freeloaders, rich and poor alike; those cynical mercenaries who consider none but themselves.

And gone, thank the good Lord, will be a self-satisfied bureaucracy whose arrogant petty-minded insularity has brought the nation to its knees.

Madam Speaker—when we ask the people of this Country to return us to this place, they should neither be expected nor asked to treat the matter lightly. If we can't be trusted to put their welfare before our own, a state of affairs which in recent years has cost the nation so dear; if we can't be trusted to speak the truth rather than hiding behind rhetoric, referring to ourselves as honourable when the world knows only too well that too many of us are not—then why would they be willing to put their lives in our hands? Indeed, why would they listen to anything we say?

We must demonstrate with our votes here today that we understand our role as public servants; that we've but one wish—to act in their best interest. In a British democracy we should be content to put our parliamentary future in the hands of the electorate, as indeed should they to put their lives in ours.'

As he looked round the packed Chamber, his mind returned to the day all those years before, when, as a young man, he'd first entered this place. He remembered the enthusiasm, the optimism, the hope that had burned so bright in him then.

"*What a privilege it is to be free to dream, Madam Speaker; free to say what we think; free to hope that we in whom the people must have cause to put their trust, might soon learn to prize that trust above everything and to honour it. I beg to support the motions before us and recommend them to the House.*"

The majority in favour wasn't as big as he'd hoped, but he'd helped to achieve what a few weeks earlier he wouldn't have thought possible. Leaving the Chamber, he walked out of the building and across Parliament Square before calling Amanda, the first snow of the winter beginning to fall as he dialled.

Looking back at the Commons, he pictured his father, Daily Herald in hand, a satisfied smile on his face, hurrying through the snow en route to the vacant seat in *the khazi at the bottom of their yard.*

OTHER BOOKS BY THIS AUTHOR

The Henhouse Roof

Born in a quiet English village shortly before the onset of the Second World War, Simon Brand's life is quickly and inextricably linked to the Clare-Thompson family and their country Estate which borders the village.

His mother moves them away after the War, and an honours degree in economics sees him opting for what proves to be a brilliant career as a business/financial consultant in the City.

At the end of a day of goodbyes in Cambridge, his eyes meet those of an exquisitely beautiful young woman through the window of a bus. They smile at each other as their buses depart, and having failed to find her in the days and weeks that follow, Simon begins to fear that they'll never meet.

He dreams about *Emily Lorenzo de Pasquale* and she becomes an absent but essential part of his life.

Later, finding himself called upon to lead a bid to save the Clare-Thompson family company, he eventually meets her, and the tragic events that follow prompt his subsequent actions and colour his attitudes for the rest of his life.

Printed in Poland
by Amazon Fulfillment
Poland Sp. z o.o., Wrocław

64068072R00145